FOUR
FIGURES
IN TIME

FOUR FIGURES IN TIME

A Novel By

Patricia Grossman

CALYX Books • Corvallis, Oregon

The publication of this book was funded in part with grant support from the Lannan Foundation and the Oregon Arts Commission.

Cover art by Kristina Kennedy Daniels
Cover design by Cheryl McLean
Book design by Micki Reaman and Cheryl McLean

CALYX Books are distributed to the trade through **Consortium Book Sales and Distribution, Inc., St. Paul, MN, 1-800-283-3572**.

CALYX Books are also available through major library distributors, jobbers, and most small press distributors including: Airlift, Banyan Tree, Bookpeople, Pacific Pipeline, and Small Press Distribution. For personal orders or other information contact: CALYX Books, PO Box B, Corvallis, OR 97339, (503) 753-9384, FAX (503) 753-0515.

∞

The paper in this book meets the guidelines for permanence and durability of the Committee on Production Guidelines for Book Longevity of the Council on Library Resources and the minimum requirements of the American National Standard for the Permanence of Paper for Printed Library Materials Z38.48-1984.

Library of Congress Cataloging-in-Publication Data

Grossman, Patricia,
    Four figures in time / Patricia Grossman
        p. cm.
    ISBN 0-934971-48-x (cl: alk paper):$25.95 —ISBN 0-934971-47-1 (pb:
        alk. paper): $13.95.
    I. Title
    PS3557.R6726F68   1995
    803' .54--dc20   95-32566
                                                                    CIP

Printed in the U.S.A.
0 9 8 7 6 5 4 3 2 1

For Helene Kendler

September

"ONE, PLEASE." Sonya nudged three bills through the little arched window. Then her fingers were stranded. She drummed them against the Plexiglas screen. "For *Zavin*," she added.

"It's general admission," said the woman.

"Well, of course. I know."

She had added "for Zavin" for her own pleasure. The name conjured what she needed—to hell with the woman behind the Plexiglas. She was a pleasant sort who made pocket money sitting at a cultural institution's admissions desk. Sonya took her in at a glance. A cloisonné brooch drew the eye to a somewhat haggard throat. In regard to their looks, some women made a deadly decision a moment. Sonya's decisions were few and simple. She did not tax her appearance with playful touches. Her whimsy was for her work.

"Step to the right, please," the woman said.

There was no need for the directive. Sonya always stepped quickly in the presence of women her own age. One swift pace in the opposite direction and she was light-years from her contemporaries.

The elevator was filled with young people going up to see Zavin. Two boys and a girl were dressed entirely in black. Metal studs, focal points in a dark field, flashed under the elevator's spotlight. Trinity in Leather, thought Sonya. Zavin would have spared them nothing. If they had visited with recorder in hand, he would have shooed them away. He would have advised them to do their homework before they pressed him for the answers that would fit neatly into their suppositions about American Modernism, or Synchromism, or Precisionism. To Sonya, he would have confided that black leather was not a cloak of many layers; it was plain morbidity. Sonya sighed to look at these children in their leather. If her bid for the Waterford bust were not accepted, she would have to teach them. Throughout her career she had turned down chances to teach really marvelous young people—students whose enthusiasm surged unchecked. Now that students packed up their zest in stiff leather and assumed the pout of high fashion models, Sonya might well have to finally enter the classroom.

The elevator door opened to the broad white characters of Zavin's name. They shimmered across the dark, expansive wall. Sonya paused over each letter, as if it were an incantation, then followed the Trinity in Leather into the first gallery. *She* followed *them,* she noted. Oh, well, why not? Hadn't she always held with the natural cycles? It was her opinion that to partake was the vital style, to observe, the cowardly one. To partake meant to permit herself to be absorbed into life's natural cycles. She had always thought she would graciously accede to the next generation. She had not imagined, though, that the generation leading the way would turn out to flash and jangle so!

Of course she had already been to the opening. But paintings at openings rarely looked the same as they did on quiet weekday afternoons. On the evening of openings, the most serious pictures became as glib as the words of the champagne drinkers who remarked on them. Except for the most offensive cases, Sonya always paid an exhibit its due by returning on a quiet afternoon. Today she walked through the galleries on slightly tipped toes. A pair of what she called her "peering" glasses dangled from a black cord around her neck. These she put on to look at pictures, removed to walk between them. She stayed well behind the Trinity in Leather. She noted, though, that they observed the paintings closely. This startled her. It was to Zavin's credit, she supposed, that his beautifully poised forms could captivate anyone. She waited for them to drift forth.

The first gallery was filled with Zavin's paintings on city themes. Of course it did not matter that "Brooklyn Bridge" or "Times Square Evening" did not resemble their subjects. Zavin had taught her that art resides in harmonious spacing. When Sonya looked at his wonderful "East Meets West," she saw that contemplation could very well exist in the bustling city. Looking at the abstraction made her smile. At the opening, she had stood next to a young art historian and told him the story Zavin had told her. When one of his students had first seen the painting, he had asked, "But *where* is East? *Where* is West?" "What do you expect," Zavin had snapped, "Buddha waiting in line at Ellis Island? It's *here*," he had said, pounding the center of his chest. In recalling this story, she had laughed heartily, but the historian nodded his head in such tepid appreciation that Sonya was obliged to excuse herself. It was often the way at openings; one way or another she was abandoned.

Now the Trinity had left and she was alone with Zavin. The only cure for loneliness is solitude, she had read somewhere, and had approached its truth tentatively, as one would a bitter elixir. But this solitude had its particular entanglements. Here she was alone with his art, a living entity of course, but not, she well knew, his incarnation. He had been gone for years. It could be said, she supposed, that by her presence at his exhibition she was observing, not partaking. Worse, she could be accused of violating one of her sturdier maxims—never harp. Whenever she found herself committing an infraction against this most precious of her credos, she would bring herself up with yet another rallying cry: Carry on! Now that she was here, surrounded by "Brooklyn Bridge" and "Times Square Evening" and "East Meets West," Sonya could not help but admit that she was taking refuge under Zavin's blanket. If she would only look at his paintings less often! Then their forms might move her as they once had, converse intelligently, as forms must. But the paintings of this afternoon had no intention of seducing her. Perhaps the opening had ruined them, after all. Sonya took the elevator down to the lobby. She avoided the eye of the woman behind the Plexiglas, as if the woman knew that Sonya's perspective on the Zavin exhibit was a privileged one and now gloated that it had betrayed her.

In the study of her spacious apartment on Riverside Drive, Sonya put on her peering glasses to read the letter from the Waterford Foundation. It was personal, but she knew at a glance her bid to do Waterford's bust had been turned down. She lay the glasses on the Barcelona table beside her and walked into her studio. There, overlooking the Hudson, she was surrounded by her busts, in the last analysis her family, the first castings of which were installed in museums and foundation lobbies around the world. These busts were her solutions to the abstract/figurative struggle, and they synthesized the two views in a manner people had applauded over and over. Her studio was peopled with busts of top ambassadors, Shakespearean actors, premier scientists. Who was this Waterford, a lesser philanthropist, to pass over her transparencies of these great men? But the occurrence had occurred, Sonya told herself, and she must respond. The interest from Zavin's trust had always needed supplementing. In all other contexts a great champion of risk, Sonya was not one to be caught drawing on her capital.

She reentered the study and sat down to respond to Otis Daley's letter, set aside two months earlier. It was an invitation to join the faculty of Rensler's painting and sculpture department. Sonya knew the fall semester was due to start in two weeks, but she counted on Daley to resolve any administrative tangle resulting from her late acceptance.

With the silent declaration, Carry on!, she went back into the studio. There she sat on her favorite chair—the Marcel Breuer "Wassily" chair, a forties innovation of canvas and steel. Facing the river, she quietly conjured the virtues of teaching. As the late afternoon sun blushed unseen over several bronze busts, Sonya watched a barge piled with tons of city refuse chug up the Hudson.

AT THE END of their freshman year, Claire had told Danny that if they were really making Art and the Computer mandatory, she was walking. He had patted her shoulder and explained that Rensler had to think about its trustees and alumni donors, if such a species could possibly exist. They had to muscle up on shit like Art and the Computer he had told her;

she had better just reconcile her delicate, neurasthenic, nine-teenth-century self to what was really going down. Now, the first day of her sophomore year, she sat in a semicircle with a group of other students and listened to Al Stosky, a computer engineer, announce the betrothal of art and technology. He rubbed his hands together and directed his roving gaze in turn to each young man in the arc of young people surrounding him. The computer now being developed for personal use, he said, would be on every one of their design tables. It would generate not only light and graphics, but sound and anima-tion. Next week, he promised, they would visit a computer lab run by three young artists who planned to use the com-puter in place of a studio full of cell painters. In the near fu-ture, claimed Al Stosky, advertising art directors would all be designing from the keyboard. The computer would both store and design type. Paste-ups and mechanicals, he predicted, would become obsolete within five years of their leaving Rensler. He was not conjuring from a crystal ball, claimed Mr. Stosky when someone gave him a skeptical look, he was de-scribing their future careers.

"When's this all gonna happen?" asked the boy next to Claire. "How do we get in on this?"

"Jesus," came a voice close to Claire's ear. It was a low roll of a voice from the row close behind.

Claire acknowledged it with a nod. "Right," she said.

Melina remained leaning ahead, steadying herself with her forearm on the back of Claire's seat. Melina Irwin had been in Claire's Foundations of Two Dimensional Design the year before. At one point she had confided to Claire her deter-mination to make films without becoming a techy. Danny had told Claire that Melina was from Greenwich. He'd told her this at the cafeteria, thrusting a spoon into his mouth, wagging it several times. Danny claimed that Rensler was so full of silver spoons it should shut down and resurface as a cutlery shop.

Claire listened to Al Stosky project a time line for the boy next to her. She pictured this boy years ahead, how he would sit for hours in front of a computer, playing cavalier games with the colors produced by microchips. She felt a miserliness swell within her.

Al Stotsky gave them the address of the computer lab where class would be held next week. He assured them if there were one class they wouldn't want to miss, this would be it.

Claire stood up to go. "So now we can all design glitzy annual reports in less than an hour and have cushy lives," she said to Melina. They began to walk out of the room. Melina looked at her sternly. Directly, though, a warm smile took over, and she cocked her head. But Claire was brought up short by the order of Melina's responses. She knew what the order meant. It meant she was merely being tolerated by someone too well-bred to take a cynical view.

"What have you decided to focus on?" asked Melina.

"Painting. Just painting."

"Good for you!" It was a common response. The purism of the painting major had been much discussed at Rensler the year before. Some people maintained that the faith of painting majors was elegant; others thought it foolhardy. "Good for you" was a versatile response. It applauded either the destiny of the successful painter or the enduring character of the one who would fail. Again, Claire felt belittled by Melina's good manners. She excused herself to claim the portfolio she had left propped against her seat. When she rejoined the others in the hall, though, she quickened her step to keep the back of Melina's head clearly in view.

Under a king-sized bed sheet on the north side of the Rollins' basement in South Orange were heaped a pile of old clothes and all of Cole's World War II mementos. On the south side were Claire's single bed and her art supplies.

Cole and Wanda had wanted Claire to attend nursing school at Wanda's old college in Pennsylvania, a complex of windowless buildings dealt out over a series of low, exceptionally green hills. Along with the nursing school's focused curriculum, these hills were meant to have a lulling effect on Claire's mercurial temper. But she had refused to prepare herself among these hills for the profession of nursing. When Wanda, herself a private-duty RN, suggested other majors, Claire rejected them. Art was it, she said. Art or no college. Cole had arranged for Claire to speak with a colleague of his at Wollman's Insurance, an underwriter who made intricate abstract mosaics from ceramic, porcelain, and glass shards. Even before Rensler, Claire had appreciated the camp of these cedar-framed spectacles, and she told her father they were great, his friend really had something, if you like that kind of thing. "And who gives you the authority?" Cole had asked, as he often did when Claire stated an opinion with conviction. By the time he explained he had introduced her to the artist to prove that people could both make art and be responsible, the enmity in the air between them was heavy. Claire had held to her original ultimatum. After several hushed conversations in their bedroom late at night, the Rollinses agreed to send Claire to Rensler. When Cole told her the news, he looked beaten. He was weary of sparring with her. Nonetheless, he stood firm on one point. He was not about to spend a veritable fortune to house Claire in a ghetto.

Among other mementos, the king-sized sheet hooded an M-16 and a semi-automatic rifle. Embellishing on the paradox, Danny had once claimed that Claire spent her time in a dark artillery cache, where she painted delicate studies of light. It was true. The basement was dark and smelled of mold and there was also a coffee can filled with bullets and slugs beneath the king-sized sheet. And light *was* everything in Claire's paintings. From her early years in high school she had obsessively studied the French Impressionists. The greatest source of pain to Claire was that for most people this style of painting was now a series of note cards in a plastic box. To her it seemed only natural that painters should forever portray people at leisure. They should use feathery brushwork over the bodices of young women dressed for a ball. With their pastel sticks, they should capture just the right measure of tone in the mums showing through a rice-paper screen. If she set herself to painting people at leisure, she had told Danny, and if the nature of the leisure was from another century, it was no business of his. It was only a shame she had to do it here in the basement in South Orange, where upstairs her mother's idea of leisure was sitting in a dark kitchen with a glass of sherry, listening to light FM, and her father's was reading an article from *The Journal of Middle Management.*

DANNY VINCENT lived in an efficiency apartment in Kollman, the subsidized housing unit Rensler had bought from the city to use as a dormitory. The building looked remarkably like his father Sal's high-rise on Coney Island Avenue. Although Danny's apartment was only one room with a pullman kitchen, it had the same gray linoleum floor flecked with gold sparkles. It had a cheap door that opened to a cement-floored balcony. Like his father's, Danny's balcony overlooked a parking lot. But where the cars in Sal's lot were American and filled with what Sal called fancy gizmos, the cars parked in the lot at Kollman were predominantly old and foreign and were not polished by their owners on Saturday afternoons. And where Sal's apartment was furnished with heavy rococo pieces on which he displayed pictures of relatives he never saw, Danny's apartment was stripped of furniture and painted white. Available wall space was given to his *retablos.*

Danny's *retablos,* based on those he had seen two summers before in Oaxaca, were painted on tin and showed scenes of village life in eighteenth- or nineteenth-century Mexico. They were votives, offerings meant to thank saints for their miracles. Regularly, the saints cured the terminally ill, mended broken hearts, filled glaring skies with rain clouds, redeemed tainted reputations, and treated the insane to holidays of resplendently clear thought. Unlike his models, the annotations on Danny's *retablos* were written in English, or English sprinkled with Spanish. "On the second *Sábado* of January 1803, *Señora* Lucia, 89 *años,* gave birth to a set of *bella* twin *muchachas.*" Danny's portrayal, in enamel colors highlighted with gold leaf, showed the birth scene, but shrouded the mother's actual delivery with a finely woven *rebozo,* its every fold lovingly rendered. The frames were usually plaster, and these Danny decorated with fluttering images related to the given miracle. The walls of his efficiency in Kollman were hung with over forty *retablos.* They had been completed during the second half of his freshman year and over the summer. When Danny moved into Kollman during registration week, he had hung them immediately. Each morning since, he had lingered in his efficiency to drink coffee, study the full effect, and take notes for new ones.

This morning, the morning of Sonya Barlow's Early Twentieth-Century Seminar, leaving his sanctum was particularly difficult. He lingered in the bathroom, inspecting his image in the mirror. His beard was progressing nicely except for the ragged growth over the corners of his mouth. He rubbed these spots vigorously. Last year Claire had complimented his beard. Over the summer, Sal had told him facial hair was for primates. Now Danny could grow it again. He smiled at the mirror. The dimple on his right cheek never failed him. He bared his teeth. When he was in junior high, he had hoped that during the night his incisors would recede to line up neatly inside his mouth. This never happened. Throughout high school he had endured the nickname Fang. No one at Rensler appeared to have noticed his incisors. At Rensler, anomalies were revered. On the strength of this grace, Danny's mouth began to open wider. Over the summer, he had done a *retablo* thanking Saint Apollonia for whitening the black incisors of a Teotitlán villager. She was the saint invoked against toothaches, the closest saint he could find for his purposes. In Danny's miniature, the villager's teeth shone in the full moonlight. Danny himself had been delivered.

At the lectern, Sonya Barlow stood in the same clothes she had worn the week before. For this, Danny gave her credit. She wore a plain, navy A-line dress and a pair of copper earrings that looked to be of some tribal design, African or South Seas. Brancusi's "Bird in Space" was illuminated to her right. "Wondrous," said Barlow. "What can possibly be said when all has been said?"

Danny turned around to see how Otis Daley, who had settled quietly at the back of the class, received this remark. As usual, his expression was impassive. Claire, sitting one row ahead, was enraptured.

After some moments of looking, Barlow added, "Of course there were several of these, and the material became the statement. The material and the setting. He once set up three of his birds in a garden in India. One was white marble, one black, and the third bronze. Each one transformed the garden into another place. Each bird was a set designer with its own unique ideas, you see."

"Gimme a break, Claire. The lady postures all over the place."
They were at Benno's, a coffee shop a block from Rensler.
Danny bit into a pineapple danish and immediately wiped
the jellied filling off his beard.

"She *lived* then," Claire said.

"She lives now, too."

"Drop her case, Danny."

He was quiet. He listened to Marvin Gaye on the juke
box. "How about Saturday?" he finally asked, then looked
away.

"The end of the month. Let's do it at the end. I've got to
paint this weekend."

Danny wanted Claire to see the Polar Bears. The club
met every Saturday throughout the winter to swim in the Atlantic. Usually the men and women just ran in and out. The
men spent most of the morning throwing a medicine ball back
and forth. The women dried each other's hair. ("The Bathers,"
he planned to say. Cezanne would've loved it.) The Polar Bears
met on the beach near his father's high-rise. Sal had told Danny
to make a day of it, to bring the girl for lunch.

"Okay. It's not cold enough, anyway. You want the screams
to rattle your eardrums. Otherwise, what's the point?"

"The end of the month for sure," Claire promised. With
her thumb, she twirled the check around so it faced them both.

The pay phone in Kollman's lobby smelled of boiled hot
dogs, someone's vomit, and pot, but it was the only phone on
the south side of campus. Danny dialed his father's number,
lay his fingers on the aluminum door handle, and scowled at
the tufts of black hair on his knuckles. "Pop," he said.

"Yeah, babe, I didn't expect to hear so soon."

"Everything's cool. I'm settled. I got the single."

"You need money?"

"Hey, you think I would call to hit you up for money?"

"I got poker, babe. Etta's coming back with the nuts."

Every Tuesday Sal had a poker game in his apartment. His downstairs neighbor, Etta Aron, bought nuts and taco chips and packaged dip. They had been neighbors for years. She ran errands for him and blushed and fluttered at his gruff manners. "Give her something to complain about," he had told Danny. Rarely had either of them voiced their appreciation for Etta, the only neighbor free to attend to Sal, who had sat in a wheelchair for fifteen years since a construction accident in 1959.

"Okay, Pop, I'll let you off."

"What'sa matter, babe? Is it the girl?"

Danny heard this as a reproof, as if he had done nothing but openly moon over Claire, whose name his father did not even know. "Shit, no. Everything's fine. I got this real grande dame type for seminar this year. You'd hate her on sight."

"You're making something of yourself, babe," Sal said. It meant they should hang up, that their conversation took valuable time away from Danny's ascent into the world of achievers.

Danny took the elevator to his fifteenth-floor efficiency, looked at his wall of miniatures that gave thanks for miracles, and flopped down on his unmade bed. Last year, winter had turned to spring and he had not taken Claire to Coney Island. Tears welled up and a pulse throbbed in his neck. Danny kicked his feet among the sheets; for several minutes he allowed himself to be the child who revels in beating out time to his misery.

DURING A STUDENT protest, Otis Daley could not remember which one, an action committee had delivered a list of grievances that included the fact that the carpet in Otis's office was much too luxurious. Otis had met with the committee to discuss the list and had compromised on several key points, but flatly refused to remove his carpet. This, he said, was where the students were still children. (Fuck you, Daley, he had seen a protester mouth.) Members of the board, potential donors, art educators from other countries, parents— all had to be shown a semblance of civility. It was no poor reflection on Rensler that he had a decent office, Daley assured them.

The carpet under fire now showed its wear. It was on Daley's list to get estimates for a new one. Not a priority, though, at the beginning of the semester. He did not have time to deal with workmen measuring the floor of his suite. Otis's calendar was full, and he did not like people bustling about when his calendar was full. He had to sit in on the classes of new instructors, evaluate proposed changes in the curriculum, and travel to several other cities to attend conferences on art education. And this morning he had to meet with the head of development, Sid Casner, to work on a new fundraiser.

When Otis's secretary Lily announced Sid, Otis went out to greet him. They shook hands inside the border of the Rensler insignia woven into the carpet's pure wool pile. Otis made a point of coming out of his office to greet staff members and visitors. No one at Rensler should endure the arrogance of waiting to be received, he thought. He had tolerated enough waiting in his own academic career. He had waited endlessly for his dissertation, a comparative study of tribal ceremonial masks, to be published by an academic press. He had waited for the approval of his professors at Cornell, and for the respect of his colleagues in the art history department of a small women's college in the Midwest. Until he had made his move into administration twenty years before, Otis's patience had been his greatest resource, but one that whittled away at the man he wished to be. Now, president of Rensler, he made no one—staff member nor student—wait without cause.

The meeting with Sid went well, as Otis knew it would. Sid was a crackerjack at development. He had a knack for raising funds aggressively, yet without offending anyone or straining the school's budget. He drew on Rensler's talented alumni. Since Sid had been on staff, Rensler had produced appeals for money that included an accordion fold-out brochure, an invitation overlaid with rice paper bearing the Chinese character for money, and a hologram in which a winsome little artist extended his beret to catch falling coins.

Each year Otis's fundraisers, indulgently known around Rensler as "Daley's Drives," took a different approach. Otis and Sid had met several times during the summer to create the concept of this latest drive. To honor Rensler's seventieth year, they had convinced some well-known alumni or their representatives to donate original art works. These would be auctioned following a two-hundred-dollar-a-plate dinner. Sid and Otis planned to do a mailing each time ten important new works were consigned. This strategy was intended to create a feeling of momentum. The dinner and auction were to be held in the spring.

Settled in Otis's office, Sid presented an appendix to the list of artists Rensler would ask for donations. "I've added some of the new faculty," he said. "What about Sonya Barlow?"

"I don't know, Sid, that seems a little mercenary at this point."

"She was pretty high profile at one time. It may be worth a little momentary discomfort. Why don't you think about it?"

Generally, it was a relief for Otis to give his approval to a plan he would personally find awkward to implement. In this case, being once removed from an action was not removed enough. Otis had observed the second meeting of Sonya's Early Twentieth-Century Seminar. His impressions were preliminary, but there was a persona there that had surely not sprung out of bed the morning she started to teach at Rensler. It had been built over the years, and Otis had the grace to respect the reasons for its necessity, even if he did not know them. "I'll think about it, but it doesn't sit well."

"I'll bet she could spare a little pastel. Or a conté study for one of the heads. Surely she did studies."

Otis generally admired the good-natured style of Sid's persistence. Yet today it was irritating. He could not approach people as Sid did. He could not approach them on any ground but their own. The path people laid to their own door was the only one Otis traveled. He thanked Sid for the new list, put a hand on his tweed shoulder, and led him to the center of the Rensler insignia. There he shook his hand again, and turned.

Evenings were a trial. Since Nora had left four months ago, there was no longer a question of an evening happening to him. Otis had to make it happen, and he was not a natural man of action. Evenings repeatedly caught him in a stupor, wandering between the living room window and the kitchen. He had to remind himself he was the president of a college— he must be someone who made things happen.

So many evenings Otis was exhausted, though. He would return home to his apartment on the promenade in Brooklyn Heights and look out the window at the procession below. Invariably, a drama was in progress. Hugely pregnant girls of no more than fifteen screamed at their impassive boyfriends.

A pack of dogs surrounded a cowering Pekinese. And there were the men. Men in tight jerseys assessed each other and then, more often than not, discreetly changed course. The men who paraded below them had been a source of contention between Otis and Nora. She had wanted to sell their co-op and move to the Island. Otis had shunned the commute, as well as Nora's prepossession. She was not aware of the number of boys who regarded each other just so slyly as they passed up and down Studio Hall's steps with their oversized portfolios or their T squares.

The dramas were there. If Otis submitted to them, they had their little fascinations. But he was greatly unsettled by his lack of discipline. After all, there were probably several civic and political meetings being held in the Heights at this very moment. There was the Heights Players, who sometimes were not bad; there was a baroque music concert at St. Anne's. Still in his suit jacket, Otis thought he should go out. He did not leave, though. He stayed home, promising himself he would start *The Varieties of Religious Experience*, as he had for so long intended. The living room walls were lined with leather-bound books. His gaze wandered over the titles, but when he got to the William James book, he did not pick it up. Instead, he recalled that shortly before Nora had left she'd had the entire library appraised. He had thought nothing of it at the time. She had always been up to something.

October

THE PROCESS of making small decisions was a great pleasure for Sonya. It might be a mango over a honeydew for breakfast, Freyhoff Brothers over a foundry in Virginia for bronzing a bust, naples yellow over chrome to stand for the slash of sunlight that fell over wildflowers in a blue crock. This afternoon it was Riverside Drive over Broadway, and there was no doubt about it. Since Sonya had begun to take the subway back and forth from Rensler, she chose the avenue depending upon the day. Today was a decidedly Riverside day. The fan-shaped leaves of the ginkgo trees were beginning to turn colors. This was not what Sonya called an anonymous observation—it was a highly personal one. After all, she had drawn and painted these ginkgo trees a hundred times from her window overlooking Riverside Park. She had seen them in every light and weather. They were her trees—she knew that in drawing them she compelled them inside her. The trees on this glorious fall day were hers, and the breeze that stirred their leaves also aroused a longing to paint them, when and how she pleased.

As Sonya watched two upper branches bow towards each other, she felt a stinging blow to her arm.

"Didn't you hear?" demanded a woman about Sonya's age.

"Why should I hear you?" Sonya snapped. Hearing, particularly these days in New York, was not the sense in which she took the greatest delight.

"Money for something to eat," said the woman. "Subway tokens."

Sonya admired the woman's economy of statement but had no intention of giving her anything. The woman wore a wool skirt, tied by a rope, and rubber thongs. Her eyes were remarkably clear. Sonya sidestepped past her.

Again, the woman hit Sonya's arm. There was not a policeman in sight.

"A quarter, for Christ's sake!" the woman shouted.

"A person has to make decisions!" Sonya shouted back. "I give you all quarters, the next week I am on the street with you. We become contenders, don't you see?" In fact, Sonya never gave any of them quarters.

The woman said nothing. She set her clear stare on Sonya's face. Gently, as if acting in a dream, she removed the Chinese silk scarf from Sonya's neck and wound it about her own. Years before, Sonya had bought the scarf as a present for herself when she had obtained a commission to do the bust of an American engineer who built bridges in Taiwan. The scarf came from the Metropolitan gift shop and was patterned with calligraphic strokes, peach on indigo. The color of the strokes did something to the woman's bright, weathered complexion—created a unity there, beautiful and appalling. It was this unity, this harmonious spacing between her colors, that sustained

Sonya's eye just as the woman turned to lumber off through Riverside Park. When she was gone, almost to 83rd Street, a wind picked up off the Hudson. It carried a chill straight down the open neck of Sonya's navy A-line dress.

Like other prewar buildings along Riverside, the decent condition of Sonya's was due to solid construction, not to the diligence of its management company. The lobby floor was marble, and ceramic tiles decorated the alcove where the mailboxes were set. When Sonya walked into this alcove, kneading her throat with the same exacting, tender touch she applied to the wet clay of a finished head, three long-time tenants were huddled in a corner. Their conspiratorial air was nothing new. The group frequently gathered in the hall to manufacture intrigue. What was different about this afternoon was that one of them approached her, violating a tacit agreement of over two decades standing that there could be no genuine business between them.

"Did you hear?" asked the one from 3-B.

It was the second time in ten minutes her hearing was being questioned by a stranger. "I imagine you're referring to a specific incident," replied Sonya.

"They got us with the red herring," spoke up the woman.

"Well. Doubtless our stories will go on," said Sonya. She opened her mailbox, and set off for the elevator. One moment's hesitation and these creatures would nab her in their web of public hysteria. In Sonya's mind, the raging fires of hell were preferable to the milieu of public hysteria.

"You gonna buy?" called Mrs. Fine.

Sorting through the mail in her hand, Sonya spotted a letter from Harrington Import/Export. She had submitted her transparencies to the Manager of Human Resources there. Never had her transparencies found themselves in the hands of such a blatantly unqualified judge of sculpture. She slit the letter open and removed it only far enough to read that another artist had been selected to sculpt Jacob Harrington's portrait. It came to her that a good part of her career had been spent fabricating character in the faces of men who bought and sold, earned and spent, spun themselves frantically around the same circle while Sonya forged ahead.

"You gonna buy?" came Mrs. Fine's voice again. She emerged from the alcove as Sonya stepped onto the elevator.

"My dear," Sonya said. "You do give yourself such permission!"

The elevator door shut. Now that the building was going co-op, its classic deco design, like the letter in her hand and the feel of her bare throat, became a harbinger of the news that real misfortune could yet envelop her.

Upstairs, she made herself some tea from the jasmine leaves she had bought in Chinatown. It steeped in a white porcelain pot whose spout Sonya had praised to many sitters and other visitors. A pure example of form as function, she had said, an altogether sensuous curve, and never a drop spills once the pot has been uprighted. Absently, Sonya stroked this spout as she reflected on the timing of what had just occurred. The horrible woman in the park, the busybodies downstairs— these were not the kinds of people Sonya attracted into her orbit. She did not believe in coincidence. What was meant by the conjunction of these little vignettes? (Weren't the best lives just a series of marvelous vignettes, the worst a series of tragic ones, she had often asked her sitters.) They were, she decided, talismans that could not be ignored. In the natural cycle of changes, she could find herself begging on the roadside. More horrifying yet, she could find herself in a printed housedress, wandering the building's corridors. If she did not buy her apartment, her world could well shrink to that of Mrs. Fine. She must not allow herself to become one of those tenants who could not afford to buy and could not afford to move. To tolerate such stasis was out of the question.

Sonya poured another cup of tea and made a decision. She would sell Zavin's woodcuts to buy her apartment. Immediately, she went to call Wiltshires, who had represented Zavin in the fifties. Roger Wiltshire had never recovered from a stroke the summer before, and Sonya did not know the new director. Nonetheless, she asked for him, and confronted the receptionist's resistance with the news that she had several Maxwell Zavins to sell. The man who eventually picked up her call identified himself as Wiltshires' assistant director. Sonya explained that she had a portfolio of fifteen Zavin woodcuts from the forties. She told him some titles, which he recognized. Oh yes, he said, they were quite indebted to Matisse's cutouts. He said she was welcome to bring them in, but their experience of recent years was that they did not turn around Zavin prints with much success. Sonya found herself speechless. She began to remind the dealer of Zavin's exhibition, but found that when her mouth opened it was clogged with the virtually palpable air of her disbelief.

In a toneless voice, the man told her she was welcome to schedule an appointment to bring in the little prints. He said good-bye.

The studio was filled with a clanking noise as heat came up the riser. Every year, heat was sent up too early in the season. It was a dry heat that irritated Sonya's sinuses a good two weeks before necessary. She struggled to lift the four windows that overlooked Riverside Park. Years of winter caulking had made a mess of her sashes. Once the building went co-op, Sonya knew every apartment would get those wonderful double-pane Pella windows. It would be a pleasure to own such windows, but if Sonya did not buy her apartment, the new windows would become a daily insult, a reminder of her unsteady toehold in the building she had lived in for twenty-five years. Sonya went to remove her portfolio of Zavin's wood-cuts from a set of drawing drawers in the corner of the studio. Just as she bent down to untie the string that bound the casing, a bright splotch of blood dropped from her nose. She turned away and another drop came, enlivening the center of a block within the floor's parquet design. She had submitted to nose bleeds from the dry heat before. All she had to do was bow her head at the wrong moment. While sculpting, she had made a joke of them to her sitters. Well! she had said. What an invasion of her privacy—what a rude trespass. Her sitters had laughed delightedly. Here was a woman who had the whimsy to feel invaded by her own nosebleed. Yet this afternoon there was no caprice, there was only Sonya and the cruel symmetry that had come of an afternoon's invasions— outside her building, inside her home, within her body.

"HOLD ON, I need to stick another fifty-five cents in," said Claire. She was at a pay phone outside a gas station off I-95. Danny's response was interrupted by the sound of the machine registering the coins.

"...*nice* of you to call," he was saying. "Nice of you to let me know."

"I know it's last minute, Danny. Sorry. She just had to have somebody, and I figured we could do the Polar Bears anytime."

"Un-huh," said Danny. "I gotta go. Sal's in the tub."

"You going back to Rensler?"

"Why? Because you're not coming out? Hell, no. I'll go myself."

"This film is gonna be great," Claire said. "We'll show you the rushes."

"I gotta go."

"Wait, Danny." Claire paused. From the phone booth she could see a wispy cloud stretch farther across the perfectly blue sky. One day pollution would render the sky unpaintable. Panic assailed her. "You mad?" She forgave herself a petulant tone.

"It's not a matter of mad," Danny said. He hung up.

It was 10 a.m. and Melina and Claire were already at Rye. Melina's 16 millimeter Bolex was packed in an aluminum case in the back of her Saab. They were going to shoot the second scene of her film about water. In the first scene, she had circled an old lighthouse on the Sound at dawn, at noon, again at twilight. A neighbor had driven Melina's Boston Whaler while she directed the shots and ran the camera, using the Boston Whaler as an aquatic dolly. This weekend Claire would steer the motor boat in a triangle between three water buoys while Melina repeatedly filmed them. Melina had warned Claire that her task would be repetitious, that she might grow tired or bored, but that afterwards they would have a wonderful dinner at her parents'. Claire, Melina said, could not imagine how grateful she was for her help. She should not be concerned about her inexperience on the water, Melina had added. She smiled and told her she had implicit trust. She so emphasized the word implicit that Claire sensed Melina had tapped into a whole invisible world of trust.

Just past the Cos Cob exit, Claire asked Melina if she could say a little more about the film. Asking this question made her nervous. Melina had a strong, rounded jaw that tended to poke forward to signal her secrecy. The buoys, she said. The buoys were mystical. Their shapes, their rhythms, their patinas—each was different, each was an archetype relating to another conception of the sea. To herself, Claire was virtually gasping for something more concrete. She said nothing. She studied her long, narrow fingers, comforted by their familiarity. Melina named a film by Stan Brakhage, asked Claire if she had seen it.

"Not yet."

"Uh-huh," Melina answered. Her voice assumed the low roll that marked her graciousness. "I'm sorry. Then I'd think you'd see a little of what I'm getting at."

Once at her parents' home in Greenwich, Melina wasted little time getting to the buoys. In the kitchen, she ran up to Luisa, her parents' Argentine housekeeper, and they twirled about in each other's arms as if they were confidantes of long standing. Claire hung back. Already, the opulence constrained her. They stood in a sort of an antekitchen with an immense butcher block table, a deep porcelain sink, a pantry built with grain bins and bread boxes and colored wire drawers fit onto tracks. Barely looking at her, Melina assured Claire that later they would take the official tour, she would show her the observatory in the north gable, but they had better get with it while they had the best light.

The buoys turned out to be a bell, a pear-shaped wooden sailor, and a cone built from iron rings. Claire concentrated on steering the Boston Whaler just the right distance around the iron cone. Melina's directions were exacting. She wanted to circle each buoy five times, in ascending speeds. Then they would proceed to the next buoy. She drew a map of the path they would take, asked Claire if she thought she could manage the boat over the imaginary lines she had drawn. Before Melina unpacked the Bolex, they did a test run. Claire spotted a drip of red enamel paint at the base of the bell, and every time the bow of the Boston Whaler reached this drip she eased the throttle forward.

Melina told Claire she was a pro, a mariner of the first rank. Her voice rose from the register that merely conveyed her graciousness. She was truly excited. She directed a smile straight at Claire, who looked down.

They both wore thick fisherman's sweaters and orange safety vests from the Irwin's boat house. At the bow, Melina braced her feet under the wooden bench in the hull, arched herself inches over the water, and supported the Bolex on her forearm. To Claire, the sight of this aplomb far out in the Sound was altogether thrilling. And the day was radiant. Flashes of yellow and white over the concentric ripples made by the Boston Whaler nearly blinded them. All afternoon they squinted and called frenzied directions to each other over the sound of the motor. Each message heard was a triumph. The serious, expensive-looking Bolex ceased to intimidate Claire. Danny would have called it obscene, would have railed on about anyone at Rensler possessing such a thing. With the sun now shining on its casing, the Bolex seemed as fitting a tool as the brush in a painter's hand, organic for its role in portraying what is lifelike.

As the shadows of the buoys on the water deepened, Claire and Melina made their last round. Claire as well as Melina had seen the changing light's effects during each convolution, and they exchanged gasps of appreciation. The bell, Melina's favorite buoy, bobbed and clanged over the ripples of the boat's wake. Claire drove through the echoes of the ancient bell. The fading sound was meant to orient them, but Claire sped towards shore with little wish to meet the familiar.

After the official tour, which included the gable observatory housing all of Kevin Irwin's amateur astronomy equipment, a wine cellar sprinkled with sawdust, and several Victorian-papered bedrooms that overlooked the Sound, Claire was led into the sunroom to have drinks with Melina's family. Seated on a chintz-covered porch swing and wearing a broad-rimmed sun hat was Melina's grandmother, Regina Cordell. She held a tall glass, half filled. A lime wedge bobbed at its surface.

Melina had changed to a short cotton knit skirt and deep green tights. Claire was conscious of her own blue jeans and black turtleneck. She suddenly saw herself as a drab stroke amid a flurry of light and airy ones. She longed to reenter in a color that would complement the sunroom's marine-blue floor, the iridescent flashes of turquoise and silver in the fins of the stuffed bass on the wall. Instead, she shook Regina's hand and then, as they entered, the hands of Melina's parents, Kevin and Selina. Claire could think of nothing to say. She thought of commenting on the deliberate assonance of the Irwin women's names, then decided against it.

Selina and Kevin put Claire at her ease. They did this without a sign of strain. Kevin, a short, trim man who had blushed with pleasure the moment he saw Melina, thanked Claire for helping with the film. He asked what she did at Rensler, and stressed that filmmaking was different in its absolute dependence on what he called team-playing. Before this afternoon on the Sound, Claire had spurned the idea of collaboration. This evening it seemed an intriguing possibility. She waited for Kevin to say more. Instead, all the Irwins made anticipatory noises as Luisa passed around gin and tonics and salmon on wedges of toast. "Thank you, Luisa," said Selina, in the tone of someone being rescued. When Melina accepted her drink, falling back on the swing next to her grandmother and crossing her legs, she shook out her hair and smiled at Luisa.

Soon emboldened by the drink, Claire began to talk about the light coming off the Sound. She compared the light on the

water to its cast in the sunroom, and remarked how both in-
doors and outdoors it must be like the Arles light she had long
imagined. Straightening to a proprietary height, Regina said,
yes, it *was* lovely. Her slurred voice was quickly supplanted
by Selina's, who said how refreshing it was that a young girl
today actually thought about the light in Arles. Claire began
to wonder aloud why it was that some regions in the world
were dominated by certain colors and lights. As she spoke, a
cat passed by and rubbed herself on the leg of the rattan coffee table. "Rebecca!" welcomed Regina.

"Oh-h-h, *fatso*," said Kevin, laughing.

Selina reared up in her seat. "Rebecca, you're not fat.
You have the perfect feline figure."

Claire looked at Melina, who looked adoringly at the cat.
Then another, sleeker cat entered and the subject of light was
abandoned. Until the north star appeared over the Sound, they
ate lobsters, drank gin and tonics, and discussed the physiques
of current and formerly owned cats. Claire had never paid
much attention to cats, but tonight she marveled over them as
if they were creatures imported from paradise.

The next morning, Sunday, Claire was filled with energy.
She knew it was possible to paint twentieth-century people at
leisure. By 9 a.m. she had already sketched out such a scene
on a gessoed canvas. The bottom right showed the bow of
Melina's motor boat, her windblown hair, her hand extending
the Bolex over the water. The middle of the composition was
worked with charcoal squiggles that would become the Sound,
and in the center distance was the bell, invisibly anchored
miles below.

In the corner of the basement were several boxes of resource files. Since early high school, Claire had diligently cut
out magazine pictures showing a wide variety of subjects. Her
water file was thick with photos of oceans, lakes, dams,

streams, geysers, even glasses of water. As she worked now, the floor was strewn with an array of water pictures, old master hand drawings cut from Dover training books, and pictures of photographic equipment from *Camera World*. The bell she had committed to memory.

Several times during the day she had to adjust the tungsten lamps to direct their glare away from the canvas. By 2:00 that afternoon, the canvas was laid with its foundation colors and Melina's illuminated hand. Claire flopped on her bed to read from a book called *The Gist of Art* by the painter John Sloane. She ate Ritz crackers and read and admired the solidity of Melina's painted hand until her return to the picture became a necessity. By dark, the painting was finished. The light on the water was not quite convincing, but Claire had captured the water's movement, the great forward movement of the afternoon before, with all the verve she had felt upon waking. Exhausted, she climbed the basement steps to the kitchen.

"Well," said Wanda, sitting at the kitchen table. "The prodigal returns. Or should I say the hermit emerges."

"Or should you say nothing at all."

From the radio on the counter, a piano tinkled out "Raindrops Keep Falling on My Head." When Claire opened the refrigerator door, a slash of light fell over Wanda's face. She wore no makeup. The light threw glints over tear streaks drying on her cheeks. Her customary green tumbler of sherry was at her elbow. Wanda never refilled this glass, nor did she ever forego it.

"What'sa matter, Mom?" Claire scraped the chair leg against the linoleum, and sat down with a loaf of rye bread and a pot of Boursin. She knew better than to turn on the light.

"You're going to eat those together?"

"I like it." Claire wished she was back downstairs. The truth, though, was that the painting had so charged her nerves with exhausted energy that she had to talk. Talking would center her.

"I'm more concerned about you," said Wanda. "We haven't had a real talk yet this semester. You haven't told me about your classes. How do you feel about your classes?"

Claire had not profited from the ritual of discussing school since the second grade when her class was made up of thirty children whose collective mission seemed to be to ignore her. Then, also at the kitchen table, Wanda had held both her hands and consoled her. As time went on, Claire grew increasingly fond of the remoteness of her classmates, accepted it as a given, and used it to cultivate a pleasure in her own company. At Rensler, there gathered a collection of students who also moved against a background of alienation. By now, her sophomore year, it seemed to Claire that they all moved together in a sort of stunned pride.

"My classes are fine. What's up with you?"

"Oh, honey. I hate to burden you."

Claire replaced the Boursin to its compartment and removed a jar of herring.

"Daddy has cancelled the cruise. He says he's worried Wollman's didn't sell enough policies this year. But *you* know."

Claire raised an eyebrow. "Go alone."

Wanda rose, turned off the radio. "I should have expected that from you," she said shrilly. "You with your black and white, pleasure and misery, alone or together. I admire your will, Claire, but you don't seem to understand. There are miles between extremes, miles between together and alone."

"Okay, Mom," Claire relented. "Stay home, then." She went downstairs to look at her painting. If she squinted, the light off the water almost worked; she could almost see the bell rocking on the Sound's current.

PEEL BACK a person's layers, Sal had said when Danny was a boy, and more often than not you will find a willing heart. As Danny grew older he discovered what generally lay beneath a person's layers was phoniness. He found this to be particularly true among those people society dubbed experts. Sonya Barlow was the perfect example. She stood dwarfed by the looming image of Hans Hofmann's "Apparition" behind her. She rose and fell on the balls of her feet as she strained to hold the class's attention. Her subject was the "prevailing thought" of the late forties and early fifties. Hans Hofmann, she said, taught that creation must be magic or the outcome cannot be magic. Hofmann said that to worship the product is death. That is the difference today, Sonya told them. Each morning today we all bow three times towards the product. Then we use all our might to erase the path that led to it. If she could accomplish nothing else here at Rensler, she said, she would like to make them all aware of this tragic difference between then and now.

Danny was struck only by her air of being the expert. Expertise had given her a tight ass, and even Sal would have a hard time finding a willing heart. No, Danny would lay bets that this old dame had never put out unless it propped up her front as the expert.

Phoniness veritably stalked Danny. Talking to strangers, his bullshit meter was off and running within seconds. Claire had told him he was too hard on people, people had to have their defenses. He could not help it, though. He was born with some odd apparatus that picked up other people's phoniness, and he was obliged to root it out in them.

He got an idea for a new *retablo*. He would paint a scene thanking Saint Camillus, one of the patron saints of the sick, for curing a villager dying of expertise. Danny could not think of a more significant or fruitful cure than this one.

"Movement and counter movement create tension," Sonya said as she pointed to the Hoffman painting. "Space is vitalized by tension."

Lost in his idea, Danny did not hear her. From the top pocket of his fatigue jacket he removed a tattered notepad and a mechanical pencil. The rest of the class he spent getting his new idea on paper.

Minutes later, on his way to get a cup of coffee at Benno's, Danny saw Melina Irwin approach with her aluminum suitcase.

"Oh!" she said. She set down the case but showed no sign of relief at the lightened load. "I thought that was you. I'm sorry about Saturday. I know you two had plans."

"No big deal."

She smiled. "What was it Claire said? You were going to visit the Polar Bears? Sounded fascinating."

What the hell did that mean, thought Danny. He knew that these manor-born types viewed the preoccupations of other classes as quaint. To be rich, Danny had long observed, was to be the perpetual tourist.

"You don't have Polar Bears in the Long Island Sound?" he asked.

Considering this, Melina narrowed her eyes. "I like that image," she said.

"I gotta get some coffee," said Danny.

"Claire tells me that you know some of these Polar Bears, that you have an inside track, as it were."

"I know some of them," he answered. "A couple live in my father's building."

There was a silence. Without a doubt, Melina wanted to be taken to them. She trusted her silence would get her an invitation. He did not take the bait. She wanted to focus her awe on the Polar Bears, to ply them with compliments on their hardiness, and on the intrepid characters handed down from their ancestors in the Russian Revolution. She wanted to pay tribute to the immigrants of the thirties, and to shyly request stories about Ellis Island. As she listened, a slender, chrome mike would be hidden under the folds of her Peruvian shawl. Danny had seen that shawl—scratchy wool with a regiment of llamas along its border. Then, trying to be inconspicuous, she would withdraw her Bolex from its carrying case and set up her tripod on the flattened shore. She would document the Polar Bears without comment, let the camera record their jelly rolls and cellulite and sagging breasts and gray-haired barrel chests. She would create a Diane Arbus in motion.

"Well," he said. "Gotta rev up the old adrenal glands. Catch you later."

Alone and pleased, Danny went into Benno's where at the counter he drank three cups of coffee and wrote notes on a variety of subjects. Towards the back of the pad, in the section devoted to phrases not to be wasted, he jotted, "an inside track, as it were."

The next morning, Tuesday, was Aesthetics in a Technocracy. The class had turned out to be mostly industrial design majors. This morning Danny skipped it. He packed his duffel bag with a change of clothes, some art supplies, and a paperback life of Saint Francis.

Danny's key turned mutely in the lock of Sal's door. When the door opened, it ushered a spill of fluorescent light into a darkened living room. The old-fashioned venetian blinds were drawn. What Danny liked about Coney Island, he had once told Claire, was that no one there gave a thought to replacing their yellowed old blinds. God invented venetian blinds for the sole purpose of depressing people, and Coney Islanders believed in depression.

The light from the hall extended straight to its object—
Sal in his motorized wheelchair and Etta on his lap, the tip of
her tongue circling his ear. They both lurched around to see
Danny with his duffel bag in the doorway. Illuminated, a dot
of spittle on Etta's tongue explained in one twinkle what Danny
should have known for years. Without shutting the door, he
turned and left for the beach.

On the boardwalk, Danny could not even feel his feet
make contact with the ground. For years Sal had had his own
refuge. (Of course he had never thanked her aloud; he had no
need of polite thank-yous.) If a choice had to be made, Sal
might choose Etta. Danny had wondered why his father had
several times told him to give a ring before coming home. He
had never bothered. Now he would have to. For the first time
in his life, he would have to ask if it was convenient for him to
come home. His own living room would not be his. The objects, *their* objects, would now be Sal and Etta's.

In the corner of the living room, beside a lacquered folding screen painted with bamboo stalks, sat their pinball machine. In junior high, Danny had played pinball in his
orthodontist's waiting room. When Dr. Sandler finally removed
his braces, thereby closing their three-year relationship, he
offered Danny the pinball machine. "The naked girls offend
some of the mothers," he explained, but Danny knew Dr.
Sandler felt bad when the incisors had once again been bared.
A high school boy from Sal and Danny's building moved the
pinball machine in his Volkswagen van. At home, Danny cut
the legs down with a hack saw and replaced their rubber nubs.
During evenings all through junior high and high school, he
and Sal had sat for hours, cheering ball bearings through their
mazes, hooting when bells rang and women's breasts lit up.
The pinball machine was chief among the objects that made
the living room unmistakably theirs. With the pinball machine,

Sal had participated in Danny's boyhood. Now the living room was Sal and Etta's. Danny knew he was being a selfish bastard. Goddamn prudish, he rebuked himself, approaching the boardwalk's end.

As fast as he could, Danny got himself to Nathan's. What he needed was two foot-long dogs in white-bread rolls, a pile of fries lost in a coil of vinegary ketchup, a shake made from a blend of Bosco and the gelatin derived from horse's hooves.

Finishing the first hot dog at a stand-up counter by the window, Danny recognized Uncle Lem drinking coffee in the corner. Uncle Lem was a Polar Bear and, like all Polar Bears, did not possess a surname. "Hey," said Danny, and raised two greasy fingers. He did not want to interrupt Lem, who was marking up the racing forms in the *Post*.

"Hey, bubala!" called Lem, "Where you been? We've been twice already."

"What? I look like a wimp?" called back Danny. "I'm waiting for ass-freezing weather!"

Lem threw back his head and laughed until the man next to him moved to another counter. Lem brought his coffee over. "How've you been, bubala? How's school? How's the old man?"

"Fine. All of it's good. Rensler's pretentious as ever, but you gotta do what you gotta do."

"Damn good school. My nephew was there for architecture in the fifties. He designs plants in the Midwest. Huge, top secret plants. Got excellent training, I hear."

Danny leaned over the counter and placed a hand tenderly on Lem's shoulder. "No disrespect intended," he said, lowering his voice, "but top secret means nuclear reactors."

Lem straightened, widened his eyes. "You college kids," he said.

Danny tried to twirl a straw around his shake. "This stuff never melts."

"So, really. When're you coming down?"

"I don't know. I was supposed to bring this girl."

"Oh. I remember. The one from last year."

Danny blushed. He could not believe he had begun last year to tell Lem he would bring Claire down. Months had passed and nothing had changed. "Well, yeah. But she's been busy."

"Throw'er up!" advised Lem.

Danny smiled. "I'll be down," he said. "I miss you guys. You think anyone at Rensler gets goose pimples? Shit, they bring out the down jackets the second the wind kicks up."

"Young people have thin blood." This was how Polar Bears promoted their singularity; they disinherited the competition.

Danny looked at his watch. "Jesus, I better go."

"Going to see your old man, bubala? You're a good boy. Always were."

Danny and Lem exchanged punches. Then Danny picked up his duffel bag and started off towards the subway. Waiting for the train back to Rensler, he flipped about in his life of St. Francis, searching for just the right miracle.

THE LARGE reception room to Otis's office, the same room where the Rensler crest was emblazoned into the carpet, served as a gallery for student and faculty work. Called the Presidential Gallery, it fell under the charge of the college's part-time curator, Winifred Dodd. When faculty members showed there, they did so to patronize the college. The students' shows were generally their first important exposure. They painted the gallery walls, hung, installed, and made neat little Plexiglas signs for their work. Beside the stenciled letters of their names they mounted statements of purpose. (The statements often surprised Otis; some included references to ancient spiritual texts.) For several days the gallery would be a mess of drop-cloths, paint, tools, and cellophane wrappers from Drake's Cakes and Yodels. By late evening of the opening, the work was hung perfectly in an immaculate room filled with sprays of flowers from Otis himself. These evening openings were high points for him. He was delighted that the work mounted on his walls inspired such broad swaggers, such vehement declarations of faith in the future.

A hanging was in progress this morning, and it could not have been better timed. Otis had come from a breakfast meeting with the Board in Manhattan. It was the meeting at which Rensler's accountant had to report the size of the operating deficit. Otis had to ask the Board for its recommendations. What was brought up was old territory. First of all, Rensler had too many financial-aid students. This had to change as of next spring's admissions round, the Board insisted. Then they turned to Sid Casner. They were pleased with his drives, the board chairman said, but it was up to both him and Otis to come up with other techniques for increasing revenue. Recruitment, insisted Brad Shaw, the newest board member. He knew that Rensler had had a piss-poor excuse of a recruitment record for years now. There was just one thing to do. Spend money to generate money. They would have to hire some top-notch recruiters and get them out there to the affluent suburbs, to the Pound Ridges and Grosse Points. At this suggestion a silence fell over the board table. It had been up to Otis to break the silence, to point out to Brad the obvious, that Rensler was set on the fringe of a ghetto and only the most tenacious suburban children succeeded in getting their parents to send them at all. Otis was obliged to report that this was the first year Kollman did not have a waiting list. Tri-state students were living at home, he confessed. Drugs, Sid had added. (Unnecessarily, thought Otis.) Again there was a brief silence, this time broken by Sid, who presented the idea for the spring drive. When he announced the list of artists who had already donated work for the auction, the Board murmured its approval. Still, it would be necessary to call an extra meeting to focus only on the deficit. Before they adjourned, Sid told them that a pastel from the beginning of Sonya Barlow's career had recently brought something at auction. He reminded them that Sonya had joined their faculty.

What a relief, then, for Otis to hear the laughter of Tito and Sandy and P.J. when he walked into his office. Briefcase in hand, he stopped at the doorway to look and to listen. Their laughter emanated from such deep reserves and rose so unobstructed that Otis could not help but think of the sound of his own meager chortles. Once, during a particularly unpleasant examination of their marriage, Nora had called his laugh anemic, had said she regretted that he had clearly never known genuine joy. He had countered that her laughter was raucous, that it always overshot its mark, that it was hyperbolic and could not be trusted to target what was truly amusing.

Tito and Sandy and P.J.'s laughter shamed them both, and Otis would be the first to admit it. He knew too that it was a matter of class. As subtly as he could, Otis had suggested to Winnie Dodd that she look just a bit harder at the work of the financial-aid kids. Their paintings and assemblages swelled Rensler's halls with vigor. Otis knew he was prejudiced in their favor. The work of the kids with connections to impoverished cultures, no matter how many years removed, always impressed him far beyond the cunning and ultra-cool statements from the suburbanites—the Greenwich and Weston and Grosse Point kids. Like the ceremonial masks that were the subject of his thesis, their work was made to scare off evil spirits. The Board did not know that Otis regarded the scaring off of evil spirits as a high art, and that he regularly sneaked forth to champion the financial-aid kids.

"Whad'ya say, Daley!" asked Tito, spotting Otis in the doorway.

"Hey," said Sandy. She bent to apply a stroke of glitter to the border of her statement of purpose. She was forty pounds overweight and never wore anything but denim overalls. "A little respect for the man."

"Care for one?" asked P.J., extending a package of chocolate donuts.

"What can possibly be so amusing? Don't you know that for some of us this is the first morning of a highly pressured work week?" That Otis suffered in the work world to keep them happy in the play world was a classic motif in his contact with Rensler students.

"You might get insulted," said P.J., an ambitious young sculptor who had opened an off-campus welding shop in his spare time.

"I just came from a board meeting," said Otis. "I'm insult-proof."

They laughed. "You had to be there, Daley," Sandy said.

"Try me," Otis said. He was not eager to go into his office.

"You know Danny Vincent? The one with the *retablos?*"

"Oh, yes, I saw them in Studio Hall one day. Great. Really quite wonderful. We should get him for here." Otis tapped the gallery wall.

"He does a great Barlow imitation," said P.J., using his sleeve to wipe chocolate from his mouth. Then he lifted himself on tiptoes, straining for greater stature as Otis had noticed Sonya do during a slide lecture. He opened his mouth to say something, but Otis put up a hand to stop him.

"You're right, folks, I might get insulted." As an administrator, he was anything but a spoilsport, yet there were unquestionably boundaries. He had a deep and forbidding tone to signal such limits, and he was not afraid to use it. Tito, Sandy, and P.J. quietly busied themselves while Otis stepped over the empty coffee cups strewn over the Rensler insignia. He went into his office. From there he called a friend in the Midwest, the president of another private art school, and asked him what they were doing to protect the status of their minority and poor kids.

That evening Otis walked home slowly. Up Henry Street, a gust of wind off the East River rushed forth at every corner. The sky to the west, over New York Harbor, was full of cloud movement. The color of night rapidly overtook streaks of orchid and flesh pink. Inside the brownstones, under ornate ceiling fixtures, people sat at dinner or moved towards one another. To comfort himself, Otis noted that these people were not configured to emphasize his loss, they were not neat little nuclear families, but were two men, or three women, or a maid and a child, or several school friends. Then, above State Street, he saw two buildings in which several people ate dinner alone, facing the television screen. For a frightening moment he wanted to join these people. He wanted to grant them the allowance that their solitude was as circumstantial as his, that like him they were genial people with lively points of view to contribute. Next, he wanted to sit down and share their dinner, perhaps talk about news in the Middle East, or the floundering management of major museums, or even how the traffic in the Heights was becoming prohibitive. He wanted to talk about anything at all. Just as Otis told himself he would have to settle for the MacNeil/Lehrer report, just as he looked up to guide himself sternly towards home, he saw Sonya Barlow. She stood precisely in the center of the sidewalk before a red brick carriage house.

"Well!" she said. "To think how we all just follow some preordained pattern. Sometimes we stray, sometimes we converge." Rhythmically, she illustrated both movements with her hands.

"It's nice to see you," said Otis. Had he detected a flash of anger? Her need for privacy was legend. According to the gossip, she was perfectly capable of taking offense at having run into Otis in his own neighborhood.

Nonetheless, Sonya volunteered, "I come here once a year or so. Zavin's studio, you know." She gestured towards the carriage house. "I believe in paying homage, don't you? Heavens, what is the making of art, if not paying homage?" For less than a second, she rose up on her tipped toes.

Otis recalled P.J.'s installation in the Presidential Gallery— an assemblage of gun and automatic rifle parts coated with car paint. He smiled. "I don't know if all the art at Rensler pays homage," he said.

Sonya whisked her fingers in the air. "Oh, *Rensler*," she said.

Otis tugged at the knot of his tie. Was he wrong to expect a nominal show of respect?

Sonya stepped closer to the curb. Otis followed.

"It is extraordinary to me," she confided, "how Zavin's work has been devalued. Museum exhibitions mean nothing anymore. They are for artist's artists, they mean nothing in terms of value. I have some woodcuts, gorgeous, elegant things, visual haikus really, and I called Wiltshires, thinking I would have them appraised. Well, I might have proposed to show the man my collection of trash-can lids. He could not turn around Zavin prints with much success, he told me. '*Turn around!*' Can you imagine a less musical term? I would expect more gentility from a used-car salesman."

Otis agreed that there was not a shred of logic to the economics of the art world. "But I did hear that a pastel of yours found its way to auction. That's quite something," he said, deliberately choosing a neutral word.

"Do you know what the artist gets for putting his soul on the auction block?" she asked. "Oh, there's legislation. There's always legislation."

Otis could not have been given a clearer signal. He would leave to Sid the job of asking Sonya to donate a drawing for the spring drive.

The door to the carriage house opened. A young West Indian woman came out with a bag of trash. "Oh, dear," Sonya addressed her. "Do you work here?"

The woman looked at them suspiciously.

"It's unpardonable of me, I know," Sonya continued, "but do you work for the Zavins? Teddy and Julia?"

"I work for the Feldsteins," said the woman.

"Oh, my," she said, turning to Otis. "Maxwell's son and his wife were living here." Then, again to the woman, "I wonder where they went. Did they sell, or just sublet?"

"I don't know anything," said the woman, and went back inside.

"Well," said Sonya. "She might benefit from charm school, don't you think?"

When a person failed to attain a goal while in his company, Otis was always respectful. It did not matter if the goal was a thought faithfully expressed, or the attention of an audience, or the satisfaction of a curiosity. Otis had come to his stance over years of observing first-year instructors. When they faltered over a point, or a student refused to acknowledge the wisdom of their advice, the instructors became for an instant utterly forlorn. For just an instant their expressions fell or their words tottered. In making his evaluations of them, Otis always overlooked their appearance or behavior in these moments. It would have been unchivalrous to abide by the bafflement his instructors revealed while so briefly lost.

So Otis was quiet with Sonya now. He did not know the details of her connection to Maxwell Zavin other than the fact he had been her mentor. But when the maid had shut the carriage house door, Sonya's eyes had cast over as if Zavin himself had slammed it.

"Would you like to stop by for a drink?" he finally asked. "I'm not far."

"Oh, it's so kind of you, but I couldn't possibly," said Sonya. She gave no further explanation.

Otis said good-bye, then, and finished his walk home. It was dark now, and the people inside the brownstones had closed their curtains. As he walked along, he thought about Sonya's disappointed expression. Again, he thought about how important it was to look the other way when people suffered unguarded moments. Suddenly, though, a slight, cold tingle crept up his spine. It was the memory of Nora, the times he had pointed out how unattractive she could be in moments of disappointment, the one dreadful time she had run to him during a crying spell and he had said her tears smelled acrid.

Near his apartment, Otis stopped off at a green grocer and bought several of the kind of pears Nora liked. When he got home he arranged them in a wooden bowl, where they stayed for a week before he threw them out.

November

SOMETIMES SONYA had to deliver a lecture to herself as soon as she opened her eyes. She would struggle into her same, battle-worn lecture as though it were a suit of armor. Its purpose was to defend her against the regrets that began to drop steadily into her awakening consciousness, regrets about Maxwell, her career, a host of small-minded acts never redeemed.

In the part about Maxwell, she told herself it had only made sense for her to stay with him throughout his marriage. She had praised the series of madonna and child pictures that Zavin had painted in celebration of his son's infancy, years before he had met her. She had compared the studies to Moore's reinvented images of mother and child. It had always been right to praise him because he was so absolutely and faithfully Maxwell. And she had praised his family because she had them to thank for her daily freedom to make choices that were unimpinged by duty.

In the part about her career, she told herself that the world was fickle, that in the late twentieth century a slow, faithful development of one's vision was destined to be trampled underfoot.

This morning no piece of her lecture succeeded in banishing her demons. It was necessary to get severe with herself. She compared herself to the women in her building, to Mrs. Fine and the others. The longer she lingered in bed, she told herself, the more like them she became.

After she drank a cup of tea and made a quick pastel sketch of one of her own bronze portraits in the studio, Sonya felt much better. The sun had emerged and she saw a young man in only a vest sweater get out of his car parked on Riverside. The thermometer outside her studio window was already up to 52 degrees. It was not likely there would be another such day until spring.

Sonya decided to call her walking friend, Irene Cone. In the sixties, Irene had been married to a research foundation chairman Sonya had sculpted. The bust, a retirement present from Jason Cone's board, was unveiled at a party in the foundation's lobby. Later, Irene came up to Sonya and praised her work, citing particularly the bronze portrait's Machiavellian chin. She kissed the tips of her fingers, then posed her outstretched hand emphatically in the air. She drained her champagne glass and divulged that her husband had just been served divorce papers that morning. When Irene giggled, so did Sonya. (She had tolerated a month of Jason's ponderous and misinformed opinions on the subject of modern art.) They became friends a year later, after Irene bought several of Sonya's pastels.

"Let's walk to the Frick," Sonya said over the phone now. "We'll meet at ten-thirty in front of the Dakota." She had not seen Irene in nine months, but long phone conversations were anathema to her. Her friends knew this. Irene declared Sonya's plan splendid. She had a nail appointment at two, she added, and hoped it posed no problem.

At exactly ten-thirty, Sonya and Irene kissed, then extended each other at arms' length. Sonya told Irene her amber mohair shawl was no less than perfect, that with the highlights in her hair it created a rapport that was purely synergetic.

Irene told Sonya she looked blooming, as usual, but did not point to any feature of her costume. She glanced down at Sonya's new pair of two-hundred-dollar orthopedic shoes, then looked swiftly up again.

The light gray shoes laced up the sides and fanned out at the toes. Sonya called them her beasts, or sometimes her dear beasts. Thanks to them, she said, her feet would survive her body by many years. The truly old ladies, she knew, shod their feet in flimsy pumps. Their ankles swelled over the sides. It was all a dance of inversion to Sonya. The old masqueraded as the young and the young were too world-weary to crack a smile and the dance went on and on. In New York, and she supposed in other places as well, the cycles had reversed themselves. But New York had been the most important place to be during her great flurry of commissions, and so she had stayed. Lately, when she traveled and people asked how she could live in New York, the city of artifice, she would point to her gray beasts. Well, she laughed, one did not have to dance, one could go to the ball merely to watch.

As soon as they reached the park, Sonya broke into a brisk pace. Irene's chin jutted forth as she tried to keep up. The skin of her neck became taut, her look of concentration seemed to direct a pallor over her face, and her fingers quivered as they fussed about the folds of her shawl. Finally, she slipped her hand in the crook of Sonya's arm. Sonya stiffened.

To passersby they became two old ladies braving their way through the park.

"Tell me, dear," Sonya said quickly, "How is Monica?"

Monica was Irene's daughter, now in her late forties. She had married an executive in Jason Cone's foundation and had two children, one in high school and one in college. The last time Sonya had seen Irene, Monica had just taken a job developing scripts on the creative teaching of mathematics for a cable television network. Sonya plied Irene with questions about Monica's career and how she fared at juggling her responsibilities. She did not have the least interest in Monica or her middling acrobatics. Sonya suffered, though, from an investigative zeal that could operate independent of her curiosity. After visiting friends, she often went home exhausted, having propelled herself light-years from her realm. Sometimes she refused invitations because she did not want to face her own discursive journeys. Yet when she was with people she asked, asked, asked. She asked in order to divert the curiosity of others, which she assumed to be malevolent. Today, all her questions about Monica were essential. Under no circumstances could she tell Irene that she now spent the finest hours of daylight teaching at Rensler.

Irene needed to rest at a bench along the way. She sat down, removed a paper bag from her brocaded purse, and absently began to toss bread crumbs to the ground. Pigeons scurried over. The birds' Parkinsonian movements repelled Sonya. She did not understand Irene's indulgence of this awful old ladies' convention; she judged Irene inexcusably lax in so giving herself up. When she looked at Irene to ask another question about Monica, she acknowledged neither the bag of bread crumbs nor the birds.

"Why don't you tell me about *your* affairs, now? Who are you sculpting? Anyone as pontifical as Jason?"

"Oh, more so, but I must never let on," said Sonya. Then, cautiously, "I've been testing the waters with my Zavin woodcuts. So far I've been told by a very arrogant young man at Wiltshires that he cannot 'turn them around.' Well, I said, if Zavin intended for them to be kinetic, I'm sure he would have provided little motors."

"Good for you!" declared Irene, slowly rising. "You know I'm a close friend of Freyda Wiltshire's." She rose and took Sonya's arm again. "Oh, dear, what has happened to that brilliant Roger's mind is unspeakable."

Sonya immediately began to ask about Roger's mind. How treatable was the aphasia? Did he have that awful gait? Had he been to the Rusk Institute? Could he read, could he reason? Most important, could he *look?* Oh dear, was it possible that after a stroke one could look at a Rousseau and see nothing but a jungle, or a Toulouse-Lautrec and see merely a prostitute? Perhaps then all the pop artists, with their just-a-soup-can and just-a-lipstick, perhaps they had all had strokes.

They came to the park exit onto Fifth Avenue. Irene wrapped her shawl tightly about her shoulders. She was short of breath. Her eyes were focused inward. She seemed amused in a private and vague sort of way. Sonya was struck with a sense of abandonment. Might she lose the responsiveness of her friends? Was this what was in store? "We can sit again at the Frick," she admonished, and rushed across the street.

The moment they entered the Frick's first gallery, a room with paintings hung on walls of embossed silk, Sonya knew it had been the wrong choice for today, a day that had turned overcast and that the lightest palette could not renew. But they walked leisurely through the rooms. They looked at "Tuscan School, the Flagellation of Christ," and at the titles of the sets of leather-bound books inside their marble-topped cases: *Queens of Scotland, Gibbon's Roman Empire, Eminent English Women.*

Irene stopped before François Boucher's scene of winter, which pictured a woman in a sleigh with a brass swan at its bow and a manservant at its stern. The misty background obscured some sort of a mill. Like "Spring," "Summer," and "Autumn," "Winter" was displayed inside a shaped frame. French and German tourists were making their round of the seasons as quickly as possible. "Oh, wouldn't you love to be *there*!" declared Irene.

"I have no affinity for mills," snapped Sonya. She grew panicked. How heedlessly she regarded her precious time by touring this dead mansion whose collection she had memorized! Why did she again and again concede to be in someone else's company when she preferred her own? "We must see the Hals," she insisted.

They went to stand before "Portrait." Irene looked about the room, at Turner's massive Venice scene and at the people who sat on a bench before it, oblivious of their heads bobbing over the canal as they spoke. Sonya honed in on the portrait's hand. It was as perfect as such a hand needed to be. She was certain it had delivered its perfection with every intention of cheering her up. Hals had posed the woman's right hand on her taffeta dress, and he had painted just the outline of a shadow around her fingers. It was a thickset hand, and it wore a diamond wedding ring. This was the right touch; her hand was loved and so it was in repose. It was not a young hand. Hals knew its age to the month. He had pinpointed it by stretching the skin the exact millimeter away from her fingers. All of this—his subject's age, her social position, the bearings of her heart—was conveyed in a few strokes.

Irene joined Sonya in her looking, then said, "I'm so sorry, dear, the time just flew. I'm going to have to catch a cross-town for my nails. I'm sure you'll want to stay."

Again, they embraced. Sonya told Irene it had been lovely to see her, they must do their little walk on the very first nice day of spring. She told her to please give her fondest regards to Monica. Then there was the slightest pause, and Sonya said, more firmly than she had intended, "If you speak with Freyda Wiltshire, you might mention I am giving some thought to parting with my Zavins."

Sonya lingered before the Hals for a moment, then left the Frick. She walked quickly through the park. She paused at the bench from which Irene had dispersed her bread crumbs. Then, Sonya had acted as though it had not happened; now she was plagued by the look on Irene's face, the yet-expectant look that could be seen on the faces of women who had for many years praised and bolstered a family and now found themselves mainly in the company of a few cats, a clique of pigeons. Years ago Irene had wanted to remarry, but remarriage had not been in store. So now the expression she had designed to accommodate was turned only on her lady friends and some pigeons, each of whose requirements were easily met. Irene's accommodating expression, Sonya reminded herself, must be tolerated as part of the natural cycle of things.

Now in a great hurry, she rushed past the bench and up the winding path towards the West 72nd Street exit. As a visual exercise, she looked repeatedly from the legs of other elderly women to her own legs. In each comparison her own legs triumphed. Yes, she thought, she was the type who could wear orthopedic shoes and turn them into a statement.

"I'M GOING to leave," Wanda announced to Claire. "It's what I need to do for myself. I feel good about it."

They were sitting at the kitchen table. The radio played "All the Women I Have Loved." The lyrics wafted through Wanda's words. Claire immediately knew that the phrase "it's what I need to do for myself" had come from the group conducted by the agency that placed Wanda on jobs. It was a new group, run by two therapists. One evening in September Claire had come home from Rensler to hear Wanda and Cole laughing together on the porch. This was unusual enough for Claire to stick her head in the doorway. Her first instinct was to ask what was wrong, but she quickly amended it to what was so funny. "Nurturing the Nurturers," Wanda had said, and they had both burst into renewed laughter. Despite its name, though, Wanda had joined the group. When Claire later asked her about it, Wanda said, "There is confidentiality to be considered here." The next day Claire repeated this statement to Danny. He was visibly worried. "What if confidentiality really takes off? We'll all be at a dead end somewhere, blabbing to a signpost."

"Jesus, Mom. You're going to *leave?* Don't you think that's a little extreme?"

"Honey. You of all people."

Claire looked at her fingers. She had privately resolved that when she entered Rensler she would stop relating to either of her parents. When she made this resolution, she imagined that their lives would simply proceed along their routine courses. "What'll he do?" she asked. "You can't just leave him."

"Of course your life will change, too," said Wanda. "It will have to."

Claire's heart began to race. She had just discovered that she could paint twentieth-century people at leisure. She intended to do so for at least the remainder of her sophomore year. She intended to tolerate no interruptions. "Bullshit!" she declared. "I'll do what I want!"

Wanda only sighed. "Look, I'm going to tell you something now," she said.

"Please don't," asked Claire. "I just want to think about painting right now," she said. "Painting's all I can think about right now."

"You're slouching," Wanda answered. "Now listen. Daddy has had someone for years."

"Right. Let me guess. Aphrodite."

Wanda pursed her lips, then said mildly, "Joke if you want. Men don't need..." she hesitated, "*qualities* to win love. It's their birthright. They provide, they attract—simple equation. The world is simple, Claire."

Looking at her mother, Claire was silent. When she was a small child, she had noticed how Wanda had to be more attractive than Cole. Each time her parents went out for the evening she had wondered why Wanda had to create a new appearance while Cole merely had to present his usual one. Wanda's clothes, it had seemed to Claire, resembled the wardrobes of her paper dolls. Not only were her several different looks authenticated by just the right accessories, but the looks themselves suggested widely varying personas. Her daily look, the freshly laundered nurse's uniform, created such a contrast to her country-club look, which was so different from her Broadway-play look, which was further opposed by her exercise-class look, that Claire could not safely identify Wanda's true appearance. It seemed as though each look was meant to disparage the other. She had always regretted the necessity of Wanda's everlasting efforts, and resented Cole's perfect immutability. The equation of provide-and-attract, Claire knew, came from Wanda's new group. Still, she had to admit it was probably an accurate equation for some.

"All right," she said. "So who is she?"

"Adele."

"Come on. What are we becoming, the ultimate cliché?"

Adele Robbins was Cole's secretary at Wollman's.

"Claire," said Wanda, "this is no time for your sarcasm. This is a time for mutual support."

Claire grabbed the salt shaker in front of her and began to nudge it in little slides towards her mother. The salt-and-pepper shakers, Aunt Jemima and Uncle Tom, had sat on this same Formica table for as long as Claire could remember. Racist, she had accused at dinner one night. A goddamn sense of humor, Cole had countered, and where was hers? Don't tell *him* about racism, for Christ's sake. Who did she think he was stationed with in Europe? Stationed and wounded with, he had boasted, and who had she bled with recently? Affection, Wanda had said mildly; Claire should understand the salt shaker merely expressed affection.

"All right, Mom. Where'll you go?"

"At first, just to Amanda's. Then we'll see."

Also a nurse, Amanda had been Wanda's friend for many years. She, too, was in Nurturing the Nurturers. She was divorced and lived in nearby West Orange.

"I'll want to see you twice a week. Once at the least," said Wanda. "I'll need that."

Claire nodded her head in agreement. "But I think I should live at Kollman now," she ventured.

Wanda rose. This evening there had been no tumbler of sherry. She looked involuntarily at its usual place at the table. She said nothing and nodded vaguely.

The light in the room had dimmed. No one had gotten up to switch on the overhead fixture. "Nocturne in a South Orange Kitchen," thought Claire. She liked this title, but imagined for it only a scene of great sobriety, of dark figures that hovered close to the picture borders. Someone else would have to paint the picture—certainly not she who painted only people at leisure, people who stretched and preened in brilliant sunlight.

Around nine one evening a week later, Claire extended her hand through the open window on the passenger side of Cole's Malibu. Together they had just carried a carload of art supplies and clothes to Claire's room in Kollman. Now she wanted to shake her father's hand. She had planned this parting courtesy, and found the idea of it thrilling. She felt a wondrous self-possession in standing outside his car, perfectly capable of turning on her heels to see him again only at her whim. A sharp wind rounded the corner from the public playground beyond the parking lot. In the distance, Claire could see two swings knock together. She heard the seat of a teeter-totter rattle against the asphalt. The wind whipped around Claire's bare wrist as she reached inside the car.

Cole's hands were occupied lighting his cigar. He wore a Russian Cossack hat that forced the skin of his bulky neck to roll over his collar. Throughout all the changes of the last week—his wife leaving, his daughter leaving—Cole had clung more tenaciously than ever to his small wardrobe. Similarly, his expression had remained unfazed. It was only Cole's coordination, his small-motor skills, that had registered the presence of upheaval in his life. Odd, extraneous movements had slipped into his simplest tasks. Although his words grew more measured than ever, his movements proceeded forth as a stammer, and Claire often caught herself staring at him. Now, for instance, he fumbled at length with two books of matches, returning from one to the other for no apparent reason.

Finally, his cigar lit, he said, "I know how sudden this all seems to you. But we'd like to take you out for Thanksgiving. You pick the place. We'll come into New York, if you like."

"You must be kidding." Her tone was as controlled as Claire could manage.

Cole yanked his cigar from his mouth with such alacrity it might have been a living thing whose survival depended upon his quick action. He flipped it around to see if it was lit. When he looked up, his eyes welled with tears, and the tears began to spill rapidly. Claire backed away from the Malibu while Cole kneaded his fists against his eyes. Then, too, he dropped and repositioned his hands unnecessarily. "Okay," he said, looking straight through the windshield. "All right, then. It all seems too sudden for me. For me it all seems too sudden."

She could have reached over to grip Cole's shoulder, but at the last moment chose not to. Once more, she opened her hand for him to shake. This was for her a foreign gesture, daring in its temerity. Yet Cole grasped her hand with both his cold ones. Claire felt a shiver in her temples. The shiver remained there, infinitesimal charges within her head, as she turned from the Malibu and went up to the first room she would live in outside her parents' house.

At 7:30 that evening Claire rang Danny's bell. They were going to the reception for the show at the Presidential Gallery. It was a mid-show reception, something Winifred Dodd wanted to try for no reason anyone could fathom. The door creaked open. On the palm that emerged through the clearance was balanced a pineapple. Various colored strokes of metallic paint shone over its sharp tips. Crepe-paper streamers trailed from its base to the floor.

"Welcome," said Danny.

Although Claire regarded her move into Kollman as a triumph that augured well for her painting, and although she virtually buzzed with anticipation, she thanked him brusquely. "He had the balls to ask me out for Thanksgiving with them," she said, stomping into the room.

The room was filled with the smell of the ammonia that Danny had used to scrub the linoleum. On the floor were several lit votive candles. They encircled a new *retablo,* one that Danny had mounted on a piece of rosewood. He started to lead Claire over, but she resisted.

"Moron! What did he think we'd talk about?"

"The Pope's position on adultery?" suggested Danny.

Claire laughed.

A cable spool that Danny had found on a construction site served as his cocktail table. He had laid on it several overlapping *mantillas.* Set over these were a bottle of wine, a plate of crackers, and some miniature cheese wedges. The cheeses were fit in a cardboard wheel. Their foil wrappers depicted Alpine scenes. More votive candles flanked the wine bottle. The table was in front of the bed.

Claire wrung her hands once and sat down. "Nice," she said.

Danny sat also. He leaned forward, balanced his elbows on his knees, and clasped his hands tightly. Pink moons with white auras appeared over his nails. "I'm really sorry about your parents."

"Look," she said. "They deserve it. I think they deserve it. You would not believe their dynamic."

"Still. Here," he said, and handed her a glass of wine. "I mean, still, it's hard."

It was just this change in Danny's tone that always put Claire on the alert. When his wit began to dissolve, as often seemed to happen after dark, her stomach tightened.

He looked at her full in the face. "I'm glad you're here."

"Just saving the commuting time—" she began, seeing from the corner of her eye his hand emerge, then feeling it on her head.

He stroked her hair. She drank wine. Each time his head came close, she lifted the glass. "We're going to be late."

"You've already seen the show."

"No, I didn't, I just ran in between classes. Anyway, I like those guys," she said. "I want to show them support. Come on."

"Claire. You can't keep doing this to me."

For a moment, it was as if Cole had issued the "can't," and Claire believed Danny. No, she was wrong, a certain behavior was required and there was no room for question. All at once, then, she remembered she was in no one's house, she was here at Kollman, she *lived* at Rensler, four floors above in a three-room suite she shared with a fashion and an interior design major. This was the first day of a life in which "can't" was not an edict, and she should not waste a moment of it. She rose in a shot. "You coming?"

After he had looked long and with a diligent unhappiness into her eyes, he dropped his head into his hands.

"I'm sorry. *Again,*" she said, then sighed deeply and walked past him. She left the pineapple where he had set it on his drawing table. The static from her sweater picked up its streamers and carried them as far as they would go.

Halfway to the Presidential Gallery, Claire was overtaken with a desire to return to Kollman, to exchange the muslin sheets Rensler supplied for Wanda's soft percale ones, to bury herself deep beneath the covers. "Show your face," she commanded herself. After all, she wanted to exhibit at the Presidential Gallery herself before she left Rensler.

Claire had a difficult time with most of the other students' work. Meanings eluded her. Personalities got in the way. Mostly, though, it was ugliness that posed a problem. Ugliness and violence. Funny how in her high school art classes the prettiness had revolted her; here it was the ugliness. Where did it come from? Why did so many of them cling to it? What did they perceive that she did not? Worse, how fraudulent did some of their huge canvases on violent themes make her delicate ones of people at leisure?

The gallery was crowded. Irises filled the room, a counterpoint to P.J.'s massive assemblages of obsolete weapon parts. These dominated the room. Okay, Claire thought, these were what she would focus on. Her father's guns and World War II mementos could have supplied parts for P.J.'s sculptures. Maybe if she related Cole's obsession to P.J.'s assemblages she would get the point. She helped herself to a plastic glass of champagne and walked over to a sculpture called "Hubris." She stood puzzling over its title. Students she knew were gathered in groups. Some waved or nodded, but everyone was involved in conversation. No one seemed to be alone. Champagne glass in hand, Claire circled several more sculptures. She examined how their parts were joined together, and rehearsed some questions to ask P.J. As she walked around P.J.'s work, though, she watched herself looking at it. Her throat perspired under the collar of her black turtleneck. She had put on earrings, little figures of a Mayan fertility goddess Danny had given her last year, and she now felt their slight weight on her earlobes. She put her hand up to twist one of the goddesses.

"I like your earrings."

It was Melina Irwin, her face flushed from champagne.

Claire had received larger compliments, ones that had accounted for more of her body. She had heard compliments that were more effusive ("I *adore* your earrings"), but she had never felt so gifted by a compliment. She was stunned at her feeling of privilege in receiving this one, and could not answer. When she finally did, her "thank you" gained definition in her throat, lost it as she opened her mouth. Melina asked her if she were all right. Claire heard herself say no, maybe it was that she had mixed wine with champagne tonight. She smiled as well as she could manage, then excused herself. On her way out, she slapped P.J. heartily on the back. He grabbed her wrist to detain her, but she wriggled away. She had planned several questions about welding techniques, but suddenly lost the energy. She gave him the thumbs-up sign, and left.

DANNY SAT on his single bed until deep into the night. He ate all the Alpine cheeses, drank all the wine, and watched the votive candles burn until they bared their flimsy tin mounts. Just after Claire left he decided where he had gone wrong with her. He should have told her about Sal and Etta. He should have said, Sure, I just found out about my old man, too. I can't the hell believe what sleazes they all are. If he had said this, he decided, she would have been his. Several times during the course of the evening he shot up from the bed, intending to rush upstairs with his new disclosure. Each time, though, he returned, remembering anew that he had stretched the parallel—Cole was adulterous, Sal was not.

Molly Vincent had left when Danny was a small boy just beginning to run freely about the house, then a semi-detached in Midwood. The connection between his running and her leaving was inexorably fixed in Danny's mind. Right about the time Danny started to charge from one room to another, banging pot lids and hooting, Molly put an ad in *Buylines* to sell his baby cradle, carriage, and layette. The woman who bought them was nine months pregnant, and she sent her husband to pick them up late one morning. Sal was at work. He came home at the usual time, but from then on it was no longer the usual home. Molly was distracted. Silences swelled between them. They were bleak and dense silences. The phone began to ring in the middle of the night. Before long, Molly left. Sal arranged that she would never see Danny again. As time passed by, Sal spoke of her less and less. Once, hospitalized after the accident in 1959, he said to five-year-old Danny, "If it had been *now,* so okay, maybe I could understand," and Danny, young as he was, realized Sal had been thinking of her all along.

But Sal and *Etta* cheated on no one. They were free to do as they chose, and Claire would be the first to point this out, to reject Danny's efforts to unite them in burden. Moreover, Claire would never admit to feeling betrayed by Cole and his secretary. She would never huddle against Danny and long for the return of equanimity between her parents. Habitually, she looked for the evidence of people's unfaithfulness. She was determined to pursue a life of solitude. He knew this about her. So each time he shot up to go to the hallway and take the stairs to Claire's room, his courage failed and he returned to his bed, to the luxury of brooding within his candle-lit room.

At three in the morning Danny got up one last time. He went to the closet to remove his duffel bag, along with an army surplus backpack. These he dropped at the foot of his bed so he would see them first thing in the morning. They sealed his pledge to himself, that he would leave this bastion of elitism, this dungeon of rarefied sensibilities, and go to Mexico.

By mid-morning on Sunday, Danny had packed what he needed. He had finished his latest *retablo,* honoring St. Peter, keeper of the keys of heaven, for admitting Consuela, the whore of Tenejapa. He was pleased. The picture had a low horizon;

the town swarmed with dogs whose muzzles pointed towards the sky, where St. Peter led the ninety-year-old Consuela to the gates of heaven. The dogs he had given a hungry look. He had titled the *retablo*, "*Perros* Look on While *la Prostituta* Gets *Suerte*." As soon as the enamel had dried, he sealed this latest *retablo* in bubble wrap and packed it along with the others in Sal's old footlocker. Then he went down to the pay phone in the lobby.

"Pop."

"Danny! What'sa matter, you're too important to answer your messages?"

For three weeks Danny had removed from his mailbox pink slips on which messages from Sal had been written.

"I've been busy."

"Don't bullshit a bullshitter, babe. We gotta talk. I don't respect skulkers."

It was true; last month Danny had skulked away. He had not returned Sal's phone messages, and there had been every hope his silence would injure. Typical of Sal, though, that rather than feeling hurt he had worked up a disrespect for Danny.

"Okay, we can talk. I gotta talk to you, too. I was thinking we could go see the Polar Bears. You probably haven't been out today, huh? Uncle Lem was asking about you."

"Uncle Lem. Christ, I haven't seen Lem in months. I figured he froze to death."

Danny paused. "You haven't been out lately?"

"I go out," said Sal. "Your old man takes care of himself."

"Right," said Danny. "Right, I guess he does."

"So get over here. You eat yet? I can get smoked herring. Bagels. Whatever. Frozen pizzas. I can get pizzas."

Danny knew who would shop for the food. "I ate," he said. "Layer up. We're going to the beach."

As the "D" train emerged from the tunnel and onto the elevated tracks, the sunlight from the Jersey side suddenly lit up the graffiti on its walls. It was a dramatic illumination, like floodlights spilling over a Busby Berkeley set. There were no diamond-studded skyscrapers or red-mouthed dancing girls, but there was the same sense of the city on parade, and the city was owned by New Yorkers in their highest good humor. There were slashes and braids of color on top of hermetic codes, on top of a street gang's coat of arms, on top of sordid haiku. The brilliant noonday sun showcased these walls—their particularly urban energy rushed at Danny's gaze. He smiled; his new mustache brushed his nostrils. This was perfect. Seeing this graffiti on his way out of Rensler was perfect. It was easy to imagine what they would say at Rensler. "Please," Sonya Barlow would say. "The primitives created exquisite symbols for each and every element in nature. What are *these*? I'm not *that* naive, dear—they are the symbols of the drug culture." Melina Irwin, her Bolex humming as she set up a talking-head shot with a South Bronx street artist, would have pestered some Hispanic arts administrator who had an "inside track" (Danny smiled delightedly at this pun) to the city's most sought-after graffiti artist. Her fifty-bucks-a-second film would run on until he made just the unwitting-yet-penetrating remark she had determined for him. This was what was wrong with Rensler, this was why Danny wanted out. All Barlows. All Irwins.

Sal Vincent had the coffee table spread with bagels, smoked herring, white fish, lox, three kinds of cream cheese spread, a plate of Bermuda onion rings, and a jar of hot peppers. A lapsed Catholic living among Jews, Sal had eaten this way for years. Now he sat beside the table, reading the racing forms from the *Post*. He smoked an unfiltered Marlboro, as usual letting it dangle from the side of his mouth, closing his left eye against the rising smoke.

"I guess you don't have to stop in this millennium," said Danny. "There's always next."

"If you were going to bring your mouth," said Sal, "you could've stayed in the ghetto."

"It's not a ghetto," was all Danny could muster. He did not want to eat.

Sal put down the paper. He folded his hands on his lap, a gesture that had stirred Danny since boyhood. For years Sal had worn a star sapphire ring, and the rays it emitted under the lamplight emphasized the holiness, the poignancy of folded hands over idle legs. When he was young, Danny had purposely looked at Sal's folded hands. He had craved the surges of pity that came upon him when he caught Sal trying to reach an object beyond his grasp, or tapping out his restlessness on the arm of his wheelchair, or gazing down at his feet. Now these gestures, or the sight of the twinkling stone on Sal's ring, were cues for Danny to look away.

"You like chives or walnut? Or plain?" Sal nodded towards the cream cheeses on the table. "I didn't remember what the hell you liked."

"Later, maybe. Let's catch the Polar Bears."

Sal waved his hand dismissively. "How many times can you watch? They go in, they scream, they come out. You find this fascinating?"

"You don't get rhythms, Pop," said Danny. It was something Claire once said to him as he looked at a picture of a series of poplar trees before a setting sun. They had ridden an elevator and walked through a dozen dim, skylit rooms to get to the picture. "This is it?" he had asked. "You don't get rhythms," she had said, making it a decree.

On the boardwalk, Sal drove his wheelchair and Danny walked beside him. When the Polar Bears came into sight, Sal made a sharp turn and parked himself beside a bench. He patted the seat beside him. As if in tribute to the Polar Bears, he lifted the collar of his parka and withdrew a stocking cap from its pocket.

In silence, they watched two men and a woman splash in the surf. There was no laughter. The men looked straight ahead. The woman watched the men. Lem was not among them.

"Maybe more are under the boardwalk," Danny said hopefully. In the past, the Polar Bears' bravado had moved him. Their bravado had lured Danny from his most inward humor. Their constant, hearty backslapping had suggested that people could live well simply by setting up small obstacles and overcoming them. But these Polar Bears were different. They displayed no reverence or wonder at entering the icy Atlantic. They were like clerks performing a duty.

Danny and Sal sat glumly, their eyes watering in the wind. "You never brought the girl?" asked Sal.

"Naah." Danny jerked his head towards the men and woman in the water. He twisted his mouth like a gangster. "Dey ain't tasteful."

Sal laughed, one snort, then lit a Marlboro. "I could call Etta later. Tell her to come down. We could play rummy. Or you two could talk. She's funny. She's funny about Poland. Lots of pigs and goats in her stories. They're bigger deals than the people. Like that barnyard you had when you were a kid. Remember? You made the animals the big deals, the people were jackshit. Maybe that's how it was in Poland for Etta."

The Polar Bears immersed themselves up to the chest. Hemmed in by small billows, they slogged along.

"Some other time, maybe. Listen. Can I UPS something to you?"

"What'ya got, babe?"

"My art. It's all in your footlocker. I need to store it. You got room?"

"Room I got. What I ain't got is a doormat that says 'no questions asked.'"

"I'm dropping out."

Finally, there was a scream. A bewigged woman in a skirted bathing suit had emerged from beneath the boardwalk. One of the men had approached the shore and pulled her back out with him. "Al*right*!" said Danny, and slammed his fist against his palm. "A neophyte."

"The *fuck* you are," hissed Sal.

"Pop. I already decided. They won't refund me for this semester, but I'll pay you back. You just gotta give me time."

"Danny. Babe. What's so wrong? Everyone else sticks it out. What's so wrong?"

"Nothing's wrong. I need to go to Mexico. It's like a leave of absence."

"It stinks down there," said Sal. "Their sewage system's got no sophistication."

"So-the-hell what! You want me to stay in the States for the plumbing?"

Sal tossed his cigarette over the boardwalk. The lit butt fell next to a Tab can wrapped in seaweed. "You're coming back? It's okay with your teachers?"

"They'll let me."

"I know you're not one of those kids who don't give a crap about their parents. What it is with you—" Sal began to explain, then shook his head.

A friend of the bewigged woman had come down to the shore. Danny had seen the friend before. She was a regular, a thin woman who made perfunctory dips into the water, then retreated to dutifully serve coffee from a thermos to the men playing medicine ball on the shore. Now she pleaded for the men to return her friend. Her voice was wrought with petulance.

"Now we're talking action," said Danny. "Let's go down."

Sal stared deeply at the waves. Danny jumped up to post himself behind Sal's chair.

"Hey! You forget the rules?" He wheeled himself rapidly ahead, stopping to wait only at the edge of the ramp. They went down to the beach together. From under the boardwalk, Lem rushed up to greet them. For a while they all talked, then Lem huddled closer to Sal to speculate about what would happen at Belmont that afternoon.

There was a commotion further ahead. Balanced on the peak of a wave was the underside of a black wig. As Danny watched, a smaller wave emptied into it. A woman with thin wisps of bronze hair began to rotate her arms in mighty circles, directing ripples like a volley of ammunition towards the guilty men. She was silent but red-faced.

Suddenly weary, Danny excused himself to walk along the shore. This was a courtesy—the opportunity for Sal to confide to Lem the heartache of having raised a son alone. When he approached the Polar Bears half an hour later, he saw that Lem had gone back to playing medicine ball over the Polar Bears' makeshift barrel furnace. Five men played and Sal sat alone, the spokes of his wheelchair sunk in the sand. As he watched Lem and the others, Sal's hands were folded over his lap. His folded hands were rendered magical, saintly, by the sunlight that sent long white rays from his star sapphire ring. Danny saw the rays from a distance, focused white lines that canvassed the beach as if in search of Danny's lost adoration. When Danny came up to his father, though, he saw Sal's expression was hard.

"A lady doesn't love you so you leave the country," Sal said, a flat pronouncement that invited no reply.

OTIS DALEY awoke far too late the morning after Thanksgiving. Too late by his own appraisal, for he usually opened his eyes just as the rising light set the bedroom's furniture into three dimensions. Privately, Otis harbored a fear of waking after the contours of the objects that surrounded him had achieved their full clarity. When he awoke late and light had already established the solidity of a new day, he felt himself to be a sorry afterthought.

Yesterday had been his first Thanksgiving without Nora. He had spent it with the Casners in Riverdale. Sid had a large family, and he had staged a Plymouth Thanksgiving for his youngest children, casting himself in the role of Squanto. Squanto and his costume had inspired an array of same-motif jokes that continued unabated throughout the evening, setting Otis, unknown to the others, on the brink of violence. He had nevertheless been polite and appreciative. Perhaps so constraining himself had led to a state of somnolence; shortly after ten a languor still pressed upon him.

When he got up, Otis made himself a cup of coffee. He had a sleek new coffee maker that could be timed to begin working while its owner slept, and also stopped dripping in mid-brew if Otis removed the carafe from its hot plate. A Rensler Industrial Design alumnus had been responsible for the coffee maker. Rensler's best product design instructor maintained that the more a product's inner workings were concealed from the consumer, the more it assumed the mystery that was part of any elegant design solution. This coffee maker, which was sold in the country's best department stores, bore the Rensler stamp; it did a great deal and showed no evidence of its effort. Even Japanese and German companies had tapped Rensler's industrial design department. Otis felt a wave of proprietary pleasure; he had had a small role in the making of this daily appliance that sat in households all over America.

Had Nora been at the kitchen table, Otis would have asked whether she could tell that the coffee maker had the Rensler stamp, and she would have answered that she most certainly could, it was such a peachy little item. Otis had no doubt this would be her response. Suddenly, he longed for nothing more than the simple reflex action of Nora's support. He brought his coffee into the living room, sat down at the mahogany secretary that overlooked the Promenade, regarded the holiday joggers with a swell of disgust, and began to compose a letter to Nora at her new sublet in Turtle Bay. The moment his pen touched the paper, longing was subsumed by the predictable rhythm of Otis's logical thinking.

Dearest Nora,

How to begin? To have begun at all is a concession, or at least you will see it that way if you insist on our every gesture, our every monosyllable, as a point of negotiation. In that context, I will flounder. Please do me the kindness of reading unarmed.

I understand that you are doing well. I hear that you have invested in a ghost-writing business and that it is taking off. Naturally, your success does not surprise me. I knew that winning you back could not be based on your retreat from challenge, nor did I ever want that. But dear, you must admit your ease in the world handicaps me. You require no protection and so have little need for the nest, or for the underside of my wing.

The young women at Rensler, the ones in their uniform of jeans and boots and plastic-buttons-exclaiming-things, would turn on me for using that phrase—underside of my wing. Who needs your wing, they would demand, the power of your wing is a male myth. Unquestionably, I have learned from them, their caucus at Rensler last spring. But the notion of all of us, liberated from myths and seeking no protection, fills me with despair. I feel the wind blowing clear through me.

Yes, you say my laugh is joyless, and I say yours is raucous. But is this really what we have concluded about each other late at night, alone in bed? Is this what over twenty years of caring partnership comes down to, betrayal by the character of our laughs?

Otis paused to read what he had written. He drank some coffee, stared absently at the runners, outfitted like deep-sea divers. What if Nora were not there late at night, alone in bed? And what if she were? To what ends did he wish to lure her from her exile back into their queen-sized bed—so that in the morning she might assure him their Rensler coffee maker was a peachy item? The empty feeling in his chest, the wind blowing clear through him, sent the candid message that his amends were suspect. He tore up the letter and began another.

Dear Nora,

It is the day after Thanksgiving and I have overslept. Thoughts of you, of us, have made me reluctant to wake. When I finally made myself some coffee and our silent voices prattled along together, we were praising the design of a coffee machine. What an egoist I have been to confuse our constant praising of all that was ours for closeness.

There is so much you shut out. And because you shut out so much, I regarded myself—the one you closed in—as elect. When you praised me, or our

*possessions, or our opinions or ethics, I always felt a
snugness that our life together met your standards,
standards which I took for granted were endowed
with a special knowingness. But our six months apart
has forced me to see myself as one among the crowd
and you as being exceptionally creedbound. Who
didn't you shut out? You commented regularly on the
young men on the Promenade, and on what you
called the vocal-type feminists, on street people who
you dared to dismiss with that obsolete reproach,
"They could get a job if they wanted to," and on
Rensler's Island Blacks and its Hispanics (you made
allowances for the Cubanos, but cast aside the Puerto
Ricans).*

*For so long all this shutting out of yours drew me
further in. The more groups you deprecated, the more
I shrank into the tight fit of your approval. I let you
malign people as long as you continued to express
satisfaction over our collection of books, or the
location of our apartment, or the design of our
kitchen appliances. And now I don't know where I
stand in my own apartment. I still love this apartment,
but my appreciation carries with it a murky back-
wash, as though it skims ahead at the expense of
something, or someone.*

*I am perfectly happy to continue the payments set
down by the terms of our separation agreement, as
this transition could not be easy for you. But I suggest
we hasten towards a divorce settlement that will
absolve us of further responsibility to each other. I
will have my lawyer draw up the papers.*

Otis moved to the loveseat next to the secretary to read
this second letter. He was amazed at its wild leap from the

first, as though years and not minutes had intervened. He sealed it, and sat tapping the corner of its envelope against his chin. On the Promenade below, a mother slapped her son's wrist so the child would drop the candy wrapper in his fist. Minutes before, while Otis was still immersed in his letter, the mother and son had walked by for the first time, and Otis had vaguely noticed the child pluck the wrapper from a trash barrel. The pattern made by his observations pleased him. The odd little symmetry of the two tiny events, the child picking up the candy wrapper, then minutes later dropping it, somehow served as evidence that his second letter was the right one.

At nearly three o'clock Otis walked down the corridor of a private school on the Upper West Side. With little desire but much urgency he had decided to take himself to a small anti-quarian book fair he had seen listed in the *Times*. Although he had some reasonable interest in rare books, he mostly needed a place to go, some mild commotion to distract him from the overbrimming energy that kept rising in him, so like passion at its inception.

The school's cafeteria had been taken over by book stalls, all numbered and bearing names: 9–*The Atheneum*, Sandusky, Ohio; 23–*Watermark Editions*, Eureka, Ca.; 41–*Pages from the Ages*, Silver Spring, Md. The browsers were decidedly Upper West Siders, a type in whose presence Otis felt much comfort. The women milled about in careless outfits of sneakers, flow-ing skirts, ribbed cotton sweaters, wool blazers, and gauzy scarves laced with metallic threads. Otis wore his usual week-end clothes—a dark denim shirt, chinos, a tweed jacket, and, what finally dated the look, smoky green desert boots. Yet Otis melded effortlessly into this scene. He might have be-longed, he might have been married to one of the hale, sensi-bly attractive women who paged through modern first editions and leaned towards one another to praise a book's end paper.

He knew what these women did: they directed Head Start programs, they wrote grant proposals for organizations researching odd genetic diseases, they edited small, left-wing periodicals, they played early music on eighteenth-century German recorders, they cooked Swedish and Moroccan meals at one another's apartments.

Such a warm sense of neutrality filled Otis when he thought about what these women did that he saw himself quite happily married to one of them. They, too, would confirm that the products of Rensler design were worthy additions to the world, yet at the same time they would work steadily at their own important but dimly appreciated projects. They could never tolerate, as Nora most certainly did, a job in which they recruited ghost writers to enliven the prose of faded movie legends or famous white collar criminals. Yes, Otis thought he could and would be happy with one of these women. He put his hands into the pockets of his chinos and began to browse in the stalls off the main aisle.

It had taken Otis all day to achieve this sense of hopeful expectation, so coming upon 20–*The Quill*, Norfolk, Va. was most inopportune. It was a double-stall, stacked with leatherbound art books, some beneath glass cases, others on open shelves. Separate colorplates had been removed from some books and were protected in acetate sleeves and placed in a bin at the corner of the stall. It was a dusty, welcoming space, and Otis felt elevated within its bounds, had even decided to buy a first edition of eighteenth-century European political cartoons, when he came upon a book whose title struck him with a cruel and dizzying recognition—*Ceremonial Masks: A Trans-Cultural Comparison*. A gray, pointillistic screen dropped before his eyes. Behind it, the stall was no longer comforting, but hazy and unreal. The women who drifted in and out were no longer appealing prospects for his future, but dreary intrusions into his present. The screen shielded him from another life, a life whose hopes had not been realized and, worse, had not been integrated into the life Otis occupied today. He could not touch the book. Rather, he positioned himself at various odd angles to it, and regarded it askance. He confirmed it was his book, printed by his publisher, a now-defunct academic press in Rio de Janeiro.

A young man in wireless glasses came over and leafed through Otis's book, revealing several of the black-and-white photographs of Aboriginal masks and, closer to the book's end, one Zapotec headdress. The young man walked away, expressionless. Otis busied himself looking through a book of Pre-Raphaelite drawings. He turned the pages slowly, trying to still his heartbeats, alarmingly thick and remote. He had so loved the research and writing of *Ceremonial Masks*. He had been so positive that from behind his scholarship and tireless citing of sources would emerge a unique and vital energy, one that would draw readers into a positive zeal to see the ceremonies Otis wrote about, to learn about the gods, and to work to preserve the ancestral cultures he had described in loving detail. He had been certain *Ceremonial Masks* would serve as the foundation for his next book, already outlined, which would focus on formal composition elements in ancient sacrificial sculpture. Rather, *Ceremonial Masks* sold three hundred and fifty copies, and the outline for the new book was rejected by eleven publishers. Otis, by then married and teaching at a midwestern college, never felt the same breathless, carefree excitement again.

The spacious front rooms of Otis's apartment were lit only by the lamps shining on the Promenade. He switched on a hall sconce and a living room Tiffany lamp. Without examining it, he put away his book of political cartoons. He placed his letter to Nora on the hall table, where he would be sure to see it for mailing the next morning. Then he sat down to write some notes for the next board meeting, the special one that would take up the problem of the budget deficit. Curiously removed from his actions, Otis wrote up a skeleton agenda. He had little hope for the resolution of Rensler's money problems. While Sid was doing the lion's share of the work, Otis decided he himself must make a greater effort to keep Rensler in the public eye. Hastily, he got out his list of faculty home phone numbers and called Sonya Barlow. When she answered, he apologized for the lateness of the hour. He asked if he could make an appointment to talk to her about a matter concerning the benefit of Rensler. Otis said it would not take long, and he would be most grateful if she agreed. She did. They made arrangements to meet during the holiday break. Her agreement was so tinged with a tone of wonder, of an adventure about to be embarked upon, that his energy rose again. He called Sid Casner, who was not home, and left a message thanking him for a wonderful Thanksgiving dinner.

December

ONE OF THE Rensler faculty had told Sonya that the Jitney was the thing to take to the Hamptons. Quieter, more pleasant than the Long Island Railroad, the brand new Jitney was certainly what she wanted.

During years gone by, Sonya and Maxwell had borrowed a car to drive to friends in the Hamptons. On the summer weekends when Renée Zavin had met her brothers and sisters' families at Lake George, Sonya and Maxwell sometimes stayed in the rented beach houses of artist friends. They did not discuss Renée except initially, when Maxwell explained that Renée never felt quite so at home as when she was with her brothers and sisters, eating rich food and speaking French at Lake George. He was too busy to accompany her on these vacations, but he frequently found time for a weekend in the Hamptons with Sonya. Even with heavy deadlines upon him (the completion of a design for the stained glass window in a Tel Aviv synagogue, a series of woodcuts illustrating a collection of Symbolist poetry), Zavin allowed time for his friends—

time for, as he liked to say with an air of heavenliness, the senses to fill.

This was today, though, and today was the Jitney. Sonya arrived at the bus with her portfolio of woodcuts. Irene Cone had arranged the visit. Ordinarily, Sonya would not see Irene more than twice a year, but when Irene described the visit to the Hamptons as an opportunity to show her woodcuts, Sonya abandoned her usual reserve of excuses.

Irene met the Jitney in her silver Volvo. Freyda, she announced, was looking forward to their little hen party. Stepping from Irene Cone's car to the Wiltshire's snow-dusted circular drive, Sonya felt a rush of annoyance. She saw no reason to demote herself to a bird simply because she was about to attend an occasion at which no man would be present.

The Wiltshire house was already decorated for Christmas. In the center of the living room a spruce tree reached to an impressive height under a cathedral pine ceiling. The ocean was the tree's distant backdrop. Branches were strung with white lights and hung with facsimiles of antique German and Swiss ornaments. Freyda invited Sonya to examine these in detail, which she did, honestly praising each but a plaster miniature of Joseph that she pronounced a lummox. On a marble coffee table was a huge bark basket piled high with pine cones and sprigs of evergreen laced with red ribbon. (This marriage of marble and bark, thought Sonya, was simply an affront.) Several hearkening angels presided from the stucco walls. The room was not at all suitable for unveiling her Zavin woodcuts. Yet this was apparently the room where they would spend the afternoon. Freyda had called a maid to bring in what turned out to be an English tea.

At Irene's prodding, Sonya and Freyda began to swap stories of the fifties art world in New York. Sitting in the Wiltshire's living room, Sonya felt obliged to validate all Freyda said. Freyda told the story of how Clyfford Still and Mark Rothko once refused an invitation to show in a group exhibit at Wiltshires because they believed that group shows devalued an artist's work. To her own horror, Sonya actually nodded her head, yes, wasn't this the most callow pose? To extend Freyda's point, she described one summer in Provincetown when the atmosphere had been so permeated by intense discussion that barely a canvas had been completed.

Privately—and publicly at Rensler—Sonya upheld Still and Rothko's refusal to exhibit for the pleasure of the affluent. Our muses are within us, she had told her students; if we take the lead from anyone but our inner voices, our work will slowly but surely corrode. Those who promote themselves have overridden their inner voices; they will never know the intoxication of true artistic freedom.

This afternoon in East Hampton, Sonya betrayed herself to nod vigorously when Freyda Wiltshire complained how silly those young abstract artists had been, how wildly talented but utterly, self-destructively silly. Yes, agreed Sonya, the crazy impulsiveness of young people often accounted for their ruin. She said this despite what she had just told her class at Rensler: "*Well*, if a young artist today can't write up a favorable profit-and-loss statement for a series of paintings, he simply won't paint them. Never mind the ideas that burn within him!"

Although Irene had invited the exchange of reminiscences, she now placed a scone on the linen napkin spread over her lap and stifled a yawn. "I heard about your peonies at auction," Freyda told Sonya. "We were all so pleased for you."

Sonya could not imagine who "we" was, but she thanked her. She thought that the large vase full of peonies was the most static pastel she had ever drawn.

"It's such a shame," Irene put in, "that Sonya must work at commissions all the time!"

"Some of them," said Sonya, who had not had a commission in three years, "are enormously challenging. It always depends upon the spirit of the sitter, you see. The more submerged it is, the more profound the challenge."

"At least you don't have to resort to teaching," said Irene. It was no surprise to Sonya that the two women took up George Bernard Shaw's view that those who could, did, and those who could not, taught. It was her own view.

"Look, my dear," Sonya said, "I took a liberty this afternoon. I brought my Zavin woodcuts. I think they would be of great interest to Wiltshires."

"Oh," said Freyda. "From the recent exhibit?"

"No. They're from earlier on. A great deal going on. Full of gesture!"

"Oh, *gesture*," moaned Freyda. "These young collectors don't care about gesture." She leaned forward. "They are terribly literal; what does gesture mean to them?"

Sonya nevertheless reached for the portfolio. What she found so irreconcilable was that the elegance of the woodcuts simply did not attract people. It was as if an entire generation had been born with no eye for elegance. Chaos and ferocity had replaced the lean poetry of several lines flying, then intersecting at precisely the right moment across a page. The Zavin woodcuts Sonya now revealed had been executed in homage to shooting stars, modern dances, bird migrations, branches colliding in a storm. They were woodcuts because their essential movements required the sharpest possible line, a line that did not touch a surface but embedded into it. Zavin had studied sumi-e brush technique under a Chinese master. Sonya had been amazed at how he had translated the taut delicacy of its rhythm into so blunt a medium as woodcut. At the same time Zavin had studied under the master, he had taken up yoga and applied his new methods of breathing to the process of sumi-e painting. The wonder about his woodcuts, then, the marvelous paradox, was that their lines were breaths—wispy meditations that did not culminate on the paper but somehow suggested that they would come to a natural death later, in another woodcut, or on another plane.

As Sonya turned over the prints, she recalled all Zavin had taught her about gesture. She recalled a long period in her life when the world was broken down to its vital gestures. It did not matter how many yachts and sunfish obscured the tugboat chugging up the Hudson; it was the tug's wake, and the wake alone, that created the gesture that became the picture.

"I can't say Wiltshires would be successful with these," said Freyda. "Although I might be interested in one or two. The storms might interest me. I think the storms might vastly improve the guest room."

Well, thought Sonya, the old dame might as well suggest I remove my heart and leave the rest of my body to rot on her Louis XIV armchair. "I'm sorry," she said. "It would be impossible for me to separate them. They are really several suites that rely upon each other, don't you think?"

"The important thing is what *you* think," said Freyda.

Sonya could not stand it when the people in power deferred. It was a pose meant to serve them while they came across as behaving with grace-under-pressure. Sonya found it thoroughly repulsive. She reached for a scone, then put it back when she felt its tired weight in her palm. Silence fell until Freyda spoke. Like her kind, thought Sonya, Freyda regarded a lively flow of conversation as the imperative constant of any gathering. "I just dread Christmas this year," she said. "On Christmas eve I'm flying to Lima." Then, for the benefit of

Sonya, "My son's an engineer there and he lives with his family right in the center of the city. The clamor is worse than you could imagine."

Irene began to talk about Monica and her family, and how they were all going to an inn in New Hampshire for Christmas; the children would cross-country ski.

The next Jitney for New York left in three hours. Just as Sonya began to seriously wonder how she would mask her contempt for these women and their trappings for that length of time, just as she was noting to herself, as she had for years, that most glowing women merely reflected the sheen from a thousand ornaments of convention, something occurred that caused them all to jump to their feet.

Roger Wiltshire, wearing a carelessly drawn gown and nothing underneath, wandered into the room. He brushed up against a brightly colored wooden sleigh ornament. A branch shook, rattling several tiny bells.

"Darling," said Freyda. The word was laden with intonation: stark fear, intimacy appalled at its own disclosure.

"There are three hooded men carrying messages of redemption in the bathroom," said Roger Wiltshire.

"Let's get back to bed, now," said Freyda. She moved towards him. "Where is Mrs. Stephens?" she asked. Then, shriller, "*Irene*. Where is Mrs. Stephens?"

"I don't know!" declared Irene, as if it were her fault the woman who was apparently Roger's nurse was missing.

Roger did not allow his wife to steer him. He turned and walked up to the portfolio of prints, still open on the marble coffee table. "Zavin," he said, and nodded, gaining recognition. Freyda cajoled, but Roger grew implacable. He closed his dressing gown and knelt before the prints. He turned each one over, fingering only the tips of their corners as he had probably done countless times before. He was silent, but the wildness that had assailed his features was slowly overtaken by a solemnity, the unreadable expression that must have for years accompanied his appraisals. He opened his mouth to speak, but speech failed him. Each time he turned over a print his expression more fully suggested the life that had abandoned him. The recovery of his deepest aesthetic responses, whether he had created them or bought them from what was sold from the critics of the day, so moved Roger that his face flushed a high color and he began to shake his head back and forth. For Sonya, it was as if Roger Wiltshire had stepped from his remote lair to take exactly what she took from Zavin's woodcuts—the primitive and essential gesture.

As Freyda and Irene led him back to his bedroom, Roger looked with incredulity into Sonya's eyes. This man, she thought, has been a victim. It was not his stroke she thought of; it was his life.

"I'm sure you need to attend to Mrs. Stephens," she said when Irene and Freyda returned. She rose on tipped toes. "If you don't mind calling me a cab, I'll just go back by the L.I.R.R." Then, because she too could convey grace-under-pressure, "I am always so impressed when I see a friend cope as admirably as you have."

In her apartment, Sonya paced through each room in succession. She switched on lamps as she went, rushed forth as if into someone's arms. In the final room, her studio, no one waited. At the corner was her clay bin, open and empty for several months. On the shelves and standing on pedestals on the floor were both bronzes and plaster casts of sculptures, busts and figures, many three decades old. Others were more recent, from the last five or ten years, and these were often on mythological themes, following her readings of Graves and Campbell and a period of closely studying Rodin. She replaced the Zavin portfolio to its drawer in her custom-made drawing cabinet. Then she sat down on Breuer's "Wassily," sprawling her legs over its canvas arm rests. The gesture so freed her from the constraints of the afternoon that she stood up to repeat it, to pivot herself in a way that surely would have compromised Irene and Freyda.

All right, she told herself, she had not done a commission in three years. She had lost that income, but had succeeded in removing herself from the hollow marketplace. Now she taught, and although there was the view that her teaching represented a reduced estate, its salary combined with the interest from Zavin's trust got her by. This was the time to start sculpting for herself again. This was the time to put aside that craving for security that becomes, she had told her class repeatedly, the noose around one's neck.

There were several coils of lead armature wire on one of the shelves, next to a sun-bleached skull of an opossum. Modeling boards were heaped in a stack on another shelf. She selected the one with the sturdiest iron support, and then began to fashion the pliable wire around it. When the armature felt right, she wrapped it around with thinner gauge aluminum wire. Then she stopped. She went to her file of supply house catalogues and filled out an order for thirty pounds of clay and grog.

The sky had fully darkened over Riverside Park by the time Sonya folded her order into an envelope. She wrapped up in a scarf and woolen cape and took the elevator downstairs. Mrs. Fine had just returned from the laundry room at the rear of the lobby. Toting a shopping cart full of housedresses, she rushed up to Sonya and took hold of her elbow. "I'm buying!" she declared. "My son's co-signing. We have an appointment with Dime Savings in the morning."

"How nice for you," said Sonya.

Mrs. Fine looked contrite. "What about you? If you can possibly manage, my son says it's like money in the bank."

"Oh, po*ssessions*," said Sonya. "They are the noose around one's neck."

She managed to get away, out to the icy December air. Up Broadway, on her way to mail her order, she thought of Mrs. Fine, ascending like a Chagall figure in a chintz house-dress to the class of the newly landed gentry. Then suddenly, ushered from nowhere, Otis Daley came into her thoughts. She recalled an appointment with him three weeks off, on New Year's Day. She was embarrassed that of all times to see him she had arranged their appointment on New Year's Day, a nationally recognized day of promise.

DEEP INTO the mid-December night Claire Rollins awoke not quite to the sound of her name, but to the urgent hiss that shore it up. Next to her bed stood Trudy, her fashion room-mate, with a Kollman security guard. Claire propped herself up on one elbow, and Trudy sat down beside her, encircling her shoulders with a tight grip. Trudy wore a Lanz nightgown, and Claire would later remember nothing so vividly as the invasion of its tiny pastel nosegays into her field of vision as Trudy spoke the words, "Your father, Claire. Your mother said he died."

Moments later, brushing her teeth in the bathroom, Claire thought how typical it was of Wanda to release the most vitally personal information to a stranger. She pieced together what had happened. Wanda had called Kollman, told the person who answered she had to talk to her daughter, it was an emergency, encountered the slightest hesitation, perhaps just the reminder that it was the middle of the night, and then proceeded to describe, in a shrill voice, the very guts of all there was to know. Wanda routinely delivered to people, to utter strangers, the flotsam of her unresolved business. Claire had often felt sorry for her mother's patients, the chronically or acutely ill who were easy prey for her tumble of excess facts. She had often laughed with Danny that in a few short weeks the poor sitting ducks had to hear more trifling detail than they had probably heard in a lifetime. Now the debris which Wanda routinely laid at the feet of strangers had turned out to include the news that Cole was dead. This news had transgressed across a chain of couriers to land flatly at Claire's nighttime feet.

At dawn, Claire rushed up to her mother at the South Orange bus depot. They clung to each other. In her mother's arms, Claire recalled the last time they had so embraced, several months before. They had drawn away when Claire realized she was too old to take refuge in her mother's arms, and Wanda saw she had no real business within her daughter's. This morning Claire held on. They both held on, listening to one another's labored breathing.

On their way back to Amanda's house, where Wanda had planned to stay until the divorce, Wanda said, "He died alone. In the spare bedroom."

"Jesus. Where was Adele?"

"Maybe they were on the outs. Mark my words, she'll disappear from the picture now."

Claire said nothing. They stopped at a traffic light.

"I bet," said Wanda, "he went off the low-cholesterol diet when he took up with her. I bet he went off the low-choles-.

terol and off the blood-thinner pills. She *accepted* him, she didn't care what shape he was in. He probably stopped trying with the tofutti, too. You may call that self-assertion, Claire, but I call it the very lowest morale."

The words meant nothing, but their tone was rich and tragic, a tone that the world owned but now lent to Wanda, clearly a widow of bitter circumstance. Wanda might have initially spilled her guts to a stranger, but now she kept up a front, and this sanguine front allowed Claire to let herself imagine what her mother really felt, knowing that her husband had died alone.

Wanda stopped the Chevrolet in front of Amanda's garage. "You don't have a father," she said at last.

"You don't have a husband," countered Claire.

This was their exchange. During Cole's sparsely attended funeral service and the days back in the old house that followed, they tried and failed to speak again of Cole. They were awkward on the subject of his "crisis," and they could not honestly deliver him from the months, years really, of torpor that had preceded it. Once, Wanda faintly proposed that Claire might like to move back home again. In a polite, almost regretful tone, Claire answered that she had better stick by her original commitment to herself.

"She fucking wanted me back *home* again!" Claire declared, clutching her throat with both hands.

Danny, who was leaving for Mexico that evening, drank Pepsi from a can and tapped his fingers on the windowsill. He had postponed his trip by two weeks to wait for a senior who was driving as far as Santa Fe.

"It's a compliment, Claire. Sal don't want *me*. No empty-nest syndrome there."

Claire plopped down on the studio bed. She had requested Danny's single during his leave of absence. Ordinarily, more senior Kollman residents would have received priority, but the Dean of Residence had indulged her because of Cole.

"You want me to leave?" asked Danny. "I could go downstairs and shoot some pool."

Claire looked at her canvas deck shoes. She slouched down and plunged her hands into her jeans pockets. She suddenly remembered Cole in the car in Kollman's parking lot, how he had fumbled with the two books of matches, how she could have put her hand on his shoulder but had not, out of miserliness. She remembered this and an upward current swept her windpipe, as if she were on a roller coaster in mad descent.

"No," she told Danny. "You don't have to leave." Then, just to hear herself say the words, "This room's officially yours for another four and a half hours."

"Right," said Danny. He wore a bright, embroidered vest. Across his back was heaven, a place of swirling clouds and floating lyres, from which Lucifer in miniature was being ejected by the sole of a foot. Danny had embroidered this vest himself, over the summer, had told Claire he would stretch and frame it and give it to her when he got sick of wearing it.

"Your dad was an alright guy?" asked Danny. "I mean besides the shit that went down this year?"

"Danny."

"*What*?" he demanded, spinning around.

"Nothing. Just the way you phrase things. Or don't phrase them."

"It's how I talk. You want a silver spoon, go to Tiffany's and buy one."

"You don't have to eat with a silver spoon to phrase a thought so people want to listen."

"So I'm not verbal."

"None of us are, if you haven't noticed. But you don't have to make a religion out of it."

"I can't believe this." Danny's voice cracked. "Your old man just died. I'm about to leave; I could get offed by guerrillas up from the Andes. Life's precarious, Claire. There you go—*precarious*."

Claire was silent. Danny stood over her. "I'm sorry," he said. "I'm gonna hang out downstairs."

Absently, Claire stared straight ahead, at his crotch. She looked up at him. "I need to get back to painting," she said. It had been her chant for years now, a focusing chant, a chant to put her on center.

Danny sat down beside her. He twisted the turquoise ring on his middle finger.

"Your beard looks good," she told him, touching it. "All filled out." She turned away.

"Wud'ya expect?" he asked. He hesitated a moment, looking at her. "Baby Huey cheeks?"

"You know, I didn't even *know* him. I mean, it was established, I established early on, that I didn't even like the man. He managed this department of insurance underwriters, okay? For the last ten years he's been writing a textbook on middle management. He talked about it at the *din*ner table, for Christ's sake, and he talked about the war all the time. Danny, it was so sad the way he talked about the war. One of those classic, pathetic, the-killing-years-were-the-best-years scenes. So I come up wanting to be an artist, and he gets livid, it scares him to death, and I get more insistent so I don't end up at nursing school with a bunch of Little Miss Muffets, and we establish this pose with each other. Me, the rebellious little ingrate and him the tyrant and bully. Things were about to change a couple of months ago, because of Adele. Things were about to change, I know it, he was going to see into himself, I felt it, I was just waiting in the background. It was okay that we both had this hate pose, wasn't it, Danny? I mean, he knew I was just waiting in the background, that I would be there for him if he called me up. He knew that, right? My father. If he would have expressed *one* self-doubt, one little acknowledgment that there are other lives in the world, like maybe that on another continent there's a Masai drummer who knows his stuff, you know what I mean? If he had *once* allowed for someone else, I would've been there in a shot. But he knew that, didn't he, Danny? He knew that if he ever got himself to the point of acknowledging, I would have been there in a shot."

Danny seemed unable to speak. Claire fell against his chest. They were quiet for a long while together. Occasional shouts came from the hall and a chord from a bass guitar seeped through the ceiling. Claire let Danny draw her in closer, press his mouth against hers. This time he was uncompromising, and she did not have enough faith in her awkward, renegade inner voice to resist when he began to slowly fondle her breasts, braless under her sweatshirt and tank top. As usual, her inner voice directed that this was not love, that for her the hand that encircled her breast must be the hand of someone for whom she felt not only tenderness but an absolute, body-and-soul approval. This time, though, she ignored her inner voice. She listened instead to a thousand outer voices disclaiming her romantic notions. She listened to the outer voices demanding that she who wanted to paint people at leisure must know, if not love, at least abandon. As Danny undressed her and then himself, as they got into the bed she would sleep in while he was in Mexico, these same outer voices pounded, first in her ears, then in her blood.

Afterwards, smoking a joint, Danny's embroidered jacket draped over her bare shoulders, one of these same outer voices spoke the single word, "thanks."

The next day, Saturday, Claire sat on Danny's bed and flipped through a book called *Painters of the French Countryside*. Danny had left for Santa Fe, where he would get a bus to Mexico City. He had pleaded with her to come with him, but she had insisted that what she needed was to get back into her painting—big time, she had said. Anyway, she had added, she was not the dropout type. Now there was a knock at the door. It was Trudy. She held onto the aluminum stand of a seven-foot-high set light.

"How *are* you?" she demanded.

"Fine." Claire looked at her and smelled nosegays.

"Oh, well. I was just concerned. Also, I have a favor."

"What?"

"Sarah, you know, my friend who wants to do theater lighting? She gave me this to return to A-V, but I have to go into town to see the new Geoffrey Beene line." Trudy blinked several times as she spoke. Claire had lived with her long enough to recognize this gesture. It always accompanied an earnest appeal. "I'm sorry," she added, "but could you?"

"Put it there," said Claire, gesturing to the wall beside her. "I'll get there when I get there."

"You're a doll," said Trudy, and turned on the heel of her velvet-rimmed boots.

Claire lifted her hand in acknowledgment, then closed the door, muttering in Danny's voice, "and you're the spoon-fed Duchess of Kollman."

The image of the pear-shaped wooden sailor in the editing box clinched it. It was Saturday, but Melina was on campus editing her film. Claire was on her way to the A-V room in Sandover Hall. She had looked to the right, inside the editing studio. There she thought she saw Melina's thick, wavy hair, wedge cut to lift just above her collar bone as she bent forward. She gripped the handle of each reel on the editing machine. So posed, her arms could have been imitating a bird in flight, and she peered intently at the tiny screen, filled with the parade of image and motion her hand had cranked out. The room was dim, but from the hall Claire recognized one of the three buoys they had filmed on the Sound back in October. The pear-shaped wooden sailor bobbed violently on the dark waves.

Claire returned the set light. There was no way back but past the editing studio. What an intensely private business, this previewing and editing of one's film. If someone interrupted her while she was painting, thought Claire, the counterbalance between the weights of her forms would surely explode into irretrievable chaos. She imagined her rage at the audacious intruder, and yet, her heart beating double-time, Claire stopped just inside the doorway to the studio.

"It looks good," she ventured from the threshold.

Melina switched off the light inside the editing box. "Hi!"

"I'm sorry. Is this a crucial point? How'd it come out?"

Melina got off her stool. "Oh, one segment was overexposed, but I'm working with the lab on it. Pretty good, actually. *You* were great. Your turns were right on the mark."

Claire looked down, then up again.

Melina approached her. "Listen, I heard. I'm terribly sorry. Really," she said, and reached out to hold Claire's hand. "Believe me."

Claire began to cry. After the first sob, she was able to stifle herself into a silent heaving, but this heaving was even worse; the pace of her grief butted senselessly against the pace of its expression. The sound that resulted was that of a trapped animal, a sound that would elicit from Melina the response Claire most feared—embarrassment. "I'm just confused," she finally said.

Melina stepped forward and held Claire's face in both her hands. "Of *course* you're confused."

Claire knew that now her eyes darted like those of a trapped animal. Melina held her close and stroked her hair and kissed her forehead. The loud beating of Claire's heart presented an awkward counterbalance to Melina's offhanded ease. If this awkwardness had appeared around the images in one of her paintings, Claire would have stayed up all night to fairly apportion the power between them. In painting, it seemed so very wrong that one form should be tortured by the grace of another.

"It'll take time," said Melina.

"I know," said Claire, consciously echoing Melina's purposeful tone. "I'll let you get back, now."

In the efficiency apartment late that night, Claire resumed her place in *Painters of the French Countryside*. The reproduction on the page before her was of Van Gogh's "First Steps," painted after a Millet. Claire had seen this picture many times at the Metropolitan. It struck her anew each time. Certainly it did not show the wealthy on holiday—this was after all Van Gogh. Yet the music and manner of the painting was all of a holiday. It showed a baby walking on unsteady legs towards its father. The baby's mother bent down, a gentle guide. The father had abandoned his work to encourage, with outstretched arms, this great new independence. Laundry dried on a fence. It was all rendered in impossibly luminescent strokes of a hundred different pale greens. Claire looked and looked. She was stuck somewhere between the picture's method and its content. Van Gogh's adamant and distinct strokes filled Claire's heart with the urgent message that she, she and everyone, must insist on all that stirred the senses. But she could not consider Van Gogh's strokes alone. She needed to examine *what* he painted—the father, the mother, the child, that constant triangle of rectitude. It was the triangle from which she came, the triangle where Danny, in time, would have her go.

DANNY STOOD for a moment before the glass front of a stall marked *Periódicos y Revistas*. What had so thrilled him about his first trip to Mexico was that, from the moment he had entered the fray at the *Terminal del Norte,* he knew that he had gone much further from Brooklyn than he had ever hoped to go. Now he stood before the newspaper stall and waited to be once again transported. First and most persuasive was the smell, the precise amalgam from two summers before—a blend of chiles, tortillas sizzling in oil, carbon monoxide fumes, and open sewers. It was these elements, apportioned in different degrees depending on the weather and time of day, that Danny had breathed in every moment of his last trip. In these first breaths at the bus terminal he gave himself time to distinguish each smell.

Next, his backpack resting against one leg and his duffel bag against the other, Danny watched. This was no Port Authority. There, the runaways and panhandlers had institutions behind them; they were field-tripping from halfway houses and SRO hotels. Here, the marginals were not buoyed up by the begrudging social conscience of the middle class. No, to Danny's way of thinking the marginals in Mexico had it better; they had *family*, family that carried them through shit times just as they themselves expected to be carried through their own spate of marginality. If they loved Mexico they loved it purely, because who could expect anything from Mexico, a mess of overturned dictatorships and upended revolutions? So Danny just stood a moment before the magazine stall, with its piles of comic-book novellas, and watched the people. A man wheeled a crippled woman who was tied to a handtruck. The rope was wound beneath the woman's breasts. She was family, maybe the man's cousin. A boy with cerebral palsy sold magic markers to a businessman. They were not family, but the businessman could have known someone like the kid— he bought anyway. An Indian woman, Danny guessed maybe Zapotec, sold *Chicles* and cotton candy the color and texture of ceiling insulation. A little girl hunched over from the weight of a baby bound in a *rebozo* sold bracelets. Danny's Spanish was elementary, but he thought she claimed the bracelets were made of eight metals and would cure a person of irregularity. All around him, people sold what no one needed. Buyers bought because they had themselves sold in bus stations, or because they believed.

Danny picked up his bags. He headed outside to find a *pesero* to take him to Chapultepec, where two summers before he had stayed in a youth hostel before going on to Oaxaca.

Squeezed next to him on the ride was a young man who read the address tag on Danny's backpack and smiled to reveal a gold rim around each of his front teeth. He had visited his cousin in the Bronx, he told Danny in mixed Spanish and English. There he had fallen a little in love with the cousin's roommate's girlfriend. Oh, yes, to him New York was the love city. The girlfriend had fallen madly in love with him, had begged him to stay. She had stolen away from the roommate's bed to come sleep with him on the cousin's second-hand sofa. Now the Mexican whispered to Danny that the roommate could maybe not fuck so well, he had himself gotten a letter from the girlfriend every day since his return. Throughout the story, Danny nodded but did not look at the young man. When the *pesero* stopped not far from the hostel and Danny composed himself with his bags on the sidewalk, he wondered for a moment what this man, Latino *machismo* incarnate, would say about two years of pining for a girl who did not return his love. He knew what the man would say: *mujer. Mujer* because Danny cried alone at night, *mujer* because he pleaded and wheedled before Claire, *mujer* because jealousy drove him not to violence but to the refuge of the bed covers. To Mexico, thought Danny looking at a display of mangos sculpted into engorged blossoms, he was just another *mujer*, maybe a *madre*, at once worshipped and spat upon for her loyalty to a nation of unworthy sons.

But hey, Danny reminded himself, he did not come all this way to obsess over how some nose-picking motherfuckers with no visible means of support tabbed up his masculinity. He walked away from the mango blossoms. He got himself set up at the hostel, and set off for San Angel, thirty minutes away on the metro.

The metro, Danny was reminded, could belong to some modernized Aztec empire. Riding on the Mexico City metro, who would guess that the government above choked its citizens with car exhaust and chemical fumes? The floors were marble. Perfectly crafted replicas of Tenochtitlán were displayed inside showcases at transfer stations. Potted palms thrived beneath slanted skylights. Station names tributized ancient history. Shale lined the tracks over which the train's rubber wheels passed at high speed, trailing an obsequious hush. Not one piece of trash lay on the shale. Men with tree-branch brooms swept among the throngs as if they were on a forsaken island. Take two pictures, thought Danny. Show them to the New York Transit Authority. Which belongs to the Third World?

Danny got out at the suburb of Coyoacan and took a bus to the El Carmen Church in San Angel. He had seen a thirty-second clip on an entertainment news show that talked about the mummies at the church monastery. He had never seen a real mummy. As boys, he and his Coney Island friends had bound themselves up in Johnson & Johnson gauze, cutting out holes for the purpose of seeing one another's eyeballs roll from side to side. They did not cut out breathing holes, which would spoil the pleasure of hearing one another's muffled pleas for release. They had spent hours discussing mummies, their tones reverent. Each had assumed his future would be too provincial to include a real mummy.

This trip to San Angel, then, was Danny's triumph. His heart beat in celebration of himself. He passed quickly through the rooms containing mural remnants to descend the basement steps. Planks had been set over the floor to preserve its ceramic tiles. The planks were rotting from the dampness. Upright wooden coffins lined the room. To look inside them, Danny had to mount a series of stone steps. The cadavers were seventeenth-century priests and nuns, preserved through some mysterious element in the soil. Sandbags to absorb moisture had been wedged inside the cases, under arms or next to groins. Danny studied each body scrupulously. Layers of decomposed skin, unrecognizable as skin, could have been the folds of some new miracle fiber. A few mummies had teeth. The jaws of some were dropped in horror, as if they had died mid-scream. Others were compliant and slack.

Danny took pictures with his second-hand Minolta. He had two concurrent thoughts. One was that he should send a picture of Sister Patricia Marie's cadaver to Rick Falzone, an old friend from Coney Island Avenue and parochial school. The other thought stabbed him in the gut—that no barrage of his enamel-painted *retablos*, whether profane or full of indebtedness to the world, could save Danny from becoming the gruesome parody of the human body before him. His legs trembled deep inside, muscle against bone. They trembled as he climbed up the narrow stone steps to the church museum and out again to the courtyard. He rested against a crumbling fountain. His legs trembled still as he adjusted and readjusted his camera strap.

Back at Chapultepec Park, Danny entered a little place with greasy plastic tablecloths. It was after three, and people ate *comida corrida*. Tables were heaped with food, but Danny just ordered eggs with salsa and a beer. Although he took out a battered notebook to sketch the mummies at El Carmen, his attention strayed to the table in front of him. It was crowded with men who spoke Spanish in a tone so furtive Danny could not make out their words. The subject, though, was clearly the waitress, a *mestiza* with jet black hair and light skin. She wore a cardigan sweater she had attempted to button over her large breasts. The gaps between the buttons might have prompted the men's voices to go undercover, but their expressions were openly salacious. Jesus, thought Danny, these Mexican women must have the skin of armadillos. He began to sketch a *retablo: Señorita* Maria Juarez thanking Saint Francis for helping her to grow the skin of an armadillo.

The waitress smiled when she set down Danny's eggs and told him to enjoy them. She smiled indulgently, recognizing him as a *Norteamericano* who would eat in an uneasy spirit of experimentation. Danny looked steadily at her face, imagining she understood that he condemned the behavior of the men at the table ahead. He was sure the waitress knew she was safe with him. That was all it took—the slightest hint in her expression that she understood Danny to be trustworthy, and he was in her sway. Other men got turned on by the curve of a breast or the shrewd narrowing of an eye. Danny's pulse began to race at the first sign that a woman trusted him. For this trait, too, Mexican men would call him *mujer*. Danny remembered all too well what had first attracted him to Claire. She had told him she loved him like a brother. He had felt first pride, then great hope, because he had made such an incredulous girl feel at home.

The waitress now pointed to the postcard of Sister Patricia Marie's cadaver. She giggled. "We become ghosts," she said. Danny laughed also. He liked this restaurant. He spent the rest of the afternoon there, sketching and taking notes in his pad, reading in a paperback he had brought about the torture techniques used in religious rites of the Middle Ages. Around suppertime he ordered another Dos Equis and two enchiladas. When the waitress set down his beer, she asked him formally how he was tonight—as if he had gone away and then returned. When he asked about her, she blushed. Moments later, placing his food on the table, she asked if he knew about the famous *momias* at the museum near Guanajuato. No, he said, but he planned to visit Guanajuato. Too bad he had missed the Day of the Dead there, she sighed.

Mexico really gets death, Danny confided in a rush of ebullience. His poor Spanish and translated American colloquialism confused her. Danny backed up to the elementary. "*Cómo se llama?*"

"Oh! *Ana!*" she answered. Gratitude flooded her tone. Awful as it was, Danny had to acknowledge that he was drawn to Ana by her excessive show of respect. In a hushed tone she asked if maybe later he would like to take her to a better place, a café in the Zona Rosa, if he would like to buy her a *cerveza* there.

As gray clouds moved heavily over the black sky, Danny and Ana sat talking at a table among others on the sidewalk. Ana said she loved the Zona Rosa for how its windows burst with styles from the rest of the world. Danny answered that this was what he hated about it, the two-bit commercialism that could make it anywhere. It was the old district of Mexico City that Danny found unbelievable. Didn't all Mexicans cherish this part of the city? Weren't they incredibly proud of their ties to the Aztecs? Ana, who only half understood Danny, shook her head vehemently, no. Old Mexico City made her want to cry. At this, her eyes momentarily clouded. It was then, when they both fell silent, that the curve of Ana's breast and the narrowing of her eye began to take precedence over her trusting gaze. They ordered two more *cervezas*.

It began to drizzle. Ana told Danny she had an uncle who owned a boarding house not too far away, still in the Zona Rosa. As she spoke, Ana watched the activity on the street. The rooms were very clean, she said. Her uncle catered to *Norteamericanos*. There was bottled water in every room. Danny reached for Ana's hand. He was not worried, as in Brooklyn he would have been, what she might think about the tufts of dark hair that grew over his knuckles. In Mexico, hairy knuckles did not give pause.

Once inside a small room in her uncle's boarding house, Ana poured Danny some water. She watched the clear flow spill into the glass as she told him her price. The water sparkled inside the glass. Danny felt himself go numb. An accelerated pulse fluttered in his throat. There was no question but that he would pay. He would pay simply as his penalty for not having suspected all along. Without counting them, Danny laid several crumbled peso notes on a cheap, ornate bedstand. It was still his first day in Mexico. He was still unused to the value of another culture's numbers, still jolted by the sight of all those thousands adding up to so little.

On his way back to Chapultepec just after dawn, Danny followed the sound of bells into a morning mass. He wandered quietly about the colonial church. His red high-top sneakers against the ancient stone floor marked him as a tourist, but no one paid attention. In Mexican churches, his presence was always met with indifference, as though he were just some part of the great design gone astray. He stopped and looked ahead. The altar was dwarfed beneath a dome that looked to be a hundred feet high. Pigeons circled beneath cracked stained glass windows. A priest in white robes chanted in what sounded to Danny like a combination of Latin and Spanish. Robed men on either side of him swung incense burners on heavy chains. Danny moved to stand quietly at a rear pew. He gazed around the church, in awe of its scale and of the homemade offerings of believers throughout the centuries. There were black Christs in dusty cases and standing mannequins like the ones he had seen in Rensler's fashion studios, except gray and cracked and draped in stiff habits. There were pictures of saints covered with silver *milagros.*

Music from an unseen organ began to fill the church. It might have been the sound of this music that signaled Danny to put aside his delight at the grotesquery of the church's holdings. He began to imagine what the worshipers felt. There was not the slightest doubt in his mind that religion was the opium of Mexico, and yet he now became a Mexican Catholic, knowing nowhere else in which to purge the disgrace of having paid for Ana than beneath the vaulted ceiling of this church.

Just as the organ held a long note, just as Danny felt a swell of despair rise in his throat, a loud clattering came from behind. The priest kept chanting. The worshipers did not move. Ah, thought Danny, they know what's going on, it's going to be a passion play! A martyr dragging chains will limp to the altar. The noise continued, but did not come closer. Still, no one turned. No one was curious. The organ kept playing, the priest kept chanting, the worshipers joined in refrain. Finally, walking on the balls of his feet in his high-topped Keds, Danny crept towards the noise.

A very old man dressed in black had unlocked the sliding door of the church's ancient rosewood repository. Offerings in the form of hundreds of peso coins spilled forth into a metal safe the old man held between palsied hands. Just like last night, thought Danny—there was no place too sacred for money to roll.

 OTIS DALEY spent Christmas day working in his office at Rensler.

Ever since he had been a boy growing up in a suburb of Detroit, Otis had felt funny about vacations. He felt they were not for him. For three summers during junior high, he had tutored inner city children in math. He had spent every summer morning in a school library with heavy wire mesh covering its windows, trying to keep fourth graders from flicking rubber bands at glossy photos of Frederick Douglass and Harriet Tubman.

Still, at age fifty-five, Otis was not clear about what he did and did not deserve. Deep down he continued to suspect a connection between performance and entitlement. He knew what some of the Rensler kids, Tito and the others, would say about this. Overdeveloped conscience, they would say. Drop it, Daley. But from where Otis stood, it seemed his circumstances never allowed for leisure time. During this Christmas vacation, for instance, Otis intended to spend a lot of time at his office because things were just not right at Rensler. First there was the deficit problem. Like so many other private colleges, Rensler would have to borrow from Peter to pay Paul, and this required the tightest of management. There was also the problem of flagging enrollment. Moreover, it seemed to Otis there had been a higher than usual dropout rate this year. Danny Vincent, for instance, that curious-looking boy who whipped out *retablos* as if he were the people's artist of Mexico and not a half-Irish, half-Italian kid from Coney Island—*he* had just dropped out.

What really kept Otis in his office on Christmas day, though, was his deep belief in Rensler. Its instructors were anything but dusty academics. The professional art world was continually pumping energy into Rensler. In the commercial disciplines, the instructors had their fingers on the pulse of things. A Broadway show poster designed by one Rensler instructor appeared on bus shelters all over the city. The fellow in charge of advertising design just taught for love; he made a hundred and fifty thousand a year designing stockholder reports and pharmaceutical ads. As for the fine arts, well, here Otis was more emotional. Despite how much technology had contributed to the making of art in recent years, Otis believed it was essential for painters, sculptors, printmakers, even for multi-media and performance artists to jeopardize their peace of mind every time they began a new piece. Old-fashioned though the belief was, he thought that artists had to keep the courage to be vulnerable, to flounder for years if necessary in order to finally say what they must. That was why he hired older artists such as Sonya Barlow—to set an example for the young kids coming of age during an age when art was fast becoming big business. They needed to see veterans of the purist school, artists who had pulled through when lean times were the norm. Artists from the trenches. Otis wanted to make sure that Rensler would always be there to support these artists. So he stayed in his office working all Christmas day.

Finally, at six-thirty, Otis left to drive into Manhattan. Three weeks earlier, after she had received his letter, Nora had called him at Rensler to invite him to have Christmas dinner with her. Typically, her tone had been neutral. She had added no more than, "I think we should see each other."

"Well," she said when Otis emerged from the elevator.

"Yes. Hello."

Her new haircut, thought Otis, was too short, cropped close to her head and shaved around her ears—like some teenage ruffian's, in his opinion. She had had one of those deliberately unnatural streaks put in. This one was a sort of purplish-red. She wore large triangular earrings with a burst of Kandinsky-like forms floating on white ceramic glaze.

"I like your earrings," said Otis.

"Thank you. And thank you for coming."

"You said you wanted to see me," he stated simply. He was in the doorway now, looking at her face for the first time. He had no wish to discuss anything with Nora but the terms of their imminent divorce, and yet his arms stretched out to enclose her. It was true, he no longer wanted to be married to her. When he looked at her familiar face, though—the smile lines around the corners of her mouth, the high, slightly protruding forehead—his attraction was simply Pavlovian.

"I thought I'd do salmon, Oats," she said, gingerly drawing away. "Not very Christmasy, but light." Oats was Nora's private name for Otis.

"Fine." These decisions had always been hers. She seemed so comfortable in making them that Otis never thought to question her. Now he said nothing. What did it mean, that she had called him Oats?

"Of course, I did make one concession," she said, and pointed to three votive candles in crystal holders beneath the leaded casement window.

"Just the right touch," remarked Otis. What was this about? For how long would he be expected to behave in anticipatory politeness? After all, what was to come had everything to do with the way Otis should now behave. And what about Nora? This light, overly delicate touch of hers; he recognized this touch from many years ago, before their marriage. It was as if

Nora had believed a feminine touch should be like the gradual alighting of a butterfly. The message this touch had naturally translated to Otis, whose caresses had been eager and full, was that he was a brute. Together, it had taken them some time to adjust to and welcome the style of each other's touch.

"Please sit," said Nora. She departed and returned with a scotch and soda, his drink. She had not even asked. This room, the meal to come, the drink, it all bore the earmarks of an attempted reconciliation. Yet Nora betrayed not the slightest nervousness. Otis knew full well the signs of her nervous distress, the audible quiver in her voice, the sudden moment when her eyes brimmed with tears before she regained control. She betrayed none of these signs now. She sat a comfortable distance away on the linen-covered sofa. She watched him with his drink.

"How's the new business?" he asked.

"Fine. Thriving, really. There's a great need, you know. People can't write. They don't want to, really. They say they do, but it's the ideas, not the words, they really want to get across. That's where we come in."

Otis nodded. He shifted his glass within the rim of its coaster on the coffee table before them. Nora drank Perrier. "Of course," she said, "I've missed several weeks in the office now. I'll be going back on Monday."

Otis looked at her. "You were away?" He could not believe they were having this little chat. It was not like Nora to delay getting to the point.

"I've had a mastectomy," she said.

There were several words in modern medical vocabulary that Otis could not hear without feeling a jolt run up his body— the vibrations from their sound somehow set off his adrenalin. For a moment, he was not sure if mastectomy was one of those words. He was unable to join the word to its meaning. In the vague attention he had paid to women's health words, he had often confused mastectomy with mammogram. Otis was unmercifully disoriented; he simply could not now remember which word carried the jolt.

Nora threw back her head and ran her fingers through her hair, an affectation from her Mount Holyoke days. "I've already had one round of chemo," she said. This time she had meant to draw attention to her hair.

"My god."

"I'll tell you this, it's every bit as grueling as they say."

"My god. I'm so sorry. I'm more than sorry. If I knew what to say...believe me, I'd say it. Why didn't you call me?"

"We go along pretending to be with people," said Nora. "We marry, we have jobs, friends, children. Then something happens and we see it's all a masquerade. This togetherness."

Otis looked determinedly at her face. He knew Nora would be wearing the best prosthetic bra sold. He flashed ahead to some time in the future when his eyes would wander from her face. No matter when this time would be, he saw it only as a moment of profound invasion.

"Interesting you said children," he remarked irrelevantly. They had decided years before not to have children. They did not believe in bringing up children in the city, and they both wanted to live in the city. In the end, they simply had not wanted children as much as their friends had.

"Well," said Nora, the vigor draining from her expression, "I'm just talking."

"I guess we're both...just talking."

Nora went into the kitchen, turning on the news for Otis to watch before she left. It was highly inappropriate, his watching the news, but Nora appeared to have planned it, so Otis complied.

She returned with the salmon. Otis helped her carry out a bowl of new potatoes and plates of Caesar salad. They began to eat, each slowly, without speaking. When Nora knocked her glass of Perrier awkwardly against her china dinner plate, Otis took hold of her wrist. He rushed around to her side of the table and held her. She was stiff; she did not hold him back.

"I read your letter," she said.

"Jesus, Nora. You know I wouldn't have sent it."

Still she did not yield. Otis returned to his place.

"Look," she said. "Let's remember, *I* left you. I don't mean to be cruel, Oats, but we have long since become strangers. I could have written you the sort of letter you wrote to me years ago. I just *didn't*," she added pointedly. "Believe me, my cache of accusations brims over."

Otis recalled his letter to her. He had been so proud of it, had applauded its liberating effect on him. Now it seemed insufferable. "I'm sure it does," he conceded. "I'm quite sure it does."

"My stand is very simple. I want to continue my life here as it has been. I don't need more stress now. I'd like to just put the divorce on hold for a while."

"Of course. For as long as you want." Otis realized he did not know what her "life as it has been" meant. He knew nothing of the details of her daily existence, which had departed so much more from her old routine than had his. It would be unthinkable to ask for details now.

Before Otis left, right before Nora opened the door to the elevator vestibule, he said, "I am here. Always here. Just call."

At 7:30 the next morning, the day after Christmas, Otis was back in his office going over some plans for the spring fundraising auction. More than ever before, the idea of vacation leisure time repelled him. Yet he could not concentrate on Sid's progress report. A wildly irrational notion repeatedly overturned in his mind. He had written a letter to Nora that he had felt at the time to be searingly truthful. Now, three weeks later, she had only one breast. Around the time Otis disclosed the worst he had perceived about her character, a precious part of her body had been cut away. Otis's attention wavered between the details of Sid's report (Old Harding had donated one of those god-awful sepia nature drawings, Sid had parenthetically cried) and the wholly visceral suspicion that his letter, his finely wrought character assassination, had caused his wife to lose her breast.

At 10 o'clock, Otis called his broker at Merrill Lynch. He arranged to sell his long-held utilities stocks, to put the money into a completely liquid account. There, he could get to it at a moment's notice.

JANUARY

THE CLAY HAD arrived. On New Year's Eve, to the screech of paper blowers unfurling and drunks yelling out the windows of their apartments along Riverside, Sonya unpacked it. After she mixed in the grog—fifteen percent was what she liked—she wedged. She laid out a large sheet of clay, about an inch thick, and stamped the entire surface, alternating one thumb with the other. She wet the grog, spread it over the clay, and began to knead. She kneaded the entire mass with the heels of her hands. For some time, she rocked away.

She adored this rocking. It embraced some of the best qualities of sculpting itself. It was both muscular and meditative. Of course, it lacked any cerebral involvement, but there were times for Sonya when cerebral involvement detracted from the animal thrill of it all. What would the art world say about this? "Oh," they would say, "*that* explains it. The light always goes out for a reason."

To override this thought, Sonya vigorously threw the flattened clay against the wire stretched across her wedging table.

Then she slapped together the resulting pieces, and rocked away again. Perhaps she rocked for too long, taken up with thoughts of Zavin, how he used to watch her wedge, sometimes drawing her, going on about the beautiful laborer—Millet's sowers, Van Gogh's potato pickers.

As skyrockets exploded in the air, sending a cascade of star sparks over Sonya's lovely river, Zavin might have been right there in her studio, watching alongside her.

New Year's morning, Sonya wanted nothing more than to get to the fresh clay in her bin. But her calendar, the brand new one with a different Matisse cut-out for each month, was clearly marked—lunch with Otis Daley. She had forgotten the appointment, and now she was furious. She wished she had left some clay for mixing, such was the need for her to pound out her frustration.

It was Sonya's well-kept secret that she abhorred responsibility. Here she was, a seventy-two-year-old woman (also a well-kept secret, easier to effect because of her exceptional complexion and taut musculature), who became a recalcitrant child in the face of obligation. Still, her defiance was sometimes a burden to her. Every time she had to do something for which she had no taste, it was necessary to cajole herself endlessly, or to pound her anger out on wet clay. This morning Sonya did a double session of yoga to lure herself into a more yielding attitude. It would be terribly embarrassing if anyone knew what she went through in order to meet the most rudimentary obligations. The luxury of living alone, though, had protected her from the necessity of exposing this and other mortifications.

They were to meet at the Museum Café, a glass-enclosed sidewalk restaurant near the Museum of Natural History. Bundled up in silk long underwear, a thick woven tunic, and a fur-lined cape, Sonya walked her brisk walk to Central Park West. There was an argument, she supposed, that the gracious thing would have been for her to have invited Otis to her apartment for lunch. She began to bristle at the thought. Why should she spend her entire morning, valuable work time, worrying over and planning just the right meal, preparing it, making an artful table arrangement, all for this man who held the absurd position of being her boss? And what if he had called this appointment in order to evaluate her performance at Rensler? Think how humiliating it would be to listen to his reproaches while they ate her wonderful vichyssoise and crab-filled pastry puffs! Sonya was so lost in conjuring this scenario she did not notice Otis just inside the café's entrance. When she swung the door open, she knocked into his arm.

"Oh, I *beg* your pardon! How clumsy," she said.

Otis Daley seemed to be in a bit of a fugue state. He smiled and extended his hand to shake Sonya's. He did not appear to have felt the blow to his arm. Sonya wondered about his deep distraction. It occurred to her that she might be fired. She rather enjoyed her classes. In her survey of modern art class she was able to share many stories Zavin had shared with her. But it was true that in her sculpture studio her students had thus far only carved the most basic shapes out of serpentine. The problem was that Sonya was a seventy-two-year-old woman who had made her life in art. Her recent appearance in the classroom was not part of the destiny she had envisioned for herself. No matter what the world thought, Sonya persisted in thinking of herself as one of those who could.

When they were seated, Otis ordered a scotch and soda. He said that it was uncharacteristic of him to drink at lunch, but today was a holiday, wasn't it? Sonya, who never drank at all, ordered a white wine. Well, she said, now they could properly toast in the New Year. (What sort of beast, she wondered, would fire someone with whom he has just toasted in the New Year?)

Otis began their appointment by telling Sonya about Rensler's Director of Development, Sid Casner. He praised his ingenuity, his tireless work habits, his deep commitment to Rensler. Then, emerging slightly from his curious state of inertia, he explained Casner's idea for a spring auction.

Sonya knew what was coming. "It's a marvelous idea, and I'm sure it will be very successful. But you know all my sculpture studies are with their commissions."

"I see," said Otis. He was quiet while the waiter placed his order of quiche before him. Steam rose and fogged up his horn-rimmed glasses. Otis veered back. "Well, I'm sorry to hear that. But haven't you also worked in pastels?"

At least he had the taste not to mention those damned peonies again, thought Sonya. "I did pastels only for a short while. They are all in private collections, I'm afraid."

This was not true. Some of her pastels were in collections, but many others, abstractions of the ginkgo trees on Riverside and the violent night storms she had drawn from the window where she and Zavin had stayed years ago in the Hamptons—these were hung in simple birch frames in her studio and living room. They set off her busts and figures perfectly, and turned Sonya's home into a triumphant collaboration between nature and human beings. This collaboration had taken Sonya many years to achieve. It was a gathering of her most articulate offspring. Their compliments to one another charged back and forth, vitalizing the air of her home, blessing it with luck. The idea of removing a single pastel appalled her.

Otis cut into his quiche. "I can't say I'm not disappointed," he said, "but it's nice to hear you're included in so many collections."

This appeared to be the end of the matter. Sonya was pleased. She lifted her wine glass to her lips and took a sip. It was pleasant to be sitting here, watching a light snow fall onto the sidewalk. She settled back to consider this man from whom she had just wrangled herself from obligation. For a college president, he was quite unimposing. Best of all, he had the good sense to give Sonya her rein, to trust that her experience would guide her wisdom in the classroom. Yes, Sonya decided, Otis Daley had a discreet soul she could trust.

"Have you been enjoying your holiday?" she asked.

"Oh. Well—"

Sonya was unsure how to proceed. She waited. Otis pushed aside the crust on his plate, looked about uncomfortably.

"Sometimes it's hard to wind down just because the calendar says we should," she said. As usual, she did and did not want to pry. She did, because as always she was dying to know what made people tick. She did not, because she had no wish for people to know what made her tick.

"Actually," said Otis uneasily, "I'm afraid it's been anything but enjoyable. My wife found out she has cancer."

Cancer was something Sonya managed to contemplate as little as possible. Years ago she had had a benign tumor removed from her breast. The scar was barely noticeable.

"To be perfectly frank," Otis continued, "it was a particular shock, because we have been separated for several months. I only found out after the mastectomy."

At the word mastectomy, Sonya flinched. She felt a throb, an insult like an actual blow to her own breast. She leaned forward, cupped her chin in her palm to let Otis know he had her complete attention.

"Well," he sighed, the fugue state appearing to overtake again, "I guess we'll just have to see. I guess it'll be one day at a time."

"Your wife must be aggressive!" burst out Sonya. "She must fight every step of the way. You must help her. The role of the mind is paramount. This has been proven. There are schools of thought. There are lectures. Have her go to one of the good meditation centers. There are diets. One must *participate*." With these words, Sonya felt herself emerge into her best self. She did not address the business of Otis's separation. Really, it was the merest trifle. And Sonya wanted also to reveal a discreet soul that could be trusted.

They spoke about Nora awhile longer. Otis ordered coffee and dessert. Sonya excused herself. She had an idea, and she needed some time for it to gel. She went into the bathroom and washed her hands for minutes. By the time she emerged from the stall, her heartbeat had picked up in anticipation.

When she passed the waiter, Sonya ordered coffee. "I have a proposal to make," she said, resuming her seat. "In connection with your auction."

"Fine. I'd like to hear it."

"I will donate my portfolio of Zavin woodcuts with the stipulation that Rensler and I split the proceeds."

Otis looked up in surprise. "What a splendid offer!"

I have broken through the fugue, thought Sonya triumphantly. "I would like to see Rensler thrive," she said. "I'm sure Zavin would have, also."

"This is terrific. I can't wait to report back to the Board. They'll be thrilled."

"I think it's a lovely little solution," said Sonya, rising. "And now, I have many pounds of newly mixed clay awaiting me."

On her walk home, Sonya fully considered what she had just done. Perhaps if she had waited, the market for her Zavins would have improved. If she had bided her time, perhaps they would have fetched their true value, enabling Sonya to buy her apartment. But as she turned onto Riverside and a flurry of snow whirled into her face, she had a startling realization. At age seventy-two and in a compromised situation, she had just made an offer whose generosity exceeded self-interest. She had made it during one of those graced moments in which a person is startled by her own unfathomed reserves.

 SHE'S JUST being well-bred. This was Danny's voice in Claire's thoughts.

Melina had asked Claire to her parent's house in Greenwich for the weekend. Danny's voice had invaded. Hey, they ooze manners, don't they? Your old man pops off, here comes the gracious invitation. Come site Orion from our gable! Ice fish in our Sound! Taste our Paleolithic wines! Split your sides on our urbane wit!

If she were being honest, Claire would have to admit that Danny would not have gone this far. He would never have said "your old man pops off." But tonight, packing a bag at Danny's single at Kollman, Claire did not want to be entirely honest. She wanted Danny to denounce Melina so she could denounce him. She had not heard from him since he left for Mexico. After what happened between them, Claire knew he had hoped she would follow him to Mexico. The very idea that she would drop her whole life to trail him around Mexico was preposterous. (What was her "whole life," Claire would have to ask herself if she were being honest. Her whole life was cast into a future in which she stood before one of her canvases and experienced precisely the sense of well-being that came over her looking at Caillebotte's "The Floor Scrapers" or Degas' "The Milliner.")

At the Irwins' on Saturday morning, Melina told Claire that she had forgotten the guest rooms were being repapered. She opened the doors to these rooms facing the Sound. In both, the old paper had been steamed off and bright Laura Ashley prints began to creep up the naked plaster walls. Huge curlicues of the old paper (those horrid gardenias, said Melina) littered the hooked rugs. Glue-spattered drop-cloths were spread over the canopied beds and marble-topped vanities.

"We'll put you with me for now," said Melina, setting down Claire's bag in her room down the hall. She closed the door before Claire could see inside.

Selina and Kevin were in China, negotiating on a collection of porcelains from the Ming dynasty. The Irwins were antique dealers with showrooms on East 12th Street in Manhattan and in Paris and Buenos Aires. They went on several buying trips a year, leaving Melina and Regina to occupy the Greenwich house together. Because she commuted back and forth to Rensler, Melina said she sometimes did not see her grandmother for several days at a time.

Downstairs in the sunroom, Regina sat on the porch swing. Claire and Melina joined her, taking up two rattan chairs with upholstered pads that matched the pattern on the swing.

"Well, dears. Tell me. Tell me what is going on in that Bohemian school of yours."

Claire found this heartbreaking. Day in and day out Regina sat alone in this big house, yet when she finally found herself being attended to, she focused on the girls' lives. Claire wondered what she did all day. She wondered what enabled Regina to get out of bed each morning and dress herself so formally. It was obvious from the smoothness of her linen dress above and below its matching belt that Regina wore a corset. She also wore nylon stockings and cloth flats dyed the same lavender as her dress. Her hair was held by crocheted netting into a loose bun at her neck, and there were magenta butterflies in repose on her ear lobes. She sat with her elbow on the arm rest and her head bent against two fingers. Claire wanted to draw her. She knew how the Impressionists would handle this aged coquette on the chintz-covered porch swing. Unquestionably, they would flatter her.

They talked together for about an hour. Claire noticed that Melina provided her grandmother with only the scantest information about her life at Rensler. Regina looked out at the Canada geese on the Sound. She talked about the courting habits of the geese in Ottawa, where she had spent her childhood. Then she said she could not wait until spring, when she could tend to her little garden once more. Oh, she declared, she simply lived for that garden! Claire noticed a stern look pass over Melina's face.

"Remember your mother with that vine last summer?" asked Regina.

Melina just nodded and fiddled with a loose reed on the edge of her chair. She said nothing, but Regina began a story. She said that last summer Selina had gotten a bee in her bonnet about a vine twisting around the mammoth forsythia by the breakwall. From morning to night, everyone had wondered who would prevail, the parasitical vine or Selina. In telling the story, Regina stressed over and over her daughter's physical power and her determination. She turned to Claire. This was how Selina approached everything, she confided. She set herself a challenge and did not rest until she overcame it. Regina's eyes flashed with pride as she told how that night, her hair a mess and her muddy shirt littered with slender yellow petals, Selina had emerged victorious. She had dragged up to the sunroom steps the fifty-foot vine she had methodically freed from each branch of the sagging forsythia. Regina paused, gloating at the girls. Her smile faded as she added, "If the vine had been choking *me* inch by inch, I just wonder. Don't you, Melina?"

Melina stiffened. She told her grandmother she wanted to show Claire Pebble Beach. They excused themselves.

Putting on her coat in the mud room a moment later, Claire said, "Jesus."

"I know," Melina answered.

Pebble Beach was a half mile from the Irwins' house. Melina explained that all the residents of the private Anchor Point paid maintenance taxes for Pebble Beach, as well as for a common duck pond she would show Claire later. The beach was a small curve of shore that had been laid with pink and gray pebbles. There was a dusting of snow now, and the dim sunlight picked up various hues of the pebbles and snow, creating a pointillistic effect. Beyond, the Sound was deep gray and rolling black shadows.

They sat on a log by the beach. "Actually," said Melina, "I think the episode with the vine was deeply sexual. I'm sure everyone, including my father, thought so, too. But of course no one would say."

With the tip of a branch, Claire sifted through some pebbles. Up until now she had used every reserve of discipline to make herself the observer. The ease with which Melina said, "deeply sexual," however, disrupted this detachment. There was no denying that the catch in Melina's voice betrayed an emotion as far from nervousness as could be imagined. Upon hearing it, Claire could not disclaim the fragile and electrifying chill that ran up the underside of each arm.

Claire had never seen dawn break over water. Quietly, she stepped out of bed and went to Melina's third-floor window. The Sound was no longer gray with black shadows. It flickered with a luminescence that could not be called white, nor even identified as highlights. The flickers were beyond the colors of a palette. They were auras. They shone the most intensely over distant ice floes, and at the tip of the lighthouse. Claire imagined the three unseen buoys: the bell, the pear-shaped sailor, the cone of iron rings. Melina, she thought, would love to film the buoys in this cold radiance.

Three sea gulls dove into the Sound, then emerged. Claire noticed a pair of binoculars on the dresser by the window, but did not pick them up to see what the gulls had caught. There was something forbidding about these binoculars; it would be presumptuous to pick them up. She returned to bed. Melina stirred, drew Claire in. "Are you upset?" she asked. "Are you freaked?"

Claire was embarrassed by the palpable beating of her heart. It pounded within Melina's serene embrace, announcing for them both how deeply within herself she really lived—a disclosure she had no wish to share. "No," she said.

"Oooh, good," came Melina's most sonorous voice. "Good." She covered them with the white chenille blanket. "Come closer," she whispered, but did not wait for Claire to move of her own accord. Never had Claire known confidence to be so graceful. "Closer," repeated Melina.

When they looked up later, the sun had filled every corner of the room.

"We did that," whispered Melina.

By all objective standards, this was the most grandiose remark, the most mawkish. Yet Claire's discipline in making herself the observer had failed miserably, and she veered awfully close to thinking it true—they *had* done that, they had made the sun rise.

At noon, Melina drove into Greenwich for eggs and fresh orange juice. Claire, against her deepest wishes, offered to stay behind to keep Regina company. She found Regina once again in the sunroom, wearing a knit dress and a matching sweater held over her shoulders by a sweater guard with hummingbird clasps. She sat perfectly straight at the glass-topped table, doing the *Times* crossword puzzle. Although Claire's own mother sat alone for endless hours in a darkened kitchen, the sight of Melina's grandmother so utterly in her own company filled Claire with pity.

"Am I disturbing you?"

"Disturbing? Heavens, no! I hope you slept well, dear." Regina did not look up.

"Yes." Something caught in Claire's throat. She had to repeat, more assertively, "*Yes.*" Then she thought she had been too emphatic. She wondered if Regina could know. There was something about her.

"Good! I'm delighted."

"And you?"

"Oh, I never sleep." Regina looked up and waved her hand dismissively.

"It's so beautiful here," said Claire.

Regina turned towards the Sound, then back to her puzzle. "I'm afraid I'm stumped. A nine-letter word for 'penitent's garb.'"

Claire was quiet. "I can't think," she finally said.

"It's nice Melina has so many guests, don't you think?" asked Regina. "I'm so pleased you are her new friend. She needs nice friends. That Shipley boy who was here last weekend—" Here Regina lowered her voice. "Do you know him?"

"No."

"Well, he hardly said boo to me, I can tell you. I believe they made it downstairs twice all weekend."

Claire looked at the crossword puzzle.

"*Hairshirt!*" Regina declared. She wrote in the nine letters. "Wouldn't *that* be unpleasant?"

Claire's thoughts reeled. Yesterday she had gotten some idea what might be beneath Regina's gracious manner. Was she telling the truth? Was there really a "Shipley boy"? Claire quickly reviewed all the ways she might broach the subject to Melina. None were acceptable. It would be awful if Melina thought she was trying to catch her grandmother in a lie. It would be worse yet if she thought Claire had assumed the right to check up on her. As they heard the sound of Melina's car tires on the gravel driveway, Regina and Claire sat amid only the sound of Regina committing words to the crossword spaces and accompanying herself with a low hum of "Oh, What a Beautiful Morning."

The plan had been that Claire would spend Sunday night and drive back early with Melina for the start of their classes Monday morning. From Sunday breakfast on, however, every time she looked at Melina's face—her rounded cheeks always glowing, the way she cocked her head when curious or amused—Claire was filled with more captivation and alarm than she thought possible to withstand. Towards the middle of the afternoon she asked Melina if she would mind driving her to the train station.

"I'm planning to submit a bunch of slides to Dodd," she explained. This week Winifred Dodd was reviewing students' slides to find artists for the Presidential Gallery. "I guess I'm nervous," Claire tried to say lightly. "I haven't really selected the ones I want to show, and I have all this Barlow reading to do and that damn convexity exercise for 3-D, and I guess I'm getting nervous. I really want that show."

Alone on the train back, Claire opened and shut Meyer Shapiro's *Modern Art* several times. Each time she opened the book its reproductions lured her into a familiar kind of thinking, the harmonious visual thinking that had become Claire's deepest habit. Each time she shut the book, all its words and pictures dimmed into inconsequence. *Modern Art* shut on the seat beside her, Claire tried to conjure the exact composition of a Matisse on one of its pages. This was a talent of hers—the ability to close her eyes and precisely recall the placement of all the images in a picture. She put her head back on the seat and shut her eyes, but all the way back to Grand Central she could see only Melina Irwin's face. The thoughts that surrounded it were anything but forms in a balanced composition; they knew nothing about push offsetting pull, restraint modulating frenzy.

DANNY HAD STAYED at the youth hostel in Mexico City until the third week in January. Most of the boys passing through had been French or Germans winding their way to Acapulco or Puerto Escondido. There had been one American, though, a fifteen-year-old red-haired boy named Tod. Tod had run away from his father's farm in Iowa, swearing his father would never lay a hand on him again.

Danny liked Tod because he was on some sort of natural speed, talking a mile a minute and pontificating in a midwestern twang on subjects about which he knew nothing. Together they had visited every church in Mexico City, and Tod would go on first about flying buttresses, then about the personal lives of Mexican priests. Danny's bullshit meter was in a frenzy of ticking every time Tod opened his mouth, yet he liked his energy and his desperation. When they had visited the Basilica of Guadalupe to watch pilgrims on their knees approaching the shrine to the Virgin, Tod had gotten down on *his* knees, had affected a trance-like expression.

Several days after their visit to the shrine, however, Tod wired his father that he would come home if he could have a TransAm with a tail fin and chrome side vents. Tod's father had sent back a one-way air ticket. Tucked inside was a picture of a TransAm parked behind three pigs, their backs to the camera.

On his own the next day, Danny had a hard time keeping himself going. Towards the end of the afternoon at the National Museum of Anthropology, his thoughts had turned bleak. They took a particular downturn while he was looking at a case of Mayan figurines, flat-faced little chieftains who appeared to be on a buzz. He stared at the rulers' faces—the tiny but dead-on wrinkles of their foreheads, their curled and sharp-edged lips—and he thought, Jesus, who the fuck do I think *I* am?

Here he stood not far from Mayan territory practically a thousand years later, and he would not be able to sculpt a face with those sublime lips to save his life. So what was the use? If he could not even approach the level of artisans a thousand years vanished, why not pack it in and become some middling drone, some sniveling son-of-a-bitch who stays up every night with a cup of cocoa and the *Journal of Middle Management?*

Danny knew there was another point of view. Look at Claire. There was not one Impressionist whose technique she could approach, and she knew it. The difference was she made mentors of them all.

So what was it with him, Danny wondered. Did he have a gargantuan ego that could not bear to be surpassed even by a Mayan ten centuries dead? Those guys probably did not even call themselves artists, thought Danny. What, *Rensler?* The Mayan sculptors were just construction grunts who whipped off a few trinkets in the lag time between building pyramids. The trinkets happened to be perfect little lampoons of rulers from time immemorial. So, yeah, thought Danny, how the hell was he supposed to *not* come up short? Who was he, but a kid from Coney Island who spent all his father's veteran's benefits on some pansy-ass art school? He never should have taken Sal's money for Rensler. He had been right to drop out.

By the time he boarded the bus to Guanajuato on the third Tuesday in January, Danny knew he would have to talk to himself in other people's voices. His own voice would not do. His own voice kept a running account of the bleak facts: He had not yet been fueled by Mexico in the way he had two summers before; he could not imagine how he had ever produced fifty *retablos* evoking heartbreaking miracles in lush colors (he could not imagine how he had produced anything); he was almost out of money and had already been passed over for two jobs teaching English; he had heard nothing from Claire even though she had his address at the hostel; he had woken to a shock of shame ever since the night with Ana.

So Danny started to talk to himself in voices less enamored of the facts. He talked first in Claire's voice, the one she used on herself, the one so driven by the mission of painting people at leisure that half the time she looked like a zealot. What was there to stop Danny from being so driven? Why were his *retablos* any less necessary to the world than her portraits of people at leisure? For fifteen minutes, as the rickety *Flecha Amarilla* bus jolted past hillside slums, Danny appropriated the exact voice Claire used all the times they had sat at Benno's giving each other pep talks.

When Claire's voice failed to do more than start him brooding again that she had not written, he just looked out the window. The bus passed a Volkswagen factory and an oil refinery. He began to make up a voice. The voice just crooned. It transferred no obsessions, no ambitions. It just repeated "it's all right" over and over. Okay, thought Danny as he watched a sleeping passenger stir, okay, so the voice makes me feel good, so what? It was as if he were defending himself against an unseen bully. This was Mexico, where the suspicion of such a voice in his head would dub him straight away as *mujer*. But the private voice kept up, "it's all right, now." It became slowly evident that the voice was his mother's. It was Molly's voice. She had crooned to him. She had said "it's all right" over and over.

The bus slowed down and turned into a town that was nothing but a dusty road lined by vending stalls. "What the hell'sa matter with you?" snapped Sal inside Danny's head. "The woman deserted you. You think she ever tried to track us down? N.G. from the word go, babe."

Sal was right. Danny stopped soothing himself in Molly's voice. Then there were no voices but those of the vendors rushing the bus as it stopped by a roadside tortilla stand. The vendors had factory-made blankets piled on their arms. They had cellophane tubes filled with honeyed peanuts, and they had sculptured mangos, flavored ices, martyred saints. They shouted out the names of their wares through the open windows and up the bus steps. Abandoned by his own voice, Danny heard only their insistent ones. He beckoned to the seller of saints, who bounded up the steps and, with a sober nod, took three times the pesos his handful of tin saints was worth.

Once Danny was settled in a cheap hotel on the outskirts of Guanajuato, he realized there was nowhere he felt pressed to go. The *momias* he associated with Ana. Diego Rivera had grown up in Guanajuato, but Danny felt betrayed by Rivera.

During his first trip to Mexico City the summer before last, Danny had discovered Rivera's murals. He had visited the National Palace and the Ministry of Education. Rivera's abilities as a draftsman, an historian, and a synthesizer of national energy amazed Danny. If only America had had an artist to do for the Hopi or Zuni what Rivera had done for the Aztec! Yet he was anything but just a history painter, Danny had discovered. He was onto himself every inch of the way. He had painted himself as a frog-eyed porker, which he was, and a five-year-old in knee britches, which he was also. During his first trip to Mexico, Danny had shot seven rolls of Rivera's murals. Back home, he had enlargements made of Rivera's portrait of the execution of Maximilian and of Karl Marx pointing towards the future. He had hung up these enlargements on the corkboard of his room at Sal's. The real blow had come several months later, when Danny discovered that everyone at Rensler was obsessed by Rivera. The art ed majors wrote dissertations. The kids who took Painting and Politics created slide shows. The students in Women Artists of the Twentieth Century scrutinized his treatment of his wife, Frida. Around the end of Danny's freshman year, Rensler seemed to be divided into camps, for and against Rivera. That's when Danny disinherited Rivera. That's when he started working on his *retablos* and stopped thinking about other artists.

Now Danny wandered the streets of Guanajuato, Diego Rivera's birthplace. Resolved not to visit Rivera's actual birthplace, Danny went instead to the market. Later, he window-shopped. Both the markets and the shops were overrun with useless articles. Half of what was sold was battery operated.

There were no piles of hand-embroidered baby blouses, as there had been in the Oaxaca markets. There were no painstakingly woven and stitched huaraches. There were no enormous sprays of calla lilies in multicolored baskets. Claire would hate it here, thought Danny. He remembered how he had described Oaxaca to her, the Oaxacans' eye for beauty and for detail. The hilly city of Guanajuato was beautiful, but its people rushed, and as they rushed they wore cheap quartz watches and Sony Walkmans.

Defeated, Danny left the markets and the side-street shops and went at last to Diego Rivera's birthplace. He paid for a ticket and passed quickly through the first floor, thinking what tight-asses Rivera's parents had been. Their rooms were cordoned off, as the rooms of parents of geniuses always are, thought Danny, and completely sterile. As in the States, he thought, money beats the guts out of style.

The rooms upstairs, though, were another story. Their vitality was that of the prodigal returned only to say "So there! Take that!" There were studies for murals, self-portraits, Cubist paintings from Rivera's period in Europe, unabashed rip-offs of practically every important artist of the twenties. Danny's heart swelled. His old proprietary feelings returned.

"Wow," came a voice from behind. A woman had just reached the top step leading to the third-floor gallery. "I can't believe there are no guards in here," she added. Her accent was northeastern American. She looked to be in her late twenties.

Another Rivera groupie, thought Danny, but not with his usual disgust. He had liked the sound of her purely American "wow."

"The Mexican honor system," he said. Then, "I wonder if Sotheby's would ask questions if I whipped this out of a shopping bag." He pointed to Rivera's charcoal self-portrait.

The woman laughed. From the diaphragm, Danny noted. Her brown hair bobbed on her shoulders. She wore several papier-mâché bangles on her wrists, all with detailed paintings of serpents or fanciful turtles or frogs. These knocked together as she raked her fingers through the back of her hair, then withdrew them and laughed some more.

Since they were the only visitors in the birthplace, they accompanied each other through the remaining galleries, the postcard shop downstairs, and the cobblestone streets near the university. It seemed also natural that they should stop at a little place that existed for the sole purpose of mixing tropical fruits within the chipped glass beaker of a one-speed blender. They lingered there as the sun lowered and a slight chill overtook the streets.

When they went outside again, Danny looked up at the rooftops starkly drawn against the hills. On an ordinary day he would have dismissed their sight as merely picturesque. Today had been so long, though, and he had seen so many miles of parched land that the sight of the rooftops against the hills exuded an eerie power, its own kind of beauty. Danny pointed this out to the woman, Robin, who said yes, the sight of the rooftops against the hills gave off something special, something truly mystical. They walked for a few more blocks, then both declared that they were hungry. She had been waiting her whole trip to have *filete a la Tampequeña,* Robin said. Would he like to join her?

AT THE BOARD meeting in late January, Otis could report that the new semester had gotten off to a good start. The number of admissions applications for next year was higher than he had anticipated. Also, Rensler had received a surprise gift from an alumnus ceramist who had made a fortune in Japan. Otis had the pleasure of announcing to the Board that Rensler could go ahead with its plans to build a new pottery studio and equip it with electric wheels and five new kilns that the alumnus intended to hand pick in Tokyo. His last piece of happy news was that Sonya Barlow had offered to donate to the spring auction an entire portfolio of Maxwell Zavin woodcuts. She had stipulated, quite fairly, reported Otis, that she and Rensler split the hammer price. Here the Board was more reserved in their expression of pleasure than Otis had hoped. The new member, Brad Shaw, agreed that Sonya's request was fair considering Zavin's stature, but that woodcuts were after all multiples, and could be worth only so much.

"Feel her out," Brad suggested. "She must have a few original Zavins, and they'd really be worth something. Negotiate a little. Tell her we could do something really substantial with half the hammer price of an original. Feel her out."

Otis could not stand Brad Shaw. The only time he felt in an awkward position at Rensler was when he disliked one of its Board members. He never knew what pose to take with regard to the nebulous boundaries between himself and the Board. He had never mastered the etiquette of this relationship, but of course he knew of several cases in which a president of a small independent college had been fired by its Board.

"Brad, I really don't think bargaining on any level would be appropriate. Sonya has been on the faculty less than a year."

After some debate, it was decided that it was better not to risk alienating Sonya Barlow, who after all did have something of an established reputation and might in fact even be responsible for some of the new applications for next year. The issue ended with the Board in agreement, except for Brad Shaw who tapped his index finger on the table for the remainder of the meeting.

As he often did, Otis left the board meeting with the notion that he was not cut out for the business end of his job. Anyone who had started out trying to excite interest in the ancestry of remote cultures, he thought, should have rightly pursued a career based on his powers of appreciation. He wondered if it were too late to start another career, if he could use Rensler as a springboard for something that would bring him more into himself.

Later that afternoon, on his way from the pottery studio where he made arrangements with two instructors for the arrival of the new equipment, Otis thought of Nora. He had told her he was always there, to just call, but she had not. Otis was ashamed that for even an instant he should wonder about the protocol in this situation. Yet protocol was of utmost importance when relating to Nora. He would rather spend time second-guessing the protocol than risk defying it. There was self-interest there, he had to admit. When he violated Nora's idea of protocol, she confronted him with an impassivity so deep as to become its own form of combat.

He decided to call. Back in his office, he dialed her work number, which he got from Information under the name of her business, Casper, Inc. The woman who answered said Nora was not in. He called her sublet. Nora picked up the phone.

"Hi. You're there. Are you all right?"

"Hello, Oats. Yes, I'm here."

"Are you all right?"

"I started my second round of chemo last week. Which would you prefer, my Raving Loon or my Camille? I can do both. I have done both."

This "have done" was a particular jolt. It meant that while Otis had been methodically adjusting to their separation—employing a housekeeper, coping with his loneliness, routinely pursuing his responsibilities at Rensler—Nora had lived through an upheaval so total as to call for the presentation of two utterly different personas. Nora, whose detractors called her "one-note."

"How do they administer it?" Otis's voice was as gentle as he knew how to make it. "Where do you go?"

"I go to Memorial. I'm on Adriamycin, the worst. I.V.—every twenty-one days."

Otis had done some reading. He knew that Adriamycin caused total hair loss. Nora had not lost all her hair, but she would.

"Do you want me to come over? Nora, god I'm sorry. Do you want to get off the phone and I'll come over?"

"Barbara's coming after work."

Barbara was a friend from Nora's Mount Holyoke days. The only time Otis ever saw Barbara was at her annual New Year's party, to which he had not been invited this year.

"That's good. What about the nausea? Are they giving you something for it?"

"So far I've had Compazine, Reglan, and Thorazine. Nothing helps. And nothing helps the vile smells and the constant taste in my mouth."

"*Thorazine?* The anti-psychotic?" Otis, panicked, hoped Nora would make a joke.

"Yes."

"Interesting," he said, then felt lame for saying it.

"They're trying everything," remarked Nora, who had always had an inordinate respect for authority.

"Are you being assertive? What are you finding out? Chemo's not the only way to go. There're vitamins, there's nutrition."

"Otis. You're aggravating me."

Aggravate. For years, Nora had used this word when she wanted to end a conversation. Otis found it an absurdly flabby word.

"I'm sorry. I won't check in like this if it upsets you. But I do have a perspective here, too."

"Perspective," Nora repeated. "Interesting word."

"Nora. You're going through hell. Do you expect me to just sit back and bide my time?"

"It's my hell," answered Nora, laughing inordinately.

Her wild laugh always made Otis feel exposed, blasting forth as it did to disclose the true flimsiness of her general composure.

"I'm dealing with it in my own way," said Nora when she had regained herself. "I would hope you would respect that."

"You can come back to Brooklyn Heights. Any time you like."

"I shouldn't have picked up the phone," said Nora. She hung up abruptly.

Otis did not know if Nora were sick or angry. He put his head in his hands. There had been so few times in their years together that he had felt he had achieved the right note with her. How many times had he managed to say the thing that she did not merely approve of, but that moved her in a way that so many people insisted they be moved?

Otis suddenly recalled Sonya Barlow, whom he had seen for lunch on New Year's Day. She was a woman who insisted on being moved. She did not give a fig for authority, his included. "Your wife must be aggressive!" she had advised. "She must fight every step of the way!"

In fact, Nora was a persistent and intelligent questioner. She never made a decision unarmed. The trouble was that she never asked the questions that would elicit uninhabitable answers. Otis could not ask them on her behalf. For his own part, he was always a bit embarrassed when presented with the intimate evidence of how others negotiated the world. Nora was his wife, but her style of asking the world vital questions embarrassed him the most. Did he now have the courage, because of her cancer, to lead her out of the burrow she had been digging for years?

Lily stepped in to ask if Otis could see Winnie Dodd, who wanted to show him slides of the work that would next hang in the Presidential Gallery. "Of course!" declared Otis in a hearty tone. "I'd love to see them!"

Winnie came in with several manila envelopes and a black leather slide portfolio under one arm. She also carried a portable light box. She smiled at Otis and set everything down on his desk.

"This is for the one-person, right?"

"Yes. We'll hang some time in mid-February." Winnie hurriedly opened the first envelope. "You've probably already seen his work. It's just terrific. It'll make a great show." She laid down a sheet of plastic sleeves filled with colored slides and switched on the light box. Together, they leaned over the slides.

"Oh, what a shame," said Otis. "We won't be able to show these."

"Otis. Really? I was sure you'd respond to this work."

"I do," said Otis, peering closer. "Terrific imagination. I love the irreverence. The funny little frames, the annotations, everything. Great. But Danny Vincent dropped out. We gave him a leave, because I'm hoping he'll come back. He's in Mexico. He must have forgotten he submitted these."

"Oh, shit," said Winnie, the "shit" a little whimper. "I think this would have been the best show yet."

"It's a shame," Otis repeated. "Let's see what else we have."

For the remainder of the afternoon they went over the slides that hopeful students had presented over the last two months. A show at the Presidential Gallery was considered the most official recognition Rensler gave. Competition was always stiff. Several graduates who had had shows at the Presidential Gallery had then succeeded in getting their work into group exhibits in SoHo.

The slides in the black case belonged to a sophomore, Claire Rollins. "Now, these are interesting," said Otis. "Strange little throw-backs. Do you think she's being facetious?"

"I think she's serious," said Winnie. "She brought them to my office a couple of weeks ago. She's serious."

"Well, she's certainly going against the grain. There's nothing wrong with that," he said, pausing over a water scene with a hand, a movie camera, and an interesting-looking buoy. "This one's very skillful," he added.

"I don't know," said Winifred. "I won't argue with the technique, but for the gallery I don't really respond to the energy." She quickly opened another manila envelope and removed the slides.

In the end, they decided to give February to a senior photographer who had dressed up nine women classmates as the Muses and posed them in some of the most sordid streets and dead ends in Manhattan.

"This has soul," said Winnie.

"Yes, it does," Otis agreed. But he had been brought back to thoughts of Nora, of the unspeakable poisons that ran through her body, killing good cells along with bad. He repeated his agreement: "Yes, there's some soul there." He knew that as he spoke the poisons rounded their course.

FEBRUARY

HER SCULPTURE had begun to claim its life. It already had a title, simply, "The Spirit." A female figure stepped off her clay base and raised her arms in the air. Later, Sonya would mount her to a second base, perhaps marble or onyx or simply enamel-painted wood. The second base, the pedestal, would be two-and-a-half or three feet high to emphasize the risk involved in the figure's embarkation. Sonya did not know where the figure was going, but she knew she was embarking upon a risk. So far, Sonya had kept the movement of the armature. The clay had not merely covered it, as was always the danger, but had extended the essence of its gesture. Sonya worked well into the night of this first Saturday in February. She had not worked so far into the night for a very long time.

At half past four in the morning, Sonya lay awake in her bed. She supposed her involvement with the figure had overstimulated her. True, this never used to happen. She had al-

ways been able to fall asleep immediately. (During their weekends in the Hamptons, Maxwell had teased her, had accused
her of lacking a conscience.) She had already tried hot milk.
She had tried Valerian, although she detested its taste. She
had even gotten up to do her breathing exercises. Still, she lay
fully awake.

She thought about the figure in her studio, about its promise. Yes, she thought, it must be exhibited. True, she no longer
had a gallery, but there were group exhibits. She began to
plan where she might enter "The Spirit." The National Academy of Design, the Silvermine Guild. Of course, the really
fine exhibitions were invitational.

Sonya tossed about under one of her most prized possessions, a quilt with a cover after a Sonia Delaunay pattern, a
splendidly controlled orgy of color, a prototype of the prin-
ciples of Synchromism. She could not help but think of
Delaunay, this namesake who never had to suffer the distaste-
ful experience of outliving the public's enthusiasm for her.
But Sonya consoled herself that Delaunay's wonderful forays
into color had made her nothing more than a successful decorator. The woman did not have a feel for the essential gesture.
And where could one really go without establishing the essential gesture?

It was after five a.m. when Sonya began to think about
her apartment. If she could only raise the money to buy it, she
would have a respectable nest egg in equity. People must have
nest eggs. Even Mrs. Fine had the lucidity to recognize this. At
this thought, Sonya became utterly dismayed. It was one thing
that the world endorsed a cheerful decorator over herself, but
that it chose to preserve the likes of Mrs. Fine was just too
bitter a pill.

Under her Delaunay cover, Sonya cautioned herself to
stop her petty thinking. Three rooms away was a sculpture

that might well end up conveying a truly worthwhile message, and damn the world if it were too materialistic to hear it. Damn the world, and damn her, thought Sonya, for betraying her basic credo, the credo she and Zavin had so harmoniously shared, that the worship of acquisitions, dead and crudely designed acquisitions, was a ghoulish devotion, a devotion entirely for the self and against life.

Surely, thought Sonya, surely she could strike a balance between the grosser capitalists and those people on the street, those men and women (Sonya shuddered) who might have spent their lives opposing materialism and now were so completely done for they thought nothing of punching out the strollers in Riverside Park. Surely it was not too late to establish herself safely yet honorably. Surely she could provide for herself a background against which to stay up until three in the morning, modeling "The Spirit." This was basic. This was not too much to ask.

Rather than give up her early Sunday walk, Sonya had taken to dressing for it in rags.

("Well, of course," she had recently told Irene Cone, "I dress like one of them and I am quite invincible. One has to accommodate.")

At ten o'clock, later than usual, Sonya was ready to go out. She wore a thrift-store parka that was by now filthy and a pair of woolen sailor pants. Even her unstylish beasts might create the wrong impression (who among them could have their fallen arches corrected?), so she wore two pairs of torn army surplus socks inside men's sneakers. She would conquer her fears. She would be in their world, not of it.

The Boat Basin, her destination of unambitious mornings, was deserted. Often in the spring or summer the boat owners and their guests hovered about the docks or tinkered with this or that. This morning, there was no sign that the house boats were inhabited. Possibly their owners were tucked under many layers of covers inside their cabins, but more likely they wintered in Florida. What a strange contingent of New York society this was! They must pay exorbitant special taxes, Sonya guessed, yet their houseboats were often in disrepair. She liked to come here and contemplate the lives of the houseboat owners. Once Irene had come with her and asked why Sonya did not bring her pastels or paints down to the Boat Basin. "Oh for *heaven's* sake, Irene," Sonya had snapped. Her tone had been so sharp that Irene had turned to look up the West Side Highway.

People passed by only rarely this morning. The wind was strong. Sonya tugged at the cords to tighten the hood of her parka. She was so lucky she had her health. She did not know where she would be without her walks. It would be miserable to be in the position of Otis Daley's wife. It was all haphazard—chance-medley—who got sick and who stayed healthy. There had been careless moments in which Sonya had included her excellent health on her roster of accomplishments, moments in which she had not only appropriated it, but had flaunted it to friends and acquaintances. Sonya always caught herself, although sometimes too late, and was ashamed. Sometimes she feared her carelessness would be avenged by the onset of a terrible illness, a grave illness such as Otis Daley's wife had. She could of course handle it, she would have to handle it with great bravery, but how fortunate to be spared the necessity.

It must be so peculiar for Otis, Sonya reflected as she began to walk north, to have an estranged wife who had cancer. She was sure he was fully alert to the subtlety of his dilemma. If she were in Otis's situation, she had to admit that she might not be up to following the principled course of action. Yet her instincts told her that Otis Daley had an estimable character, and she felt sorry that he might be in for a long and difficult struggle. Wouldn't it be nice, thought Sonya, to have him up for a light supper? She could make her lovely seafood crepes, an endive salad. Of course, she would have to put away her pastels, the ones she told him were in private collections, but she could replace them with an old colleague's work, now in storage. They could have a thoroughly pleasant evening. It was true that rapports floated about the universe. Rapports wandered the universe and lit down with exquisite grace at whim.

Sonya turned onto West End Avenue. A man wearing only a woman's ragged raincoat and walking with one crutch stepped into her path. "Gotta light?" he asked, craning forward to peer inside Sonya's torn nylon hood. He put out his hand, palm up.

"For heaven's sake, *I* don't smoke!" snapped Sonya. Her voice was full of indignation. The man just shrugged and hobbled away, not in the least ruffled at yet another blue blood gone the way of the world.

"Otis," she said, gazing out at the gray water of the Hudson. "Sonya Barlow. How *are* you?"

"Well, fine. I'm fine, thank you." His tone was quizzical.

"It occurred to me you might like to see Zavin's woodcuts next weekend. I thought, wouldn't it be lovely if you came up for supper and I could show them to you?"

"That's a nice idea," Otis agreed. "But I was looking forward to seeing them in the presale exhibit. Did I mention the presale exhibit? We're having it in Manhattan, along with the auction. One of our alumni owns a gallery, and Sid got him to donate it for an entire week."

"Oh, how clever," said Sonya.

There was no sound on the other end of the line.

"I never stopped to consider how much work must go into planning something on this scale."

"Yes, Sid's been busy. We're awfully appreciative of your contribution. The Board is just delighted with our arrangement."

"I think it will work out well for both of us. You know, I never collaborate, and this is a collaboration of sorts."

"We're all the more grateful, then."

"Well," said Sonya, "I'd love to have you just for supper next weekend, then." Her tone was an explosion of forced vigor.

Otis cleared his throat. "That's kind. But I've been invited out of town next weekend. I often go out of town on the weekends. But it's kind of you."

Quite by accident, Sonya caught her reflection in the hall mirror as she passed by to hang up her parka. Her reflection was too appalling to bear, but she returned to examine it once she had changed into the cotton tunic she wore when she sculpted. As a young woman, and still into her middle age, she could stay up all night and show no effects. This morning, though, there were dark stains beneath her eyes. The skin below her prized high cheekbones was sunken, nearly collapsed, she saw, and deeply creased. A tightness about the corners of her mouth revealed a woman too much of this world. It was clear as it had never been that she was seventy-two years old. She was at least fifteen, maybe twenty years older than Otis Daley. It occurred to Sonya that he might actually know it.

In the studio, "The Spirit" stood where Sonya had left her, swathed in layers of wet cheesecloth. Sonya unwound the layers by holding the tip of the cloth and slowly circling the figure. The volume and shape of the figure's torso was the most clearly established. The crease that ran down her vertical axis, from between her breasts to her groin, suggested her physical power. Although Sonya had yet to form "The Spirit's" features, her raised chin made it clear that she was quite up to whatever risks would come with her embarkation. And why shouldn't she be, thought Sonya. She is young. Her new beginning, whatever it was destined to become, would certainly embrace people and adventures.

Now that she had looked into her mirror and seen that she was seventy-two, Sonya knew her own embarkation would be different from her figure's. The future she embarked on might not teem with people. Her future would assuredly include adventures, but the adventures might not be rich and meaningful as in the days of sculpting premier scientists and statesmen, in the days of wedging clay while Zavin drew her, in the endless and meandering summer nights with the Provincetown artists. Her future might be spent alone in these rooms she did not own. It might well be spent in increasingly smaller rooms that she did not own.

If she succeeded in exhibiting "The Spirit," it would not be merely a step in the slow budding of her exposure to the world, for where would she go from there? Yet even if her future adventures turned out to lack apparent purpose, Sonya would participate in them as if they were an embarkation. Of this she was absolutely certain.

For now, though, she must do something out of the ordinary. She must rewrap her figure, take off her sculpting tunic, and go to sleep. It might be the middle of the afternoon, but she must have a deep and luxurious sleep. She must sleep and wake up herself again, a vital woman with always a sense of beginnings about her, a discriminating woman who refused most men and was herself refused only in favor of the most pressing obligations.

CLAIRE HAD gotten no mail for weeks, but on the second Tuesday in February she opened her box to find two letters she had been expecting.

The first was in an envelope marked with the Rensler insignia. She opened it right by Kollman's bank of mailboxes. It was a form letter, personally signed by Winifred Dodd. "We are happy to have had the chance to consider your work for the Presidential Gallery. Although you were not chosen for our upcoming one-person exhibit, we hope you will submit your slides again in the near future."

Minutes later, the silence and emptiness in Danny's efficiency overwhelmed her. Despite the many canvases stacked against three walls, there was such an acute sense of nothing there that Claire feared the room's sterility, the coldness rising off its gray linoleum, would prevail over her own presence. Recently, she had been having trouble establishing herself in rooms. During an unguarded moment she had described this phenomenon to her mother over the phone. Wanda had said it was natural when she considered that Rensler was not her home.

Claire knew the empty feeling had nothing to do with being away from South Orange. The feeling had to do with Melina. Melina was dangerously cavalier. She made torrid declarations with ease. She could praise Claire and fresh-squeezed orange juice in the same language and tone.

On her way to Kollman one evening last week, Claire had seen Melina and a tall boy getting into the Saab. They did not look happy—they opened the doors and got inside without looking at one another—but even their swift and automatic gestures, the reflexive way they fell onto the Saab's high seats, suggested the intimacy of mutual habit. Was this "the Shipley boy"? The sight of them together had knocked the wind out of Claire. For several days afterwards she had forced herself to think of nothing but getting the show at the Presidential Gallery.

The second letter was postmarked Guanajuato, Mexico. Claire got out a Tab and settled down at the round table in the kitchenette. She opened the envelope and removed several photographs. There were black Christs on the cross, the baby Jesus swaddled in varnished gold lamé, meticulously woven straw altar boys. Claire smiled. When she unfolded the letter, a tiny tin saint fell out.

> Hey Claire,
> Check these out. Not exactly Barlow's "elegant solution," huh? So it's been good. Been wandering the one-hog towns and crashing sacred ceremonies.
> Money is getting tight—I couldn't get a teaching gig in Mexico City, so forget it here. San Miguel is next, and everyone already speaks White Man. I may have to come back earlier than I thought.
> I'm hitting San Miguel with this woman Robin. She knows some jewelry-makers there, Mexican. She works with them.
> I talked once to Sal, and he's okay. It's weird being so out of touch.
> Hope the moats are still up at Rensler Castle. There's a backasswards ratio down here—the more Godless a place, the more churches there are. We all need a few moats. Keep yours in good shape.
> Blessings,
> Saint D

Claire had no doubt that Danny was having an affair with the woman named Robin. With Danny, an allusion was a

whole story. Well, what did she expect, she reproached herself. From Danny, from Melina, from the Presidential Gallery?
It took some sense of authority to expect; like Cole always
said, who gave her the authority?

Claire got up and lined some of her canvases face out
against the wall. People took pleasure, bowls of fruit suggested
domestic serenity, light twinkled over expanses of water. The
pictures meant nothing. Claire stared at them and burst into
tears.

Later she switched on the black-and-white portable television Wanda had given her. Until dinner time, she alternated
between soap operas and game shows. Then she walked
bleary-eyed into the dining hall, stood in line, and pointed to
one of the steaming vats. A silent old woman who had been at
Rensler forever and was about Regina's age scooped lasagna
onto a styrofoam plate and handed it to Claire. She sat alone
to eat, reading the poster that described the Heimlich manuever
on the cinderblock wall across her table. She scrutinized its
every aspect, in the way she sometimes did with mundane
things during moments of irrecoverable hope.

The next Saturday at noon, Claire sat with Wanda in a
suburban diner. Claire drank coffee and flattened leftover pie
crumbs with the underside of her fork while her mother ate a
Greek salad. Wanda had joined Weight Watchers and lost ten
pounds, although she did not need to, had started a exercise
class and gotten her hair tipped. When she'd picked up Claire
at the bus station, the contrast between their appearances was
so startling that neither of them said anything.

Wanda sat eating with a new delicacy. "I wish you'd let
me take you shopping. Does everyone at Rensler wear black
all the time?"

"Most people do."

"Well, I can't understand the statement you're trying to make. I mean, I can understand it, I just frankly don't care for it."

Claire looked around the dining room. There were many women wearing pastel-colored synthetics. "These aren't colors," she said. "You call these colors?"

"Claire, there's no need to take that tone. And you don't have to choose the worst examples to make your point. It makes you look foolish. You know there are plenty of decent colors in the stores."

"I don't mind the way I look."

Wanda pushed her salad plate aside. She had eaten all but three rectangles of feta cheese and some olives. Claire speared one of the olives.

"We could at least get you some colorful scarves. There are wonderful scarf designers. And there're sales now."

"I don't need scarves. But thank you."

Wanda signaled the waitress to refill her coffee cup. "*I* should be the one to wear black," she said, then leaned forward and lowered her voice. "But I have to tell you, sweetie, I feel just fine. More than fine."

"Really? Do you really?"

"Absolutely. You know, I'm still in Nurturing the Nurturers, although you'll be glad to hear we don't call it that anymore. We don't call it anything. The girls there have been wonderful to me. Only one of them is married, and her husband is a doctor so she's developed plenty of outside resources. That's the key, honey, outside resources. I can't stress it enough."

Claire just stared at her mother, whose social life for years had followed the path designed by Cole—annual dinners to welcome new country club members, summer picnics on the grounds at Wollman's, an occasional show in the city.

"I worry about you that way. You with your painting. It's an *inner* resource. Now don't jump down my throat, there's nothing wrong with an inner resource, but, well, to bend a phrase, you can't take your inner resources to bed with you."

Claire felt her pulse begin to race. This was one of Wanda's openings. Since Claire had been in junior high, Wanda had stopped asking direct questions. Rather, she provided openings.

"So what do you do? I mean, how has your life changed?"

"Well, for one thing I go out all the time. You know how your father was about that."

"Where do you go?"

"Oh, you know. To Weight Watchers. There are some women there with fascinating stories. And I plan things with the girls in the other group. Some of us are going down to Atlantic City at the end of the month. That may not be my thing, I'll see, but the point is, how *can* I see, how can I decide how I want to live now, if I don't do these things?"

"That's good," said Claire. "Really. I mean it."

Wanda beamed. "And I'm redoing the den, getting rid of that terrible recliner and hassock that I hated for years. I'm going to make that house mine now. You want more pie, honey?"

"Come on, *two* pieces? What're they telling you in Weight Watchers, stuff the other person?"

"Well, I guess you're all right. You don't look well, I have to tell you, you look terrible. But I guess if you can snap at me, you're all right. You know, you'd get better rest at home. None of that terrible screaming in the halls."

"I sleep okay."

"Well, why don't you at least let me buy you some scarves, then? You could drape them over that," she said, referring to the black jersey that Claire had been wearing for three days straight. "They would pick you up a little."

They left the diner and went to Bloomingdale's, where Wanda bought three silk scarves for Claire and a flowered rayon one with fringes for herself. All afternoon, nothing more was said about Cole. They went to a movie. Claire ended up staying the night and the next morning they had brunch at the same diner. Then Wanda drove Claire to the bus stop. It was raining, so they sat in the car waiting for the bus. "What did you do with his clothes?" asked Claire, just to say the word *his* and have her mother know who she meant.

On the bus back, Claire thought about the first time she had dreamed of leaving home. There had been a basis for her dreams. Her first visit to the Metropolitan Museum of Art had fixed in her mind an unshakable notion of the feelings she could have all the time if she lived in New York City. She had been only eight and had gone with her school class. They had gathered in the Great Hall, and for the first time in her life Claire had breathed in grandeur. The flowers alone rendered every bouquet she had ever seen paltry and sentimental. For their sheer number and brilliance, the flowers announced to Claire that she stood at the entrance to a kingdom. When she and her class went up the stairs and wound their way through the galleries, the other students shoving and snatching one another's name tags, Claire had hung back and gaped at the pictures within their gilded frames. The function of these frames, Claire had been convinced, was to celebrate the images within them every moment of the day. And she fully saw how some of the pictures deserved such royal attention. She did not like the ones that showed horses rearing against a moody sky, and she vaguely feared the equally dark still lifes that showed dead partridges and aged cheeses. But the light pictures, the ones her teacher had called Impressionistic, deserved their gilded frames. The people in them were the most relaxed people Claire had ever seen. The landscapes they picnicked in were dashed with light from the finest moments of the day. It was as if those particular moments, and not the artist, had held the paintbrush. Claire had returned from the Metropolitan convinced that if she lived in New York those same moments would hold the brush that would record her days.

Now, finally, Claire had moved to the city, but a record of her days would have to include every feature of her landscape, even the parking lot of Kollman Hall, which was littered with broken glass, fast food containers, bottle caps, and massed splatters of pigeon droppings. Loops of spiked wire were affixed to the parapet of Kollman's roof. Twenty-four-hour security guards patrolled the lot and lobby; they held walkie-talkies and wore night sticks. When Claire returned from South Orange, it was still dark and rainy, and she crossed this parking lot alone. She had only lived at Kollman a short while, but already her walk was that of someone pursued. Already, the outdoors was only the place she passed through to get where she was going.

As she waited for the elevator, relieved to be inside, Claire opened her one piece of mail from the weekend. It had no return address, and she did not recognize the handwriting. Inside was a card printed with one of Jim Dine's hearts. Only at Bloomingdale's with her mother had Claire been reminded, by all the garish hearts, that it was Valentine's Day. The message inside her card said, "Let's get together. *Soon.*" It was from Melina.

As Claire opened the door to her efficiency, a thousand questions assailed her, but her paintings, still face-out along the walls, were so beautiful she could have put them in gilded frames.

THEY HAD been in San Miguel for almost three weeks. One of Robin's jewelers had found them a cheap room near the *Instituto Allende*, where Robin was taking a photography course. At first, this photography course bothered Danny. He thought he had come very far to be back at Rensler. When he hinted at this to Robin, she put her arm around him, flicked a mass of wavy brown hair over her shoulder, and told him, "One thing we all have to learn about relationships—we're not the other person." This had struck Danny as infinitely wise.

Nonetheless, Danny's days had come to belong to Robin. In the mornings, he went with her to her jewelers. Nearly a dozen of them supplied her with the jewelry that she sold from a concession in Quincy Market in Boston. But in Boston, Robin had recently quarreled with the managers of some nearby concessions. Several weeks ago, she had decided to move to New York, as she had been hoping to for several years. "Isn't this amazing timing?" she asked Danny after they had been together for a week. He had instantly seen that yes, it was amazing timing. Robin had already gotten a license to put up a table at an outdoor market in SoHo. The trip to Guanajuato had been an excursion for her—she had already been working with her jewelers in San Miguel for several weeks. Now she had returned with Danny to take the course at the Institute (she always took courses, she told him, wherever she went) and to check up on her jewelers.

Many of Robin's jewelers were Mexican Indians who worked quickly and with skill, only slightly varying the designs they had worked at their whole careers. Some fashioned tough leather tubes, then bound them together with bands of brass or copper. Usually the leather bracelets had stones or fired pieces of clay set a little askew at their centers. Other jewelers worked in silver, and had moved to San Miguel from Taxco. They copied the designs from the workshops there, turning out with remarkable speed rings and earrings and pendants that Robin admitted were pure pablum. She worked easily with all the Mexicans, giving them her quotas and seeing the quotas met. She spoke to them in Spanish, but they rarely discussed money. Their arrangements apparently stood firm. Danny knew she paid them in American dollars. On this trip, Robin increased their quotas. She told them she wanted to start out in New York with a hefty inventory.

The rest of Robin's suppliers were North Americans who had learned jewelry-making at home or at the *Instituto Allende*. Their designs were more ambitious; they rambled into Latin American mythology and folklore. They experimented with materials. Their work had an urbanity and a lightheartedness about it that the Mexicans' lacked, and Robin had sold a great deal of their jewelry. It was a New Yorker who had made the papier-mâché bracelets Robin wore, and a woman from Salt Lake City who made the necklaces of miniature ceramic skulls she also wore. Their work, Robin confessed to Danny, drew a whole other contingent of shopper to her stall. It was the combination of these two contingents—the field-tripping suburbanites dying for expensive novelties and the high school kids dying to look like Mexican peasants—that kept her solidly in the black.

Robin had a difficult time with her North American suppliers. They argued quotas. The North Americans insisted they were artisans—they had acquired their skill and did not have it in their family blood like Robin's Mexicans did; they could not just crank it out. They argued price. They demanded to know Robin's profit margin, an unheard of request from the Mexicans. They wanted contracts. When Danny went with Robin to the North Americans' studios, he stood in the background and watched the sparks fly. Robin strode up and down the floors of their shabby, sun-filled studios, angrily shoving up her forearms the bangles of their design. She threatened to stop representing them, to deprive them of the opportunity to enter the New York market. "I produce for you!" Robin insisted, and spun off the numbers of each of their designs she had sold at Quincy Market. Once she found a design that sold strongly, Robin was furious when one of the North Americans stopped making it and presented her with an entirely new design. If they were going to have contracts, Robin insisted, then she would have a clause which obligated them to continue to produce high-volume sellers. She was not playing Catherine de Medici here. If she lost them, she lost them; talented jewelers were a dime a dozen in San Miguel.

In the early afternoons, while Robin was in the darkroom at the Institute, Danny wandered about town. The facades of the colonial buildings along the narrow streets opened up to art supply stores and "*supertiendas.*" There was a deli and an English-language bookstore. Mexican girls around the *zócalo* sold the same leather jewelry that Robin represented. Everywhere posters in English advertised Spanish lessons, therapeutic massages, poetry readings, and the services of healers. Bus loads of retirees from the Sunbelt invaded the plant-filled courtyard restaurants where Danny drank beer; one among them was always popping up to snap pictures of their group at lunch.

One afternoon Danny returned to the room early. When Robin came back from the Institute, he said, "I think I gotta get outta here."

"Baby! What's the matter? Are you sick?" Robin put down her camera equipment and rushed over to touch Danny's forehead.

"It's just not my style, you know what I mean?"

"It's not for everybody," said Robin, her voice growing shrill. "I can appreciate that. But this is my supply center."

"I know," said Danny, and could think of no legitimate argument to rush her. A week ago, Robin had told Danny she thought she was in love with him. She had told him he had just the kind of irreverence she needed in her life; too many people took themselves too seriously, even *she* sometimes took herself too seriously. She had been honest with Danny. She had told him she was thirty-two and had been divorced for six years. She told him she had recently broken up with a man in Boston, a stockbroker her own age, that they had just clashed about too many "value things." She was not specific.

Danny was deeply flattered that Robin was in love with him. In less than a month, she had had a consummate influence—the imbroglio with Ana seemed to have happened ten years ago, his fixation with Claire an eon past. Danny's evident self-consciousness seemed not to bother Robin. She devoted herself to building his confidence. She said she adored hairy men. She told him that she thought the incisors that protruded a bit from the rest of his teeth were distinctive, a real character mark. She praised his build. She gave him silver belt buckles and wrist bands from her jewelers. She presented him with a ring in the shape of a serpent; it coiled around his long middle finger, obscuring the tuft of black hair.

Without saying a word, Danny and Robin knew they would return to New York together. Robin would set up at her SoHo market. Danny would decide what to do next.

"Maybe I'll just go ahead early," Danny said. "I'm almost outta dough anyway. And I hate this place, I have to tell you. All these Scarsdale babes walkin' around on a quaint-high." Danny knew he was taking a chance. He knew that Robin counted the women he described among her best customers.

Robin settled back against his shoulder. She circled her hand beneath his T-shirt. "Just deal with them, baby," she said. "They're part of this world, too."

Danny was quiet. He turned to watch the electric fan that rattled on the floor beside the bed.

Suddenly, in a burst of energy that did not seem consonant with the languid air of their little room, Robin shot up and straddled Danny. She pulled her blouse and camisole over her head, but kept on her necklace of tiny skulls. Pushing up his loose T-shirt, she rubbed both her hands back and forth from his silver belt buckle to his shoulders. Her motions were smooth and wide; she bent her head to let her hair trail along Danny's abdomen, its mass sweeping over the coiled tufts that grew haphazardly over much of his body. Her skull necklace clinked against his silver belt buckle. Danny hooked his thumbs through the loops at the waist of Robin's jeans. He tugged hard. She arched up in surprise, but her flushed eyelids dropped. "Wait," she whispered, "wait just one minute."

Robin jumped up and hastily removed the rest of her clothes. Watching her, Danny did the same. In the corner near the doorway was the tripod she had borrowed from the Institute. She set it up at the foot of the bed, affixed her Nikon to it, and fiddled for a moment with the Nikon's automatic timer.

"All right," she said, back at Danny's side in an instant. She looked up to make sure they were both level with the camera's lens. He looked up, too.

Two days later, after Robin returned from the darkroom, it began to rain for the first time since they had arrived in San Miguel. The rain was torrential; streams of red water and mud rushed between the cobblestones of hilly streets and between the rows of corrugated roof tiles. Rain filled abandoned fountains in disrepair so that water poured over their sides and through their cracks. Danny was miserable in his idleness. He had not decided what would be his next step in life, but he did not want to stay in San Miguel another moment.

He went with Robin to a café where the electric lights flickered and then went dead. It was the middle of the afternoon. With each sip of muddy coffee Danny became more distraught. In five minutes he presented her with a plan of how they could get out of San Miguel the next morning. She listened in silence, poking at the large sugar bun before her, wiping her fingers, poking the bun again. Then she said okay, it was not optimal for her, but she could see it was necessary for him. They spent the rest of the day and evening shuttling between her jewelers, getting boxes and packing them with what the jewelers had so far turned out. In the last two boxes Danny packed most of what they had brought to San Miguel—some clothes, books, notebooks, all their camera equipment, and Robin's photographs from the Institute. Early the next morning Danny borrowed a handtruck from the *supertienda*. He carted boxes back and forth to the post office. He sent the boxes to himself, care of Claire Rollins at Kollman Residence Hall. Later, he could explain to Claire. She would be pissed, as always when she was confronted with an inconvenience, but he knew she would just pile the boxes in the hall and forget about them. If he shipped the boxes to Sal, Sal would glare at them all day. Later, he would ask questions for which Danny had no answers.

While Danny sat in their room awaiting her return, Robin hired one of the North Americans to become what she called a shop steward. She chose a Californian who was friendly with the Mexicans who worked for her. He had a mighty build and a taciturn expression. Danny suspected that they had been lovers—that their affair had prompted her firm stance against getting close with employees.

Robin had borrowed a typewriter to write an agreement between herself and the Californian. He was to see to it that her jewelers completed their present quotas on time. He was also to do quality control based upon standards she set down in the agreement, and he was to ship off the remainder of the jewelers' quotas to her at an address she would provide later.

While Robin was gone, Danny read some from his book on saints and his book on medieval torture techniques. He read about bloodletting until he felt a prescient sense of himself returning. He glimpsed his old beloved self, skewed and irreverent, the same self that Robin had declared she needed.

Thinking over his trip, Danny could not imagine how at the National Museum of Anthropology he had gotten so down on himself. He could not believe he had plummeted because he could not compete with a Mayan ten centuries dead. When he thought of that unknown Mayan now, he wished only that he could meet him, could shake his hand and ask how he had managed to sculpt those fine-edged, snarly lips, how he had so captured the chieftain's conniving heart.

As Robin walked into the room, it suddenly occurred to Danny that he had come to Mexico with little hope, but that he was leaving it with a woman who had changed her plans simply out of respect for his vague desires. He grabbed Robin's hand and ran with her down the stairs, out to the road, and all the way to the *zócalo*, where a battered Volkswagen became the first in the chain of vehicles on their long journey home.

THE MUSES disgusted Otis. Contrary to what he had told Winifred Dodd, he did not find them soulful. The photographer, a burly senior who was ubiquitous with his two cameras and their endless array of lenses, had posed nine half-dressed female students at some of the worst sites in Manhattan: an East Harlem scrap yard, the fire escape of a dilapidated Chinatown tenement, a needle-ridden tunnel near Riverside

Park. Each student held up some prop to represent the art or science over which she presided. Otis felt manipulated whenever he passed through the gallery to his office. Moreover, he was humiliated for the female students who doubtlessly thought they had contributed to a serious statement. He had no idea what had possessed him to agree with Winifred Dodd that this young man deserved a show at the Presidential Gallery. Really, they should have selected the Impressionist imitator. At least she was honest.

As soon as Otis entered his office the last Monday in February, he glanced at his calendar to find out when the senior's show would be dismantled. There was another week and a half before the muses came down.

While flipping through his calendar, the printed heart encircling February 14 caught Otis's eye. Every year for twenty Valentine's days he had presented Nora with an increasingly uncommon flower. During the last several years he had shipped to her a different species of exotic orchid, which he had ordered six months in advance. Nora had always been delighted to receive this one expensive flower. Without fail, she had called him at his office the moment it arrived. This year the flower had come as usual, addressed to Nora.

For days, Otis had tried to reach her. Friends of theirs were celebrating their silver wedding anniversary, and Otis needed to know what to get. Something in silver would not be right, as these people had contemporary Japanese decor in their New Jersey home. He knew Nora would make a stream of rapid-fire suggestions, all terrific. She would not mind being called for this purpose. Always, she had been the one to match the etiquette with the occasion. (It did not seem fair to Otis that overnight he was expected to forego all the ways in which Nora, at such small expense to herself, smoothed his uncertain edges.) For days he had tried to reach her from his office and from home. He could not feign casualness while calling from home; her luminous Valentine orchid sat on the rosewood sidetable beside the telephone. Otis had drummed his fingers on the tabletop while he stared off, half-accusingly, at the South Ferry across the East River. Whether he called from home or from his office, neither she nor her machine picked up.

Finally one evening Otis drove directly from Rensler to Nora's sublet in Turtle Bay. When the doorman announced him, there was a short silence before he nodded and told Otis it was all right to go up.

Barbara Ziegler met Otis at the elevator. Otis had not seen her since her New Year's party the year before. "Is everything all right?" he asked her.

She did not look at him directly. She had grown and permed her hair; it floated out from her head in some sort of Nefertiti style. Her lipstick was russet and her cheeks were gaunter than Otis remembered. "Yes," she said. "There's nothing to worry about."

"Nora hasn't been answering."

"She's not here."

Otis stood awkwardly beside a potted rubber plant in the hallway.

"Would you like to come in? I'm staying here for now." Barbara led Otis into the room where two months before Nora had told him about the mastectomy. The room looked the same, except for a blue ceramic ashtray filled with russet-tipped butts and a pile of fashion magazines next to the sofa.

"I'm staying here while my new floors are being laid. Then I'm flying out to Denver."

Barbara Ziegler worked for a video distributor, for which she sometimes traveled. It was typical of her to use the self-important phrase "flying out." It was typical that she filled

Otis in on the predictable progress of her life while vital changes and questions concerning Nora's hung in the balance.

Otis felt under no obligation to make small talk. "Where's Nora? Why isn't she here?"

"She's in Malibu."

Nora disliked California. She was fond of quoting Gertrude Stein, "there is no *there* there." Otis wondered if perhaps Nora had taken his advice, if she had gone to California for some alternative treatment.

"She'll be gone several months," Barbara added. "Why don't you sit down?"

Otis sat, looking at the carpet. His flannel pants and polished moccasins presented a striking contrast to Barbara's crimson tights, her pointed, metal-tipped cowboy boots.

"Would you like something?"

"No," said Otis. "I'm sorry this is so awkward. I find it difficult being in the position of asking you about my wife."

Barbara slipped off her boots and folded her legs beneath her on the couch. She leaned back and smiled, her expression a studied combination of intensity and patience that set Otis's teeth on edge. "What would you like to know?"

"Naturally, I'd like to know why Nora went to Malibu."

Barbara nodded soberly, as if evaluating the worthiness of Otis's question. "Well, the truth is—" Here, Barbara paused to look about the room.

"For Christ's sake, Barbara!"

"The truth is she has fallen in love. With a stunt man whose book Casper was ghosting. He's almost seventy, but you would never know it. Are you all right?"

"Yes, of course." Otis would not think of giving this woman a shred more power than the horribly imbalanced circumstances had already meted out.

"They're going to try living out there, in his beach house. Nora'll keep up the rent here."

"What about the business?"

"There's some talk of opening up a California office. Everything's premature. Are you all right?"

Otis guessed the stunt man would contribute to Nora's support, just to tide her over. He was struck by the idea that he and the stunt man were engaged in a blind collaboration. Together, they bought Nora new beach wear. Together, they took her out for dinner.

Otis leaned forward. He wanted to leave. "I know you were there for her during the chemo," he told Barbara. "I want to thank you for that."

"She's quit the chemo." At this, Barbara's voice wavered.

"Isn't that dangerous? My God, that's *dangerous*. I think she should try other therapies, but in addition to, not instead of! Didn't you talk to her?" Otis looked at her, this friend of his wife's. As much as anything, he wondered where she stood with respect to being the harbinger of so much painful news.

"She was miserable. She was like a dying dog. No one should have to go through that. Can you imagine that she had her breast removed and was put on that barbaric regimen all inside of three weeks? It scares the living daylights out of me and every woman my age."

"But how can they get it all if she quits?"

"Sweetie. I don't think they're going to get it all. There was plenty of lymphatic involvement. More than she said, I'm sure."

Otis did not respond. Although he allowed that Barbara's endearment was intended to soften the blow, its brashness lingered in the air. He put his hands over his ears and cradled his head. He had assumed this pose since childhood, always during moments gone wild, moments that deftly escaped the province of logic.

"Well," said Otis, standing up, "I'm glad that you were here."

Barbara walked him to the door. Her pace was tentative, and Otis was obliged to imitate it. In the lobby before the elevator she said, "I'd love to see you sometime. We've known each other a good long while."

As she leaned against the wall beside the rubber plant, her russet lipstick still fresh and her hair a sculpted mass off her head, Barbara Ziegler could have been a flat and angular figure painted on an Egyptian vase; consequently, Otis was startled to hear words coming from her. He did not answer. He just left her standing there, her lips moving as she suggested they get together when she returned from Denver.

Otis decided to take the low road for a while. He could freely admit to himself that this decision was born out of his own hurt and confusion, that he was resorting to self-protection in an unhappy time, falling back into old patterns of passive resignation. He freely admitted this, yet did not care to push himself beyond it. In taking the low road, he simply stopped trying to reach Nora. He did not attend their friends' silver anniversary celebration, but he sent a dozen roses. Further, when he passed Sonya Barlow in the corridors of Studio Hall, he did not detain her with Rensler business, as he might have. Not wanting to be reminded of the lie he told in connection with her supper invitation, he rushed past as if on a pressing errand.

The most pointed example of Otis taking the low road came when the Board disagreed with his proposal to turn two recent alumni bequests into endowed places for minority students. "First of all," Brad Shaw had argued, "I'd like a definition of just what minority *means.*" This was said so contentiously that Otis was filled with weariness. He had no interest in having an argument about cultural populations with the Board. He had no interest in hearing them defend their liberalism in every way short of funding two spots for students who would otherwise not be able to attend Rensler. Otis knew the Board was not going to relent, and he could not bear the thought of all the self-justifying bluster he would have to put up with if he tried to win them over. He decided he would not try. It was therefore quickly voted that the bequests would be used to hire two top-notch recruiters who would travel to Bloomfield Hills and Palm Springs, to Highland Park and Santa Barbara. Through untold powers of divination, these recruiters would attract just those over-privileged youngsters who were convinced that a true artist was marked by his or her ability to thrive in seedy surroundings.

As the meeting broke up, Otis exchanged hearty handshakes with each board member in turn. He was the first to leave. Behind him, he heard mingling far-pitched voices and the sound of backslapping.

MARCH

ALL THE WAY home in the taxi from Freyhoff Brothers in Long Island City, Sonya kept pursing her lips. Periodically, she also shook her head. She had gone to talk to Irv Freyhoff about the bronzing of "The Spirit," which art handlers had delivered several days before. She was told Irv Freyhoff was dead. His brother Dave had retired to Phoenix.

"The Spirit" had turned out to be one of the most promising of Sonya's progeny—a bold figure whose correct anatomy established itself through passionate gesture—her raised arms, her one uprooted leg. Although she would never say it aloud these days, Sonya regarded "The Spirit" to be a highly feminine work of sculpture. Again, this was because one noticed the details of correct anatomy only after "The Spirit" had made clear her essential connection to the moment in which she lived. Yes, Sonya thought, this was feminine. Too many figures by men rippled with muscle, and so much of this musculature was hyperbole. Maxwell, who had not been a sculptor, had had enough objectivity about his sex to realize this over-pronounced brawn was a problem in many figures by men. Maxwell would have been delighted with "The Spirit" in whom charged emotion and solid physique so adamantly merged. He would have smiled as if at his own triumph.

At Freyhoff Brothers, however, "The Spirit" was just an-other lump of clay over which to pour plaster for a mold. It did not matter that Sonya had taken her work there for years. It did not matter that Irv and his brother Dave had cast Sonya's top ambassadors, her Shakespearean actors, her premier sci-entists. Once nearly twenty-five years ago an apprentice at Freyhoff's had done a poor job on a cellular biologist. As a result, Sonya had taken her business to a foundry in Virginia. When Irv and Dave had offered to personally recast the biolo-gist, Sonya flew back with open arms. She felt better knowing her sculptures were just a subway ride away. Her beloved busts, her exhibition pieces, all had been safe at Freyhoff Broth-ers. But now Irv had died. In the three years since Sonya's last visit to Long Island City, Irv had died and Dave had retired. The young apprentice who had botched her biologist now ran Freyhoff's. He had come to have gray hair and wear bifo-cals. He told her the foundry business was endangered. Now there were polyresins. Now there were materials and tech-niques by which sculptors could themselves make their works permanent. User-friendly techniques, he had added sarcasti-cally. Who casts in bronze anymore, he asked.

It was of no concern to the apprentice, thought Sonya as she fit the key into her apartment door, that she was spending a fortune on the casting of "The Spirit," and the figure she had worked on every night and every weekend for two months would emerge from Long Island City buffed into a glowing obsolescence.

After Sonya returned from her Sunday morning walk, just as she hung up her thrift-store parka, the phone rang. It was Irene Cone. Sonya was annoyed to hear her voice.

"I'm calling with some rather mixed news," Irene said. "Roger Wiltshire died last week. Had you heard?"

"No." All this dying. Sonya was afraid she sounded outright hostile.

"Before he went, he had several days of extreme lucidity. Freyda and I found it chilling, but the doctor said it happens. There are medical explanations."

"Isn't that interesting."

"During this lucid period, dear, he advised Freyda to buy your Zavin portfolio for Wiltshire's. She wouldn't have necessarily trusted his advice, but he had already made several very astute recommendations regarding his own affairs. His affairs after he was gone, that is."

"Oh, *Irene!*" Sonya resorted to the same nasty tone she had used the time Irene suggested she paint a picture of the houseboats on the Hudson.

"She wants to schedule an appointment with you. I think you'll be quite satisfied with what she'll offer. More than satisfied, I think."

"And Freyda Wiltshire couldn't call herself?"

"Have some compassion, dear."

"Tell her tomorrow night at eight, then."

"I'll be happy to do that for you. And how are *you?* How is your work?"

"My work is fine. Trouble at the foundry, but my work is fine." Sonya was glad for the opportunity to mention the foundry. "In fact, I'm expecting a call from them, now. I hope you and I will see each other for our spring walk. I look forward to it."

Of all the Greek goddesses, the nine Muses were the most special to Sonya. She was disgusted that some little Rensler swellhead had posed them in sordid settings. He had then rendered the scenes in silver gelatin, as if by so crystallizing the edges of his images he would elevate them into art. That he should pose Erato in what was clearly a den for drug users was the most tasteless of what one could expect from a mediocre sensibility. The only reason Sonya had stopped to look at the photographs at all was that she had to compose herself before she confronted Otis Daley. The horrid photographs, however, reinforced just how necessary it was for her to leave Rensler.

Sonya took a deep breath, then strode up to Lily's desk to announce her arrival. This morning Sonya wore a bas-relief pin that showed a lark in ascent. The angle of its flight against her navy blue A-line dress projected the lark towards Sonya's raised chin. Ever since her completion of "The Spirit," Sonya had held her own chin higher.

Otis walked around his desk with his arm outstretched. "Please. Sit," he said, and gestured to a suede chair whose lines did not impress Sonya. She thought his voice sounded fainter than she had last heard it.

"This is enormously difficult, and you will think ill of me," Sonya said. "My circumstances have changed. I must repeal my offer."

"But I've told the Board. Everyone responds to the work of Maxwell Zavin. If you had seen their genuine pleasure—"

"I'm terribly sorry. To be so untrustworthy causes me great pain. But between my own survival and the pleasure of your Board, I must say...well, of course you know what I must say."

Otis looked down at his hands folded on his desk.

There was a framed picture on his desk, the back of which faced Sonya as she sat in the suede chair. It must have been his poor wife. She had to suppress an urge to walk around to Otis's side of the desk to get a look at her.

"Of course your own security must be your top priority," said Otis.

"I have to be perfectly frank in telling you I am not at Rensler to provide recreation for myself. You and your Board may well think that my exhibition record and my years of commissions have set me up. Obviously not. I don't enjoy sitting here today."

"Please, you don't have to—"

· Perhaps Otis Daley's soul was too discreet. Sonya felt her cheeks flaming. Like all of them, these great art fans who cheer you on and praise you to the sky, they don't really want to know.

"Those awful, tawdry places in the photographs out there," said Sonya, gesturing in the direction of the closed door to the Presidential Gallery. "They are menacing to me in the most personal way. Why should I think, in this city that is crumbling around us, that I am so light, a delicate blossom that will float to the top? Day by day, if you haven't noticed, there is nothing left to float *on*!"

"I have noticed," said Otis evenly. "Of course we've all noticed. That's why we have to raise funds as aggressively as we can. That's why the auction's so important. You must remember Rensler has no endowment."

"Have you noticed in this discussion, that the territory you protect is far more expansive than the one I protect? And yet you expect me to turn mine over to you. It's quite feudal, really. It is quite lord and vassal."

"It's nothing of the sort." Otis's tone was severe. "It is simply this: On New Year's Day you made a very generous offer and I accepted. If you need to now withdraw that offer, I perfectly understand. I will let the Board know at our next meeting. Sid has been very successful in seeking donations. I don't see a problem." Otis stood up.

Sonya trembled as she stood also. She made herself look openly at Otis's face. It now occurred to her that he might think the entire bungle had come about because he had refused her invitation to lunch. Her cheeks burned all the more.

Otis opened the door and walked Sonya out to the Presidential Gallery. Standing on the Rensler insignia woven into the worn blue carpet was Claire Rollins, a young sophomore in Sonya's twentieth-century art survey.

"Claire!" greeted Otis, his tone now hearty. "Thank you for coming. How would you like the next show here? Another one-person? Winnie was going to write you, but I said, no, have her come in."

Although Sonya should have walked straight past them and through the gallery, she stood unmoving next to Otis. She watched Claire's face as she took in the news. It could have been her own face, so many years before, when she first heard that the most personal of her convictions would be mounted for people to see. It could have been her face when she first perceived there might truly be a link between what she and utter strangers held dear. Claire Rollins's thrilled and anxious expression was identical to Sonya's so many years before. It was Sonya's expression the moment it seemed possible that the great, collective vision of the ages might come along and acquire her own vision, might casually sweep her vision into its wake.

For moments Sonya stood alongside Otis, foolishly beaming with him at this young student who, rather than look back at them, dropped her slide portfolio and bent down to retrieve it.

Someone had posted a handwritten sign on the rear wall of the old and tarnished brass elevator in Sonya's building. "For those of you who don't know," it read, "Mrs. Fine, a long-time resident of this building, passed away last week. Many of us in the building knew and loved her. There will be a memorial service at Riverside Church tomorrow at 2 p.m."

Of course Sonya would not go. Whatever she was, she was not a hypocrite. Still, the posted notice had set her heart pounding anew. She tried to calm herself. Once inside her apartment, she changed into her leotard and assumed a full-lotus position at the center of the beautiful kilim that Zavin had given her nearly three decades before. Her pulse still raced. She closed her eyes and tried to clear her mind. She guided her thoughts outside the confinement of self, let herself become just another among the plaster and bronze figures that peopled this room. As if the whole room were a frenzy of converging forms, Sonya imagined herself the one resting place that made the composition work. As a result, her breathing stilled. Sonya began to waft through a lovely calm, a calm broken by the unbidden, raspy sound of Ida Fine's last words to her: "It's like money in the bank."

SEVERAL DAYS before Claire got her show at the Presidential Gallery, fifteen boxes from San Miguel had been delivered to her apartment at Kollman. They had arrived without notice. Claire slit open the first one with her mat knife. Inside were several Nikon lenses. Below these was a clasp envelope, open. Claire removed a handful of 8 x 10 black-and-white photographs. Their weight in her hand surprised her. The pictures had been taken with the whole array of lenses: wide angle, zoom, fish-eye. They showed Danny with a woman—doubtlessly Robin. They showed Danny's buttocks, the hollows in his contracted muscles as he bent over her. They showed indistinct planes and limbs at right angles. They showed the woman's hands posed in the shape of a pedestal for some precious object—a Faberge egg, the Hope diamond; her fingertips were a mount for Danny's erect penis. Some pictures showed her face, along with Danny's, laughing hysterically into the camera. The skin around Robin's eyes was tighter than Claire would have thought. Danny's was a face so delivered from the grim labor of trying to sell his love that Claire did not recognize it. Through the grainy surface, his high-spirited expression was clearly that of a person at leisure. Its appearance stabbed Claire first with guilt, then fury. She opened two more boxes. Trays of jewelry were piled inside each. Gaudy, she thought, and closed the lids.

Minutes later, Claire called Sal Vincent and found out that Danny had been home for two weeks, that he was staying in Coney Island with his new girlfriend. Claire had never met Danny's father, but she had no trouble telling him that fifteen boxes had arrived at her room at Kollman Residence Hall. If Danny did not have them out in one day, she would leave them stacked in the parking lot.

Three hours later, Danny appeared. He stood at her threshold in his denim jacket with the embroidery of Lucifer's expulsion from heaven. He held onto the bar of a hand truck stamped with Kollman's name. "Hi."

"Goddamn you."

"Talk about a restricted vocabulary."

Claire took some pleasure in the fact that Danny's face was crimson. "You dropped out. This is not your room. You can't just use it as a warehouse."

Danny strode past her. He began to pile boxes onto the handtruck. "Hi!" he said in an enthusiastic, high-pitched voice. "I'm so glad you're back! How was Mexico? Have a beer. Tell me all about it."

"Danny, I don't have time. I'm painting, okay?"

Danny stopped loading the handtruck. "What'sa problem?" His face was still red.

At a furious pace, Claire rattled a brush inside her turpentine jar. "I'm going through a confused time. I'm letting some things gel. Just respect that, okay? Please just take these out of here. We can talk later."

Danny banged around in silence, loading boxes and taking them to a freight elevator. When he left he said, "I'll be at Sal's. When you're gelled." The door shut behind him, and Claire threw several brand new acrylic brushes to the floor.

To celebrate her upcoming show, Claire went with Melina to Essie's, a lace-curtained café two blocks from Rensler. It was the warmest night in months, an anomalous night, a prevision of spring. A rope tied to the window gates held Essie's front door open. Incoming breezes stirred the curtains and brought with them a faint smell of tar from newly filled potholes outside. It did not matter to Claire that the smell of tar was acrid. What mattered was that it was warm enough for the outside to be admitted inside, for the candlelight and street lights to merge in her field of vision, for the people on the sidewalk to see Claire and Melina inclined towards each other.

Since she had received the Jim Dine heart for Valentine's Day, Claire had seen Melina twelve times. Twice they had stayed in Greenwich. The second time Regina told Claire how glad she was Melina did not bring the Shipley boy around anymore; she had never cared for his sullen manner. The other times, they had stayed together at Kollman. Melina's Peruvian shawl now hung full time in Claire's closet. When alone, Claire sometimes opened the closet just to look at the llamas along the shawl's border. Although they filed workmanlike across its vast hem, their countenance grim, the llamas became for Claire ushers to a future she had never contemplated—she, who had so minutely imagined the scenes of her life ahead.

They drank wine. Claire told Melina she would like to take her to the south of France, to Provence, to Arles; she would like to paint her in legendary light. Melina laughed. While that sounded lovely, she said, Claire would probably not find her as complacent as the models from the days of the Impressionists.

Claire fell silent. The thought that she had offended Melina, had possibly angered her, left her stranded. Ever since she had met Melina, watched her aloof response to the more vulgar of their classmates, her grace in critiquing the work of inferior artists, her offhand and gentle mocking of her parents' wealth, Claire had felt in her sway. She was in awe of Melina's social ease, and felt sure Melina would always be more tactful, more correct, than she. Again and again, she found herself in the position of requiring Melina's pardon. Suddenly she wanted to be back at the efficiency, alone.

"Sweet Claire," said Melina, seeing Claire's downcast eyes.

Claire looked up nervously. There was vastly more wanting within her, and she could not hide it.

They spoke of Claire's show, how she would hang it. They discussed Melina's new quandary—would she focus on documentaries or dramatic shorts? Melina complained that both fields were dominated by men with streaks of megalomania. At this turn in the conversation, Claire began to feel restored. A tiny but perfect point of longing, a nucleus, began to swell.

Melina ordered a blackberry cordial. Claire sat back. After their dinner plates were cleared and the cordial sat before her, Melina said, "I talked to home today. Grammy's in the hospital."

In the Greenwich house sunroom a week earlier, Claire had played double solitaire with Regina. Regina had worn her magenta butterfly earrings.

"What *happened?*"

"My parents came home yesterday morning. Last night, Grammy swallowed half a bottle of Dalmane. We don't know where she got it. Not from her doctor."

"My god. Do you want to go?" Claire pushed back in her chair. "Shouldn't you be home?"

"It's happened before. I don't want to go home, I want to be with you. My mother's furious. With me, too. Of course Grammy did it to punish them, they were away for two months. But she told my mother I've been gone most of the time, too. I think I'd better stay clear of there for a few days."

If she and Melina had spent twelve nights together, Melina must have spent other nights over the past two months somewhere else. When she looked at Melina's face, she could no longer focus. "I think you should go back," she said. "Really."

Melina bit her lower lip while considering her response. Her smile was tentative. "I'd love to stay with you. Don't you want me?"

Again, Claire looked down. Unlike Melina, Claire was for the first time making love in a way that society, at its kindest, distrusted. Added to this, Claire did not altogether trust Melina. Were they to stay together, Melina would steal her focus. Far more capable than Claire of dismissing the expectations of conventional society, Melina would just keep approaching. Like the waves that had slapped against the Boston Whaler idling in the Sound, the rhythm of Melina's approach would lull Claire. Then, suddenly, Melina would retreat. Claire would be left without her precious ability to focus, the ability she counted upon to earn her the life of an artist.

Melina cocked her head slightly to one side. She cradled the bowl of her cordial glass between two slightly freckled fingers, then tipped it in Claire's direction. "Don't you want me?" she repeated.

Claire opened her mouth to say something about trust, the Shipley boy, what she required from someone for whom she would trade her solitude.

Melina waited. Her attention was fully upon Claire.

"Of course I want you," said Claire. "I thought you might not want me."

WHENEVER THEY went out together, Danny and Robin wore mythical symbols. It was just something that happened. Tonight, standing outside the Presidential Gallery, Danny wore his serpent ring and a belt with an ivory unicorn head inlaid on a silver buckle. Robin wore papier-mâché earrings in the shape of Pegasus.

"Let's just hang out here for a minute."

"Danny. You're nervous."

At this, Danny pinned Robin against the wall and kissed her. Robin did not respond except to repeat, when Danny finally released her, "You're nervous."

He led her by the hand. A wall bordered by a column of glass bricks had been installed at the entrance to the Presidential Gallery. Someone had painted the wall dark blue, indigo. *People at Leisure* extended upwards in a peach-colored flowing script. "Jesus," said Danny. "All of a sudden Daley's puttin' on the ritz."

Although most of the paintings were framed only by one-by-twos nailed into their stretchers, a few had gilded frames. Danny decided Claire must have found these or picked them up at an antique shop. Molding frames out of plaster was *his* thing; she had always been envious. He recognized most of the paintings in the room, but some she had done when he was in Mexico. One, of a group of people drinking wine in a poppy field, she had been completing the day he picked up Robin's boxes.

Danny merely scanned the pictures. At this opening, the people interested him more. Barlow, for instance. He was amazed to see her at a Rensler thing. She did not give two shits about the place and everyone knew it. Yet here she was, in a corner with Jake Winter, the Illustration II instructor who had learned to airbrush so he wouldn't have to learn to draw. Here she was, Sonya Barlow, who would flunk you if you had heard of Claes Oldenburg but not Camille Claudel, Richard Serra but not Gaston Lachaise. Here she was straining on her toes to listen to a guy famous for the airbrushed image of a merry weasel family—the mother, father, and baby who had survived an entire decade on a sugared-cereal box.

"This is great," Danny told Robin. "This is really great." He led her to the long table at the rear of the gallery, where they were served champagne. His hand sweated in Robin's, but he did not let go. He began to see people he did not want to see. Daley was over by the painting of the boat and the hand holding the movie camera. Danny had heard that Otis Daley was really into his *retablos,* that if he had not dropped out he could have had the Presidential Gallery himself. He had heard that Daley was sad when he'd left Rensler. Danny knew this disappointment was not a pose. Daley was all right. Danny suspected that Daley, like him, had no use for the sil-ver-spoon kids.

Danny had primed himself for this opening. It was not like he had returned without a pot to piss in, he reminded himself by the champagne table. Robin was with him. Everyone would see her obvious love for him and the fact that she was older—confirmation that Danny Vincent had all along required something out of their reach. But when Danny looked now at Otis Daley, this reasoning was exposed as mere rationalization. Daley was a good fifty-five years old. What would he care if Danny had won over a thirty-two-year-old entrepreneur? Otis Daley would focus only on what Danny had lost.

"Don't you want to see the paintings?" asked Robin.

"Nah. I've seen them. I'll stay here."

"Uh-huh. What's going on, Danny?"

"Nothin'. I've just seen most of them, all right?"

"Uh-huh. What are we doing here, then?"

"Come on, babe. I thought you wanted to come."

Robin pulled her hand away. She walked towards Claire's first painting, the one nearest the entrance. It showed three people picnicking on a city rooftop. Danny remembered when Claire had painted the picture, the last one of her freshman year. She had sneaked onto Kollman's roof and made charcoal studies of the brownstone and tenement rooftops across the way. Danny had liked the painting that had resulted. "The edge of leisure," he had complimented her.

"Wait," Danny called after Robin.

She waved back at him, a violent gesture. Her Pegasus earrings quivered.

"Jesus," Danny muttered. He drank more champagne. He looked around for Tito and Sandy and P.J., and spotted them talking to Melina Irwin. She pointed out something in one of Claire's paintings. Melina was wearing make-up and a purple silk shirt. Others would think she looked great. He could not stand the way she beamed. Tell her that her best friend had just been sentenced to purgatory and she would beam.

Suddenly a hand embraced Danny's and squeezed. He was going to be cool. He would not squeeze back. When he turned around, though, it was Claire who held his hand. "Danny Vincent, this is my mother, Wanda Rollins."

The champagne made Danny's mouth feel dry and taste rancid. Before he could answer, Claire had released his hand and put her arm around his waist. She had leaned so far into his side that his arm naturally fell around her shoulders. He extended his other arm. "Nice to meet you, Mrs. Rollins."

"What an interesting-looking young man," said Wanda as if Danny were not there. "A real flair. A real style."

"That's a new one," said Danny.

Claire laughed and pressed her outstretched hand on Danny's stomach, above his unicorn belt buckle. The pressure was strong; Danny understood it as a threat. He felt a piercing pain above his eyes—the champagne. A few days earlier he had figured out that Claire had seen the pictures of Robin and him. Compelling him to take part in this masquerade for her mother was Claire's retribution. He did not know the purpose of the masquerade, but it increasingly attracted him. He kissed Claire above her ear. "Great show, isn't it?" he asked Wanda Rollins. "This is great for Claire. Most people who get this space are further along than sophomore year."

From the corner of his eye, Danny saw Robin leave the gallery. "I gotta ask Tito something," he said. "I'm sorry I can't stay longer." He took Claire's face between his hands and, as Wanda looked on, kissed her on the lips. "You gonna talk to me from now on, Superstar?" he shouted, fleeing the room.

He did not overtake Robin until she reached the Rensler gate, on her way to the street where Benno's, now dark, stood on the corner. He pulled her by the arm, then easing up on his grip, kissed her fingers. "All right, I'm an asswipe. I know, a real asswipe. Hate me."

Glossy photos of Rivera's portraits of the execution of Maximilian and of Karl Marx pointing towards the future still hung on the crumbled corkboard above Danny's bed. Alongside them, draped over pushpins, Robin had artistically arranged several of her necklaces. Sixteen floors below, Robin's boxes were stored in a locked compartment between Sal's vinyl Samsonite luggage and Danny's old Schwinn. Robin had a van. Every morning she loaded up boxes and took them to the SoHo market. Every week a new shipment from San Miguel arrived in Coney Island. Sal was impressed. A smooth operation, he said.

Danny had gone back to making art. He made cadavers out of plaster of Paris. Every day he had to vacuum the dusty plaster footprints from Sal's beige acrylic carpet. Sister Patricia Marie was propped up against the living room hutch. Her habit, thick folds of half-shredded gauze, was as white as the rest of her remains. Two spots of gold gleamed—one tooth and the crucifix around her neck.

Every morning on his way to make coffee, Sal Vincent had to roll past the body of Sister Patricia Marie. This morning Danny sat next to her, reading the paper.

"If it were up to me, babe," said Sal, "you could stay forever. I don't give a shit, you're my kid. I don't understand the point of this stuff, but I figure you know the point. I'm not offended, why should I be? But Etta—that's a different story. She wonders what'sa matter with you."

"Since when do I have to prove myself to all of Coney Island?"

"You gotta get yourself a job, too. What man lives off a woman?"

"We got a deal. Soon as she can afford it, she hires me."

"What man works for a woman?"

"Come off it, Pop."

"Listen, I told you, it's not me. It's Etta."

Danny looked Sal straight in the eye.

"The fact is, not like I'm even awake here, but now's as good a time as any." Sal paused to light a cigarette. "The fact is, we're married."

"Jesus. Why?"

"Whad'ya mean, *why?* Decent women want it. So she gave me a choice, you know, marry her or forget it, she would move to Florida. I can't stand Florida. So it happened while you were gone. The fact is, she's supposed to move in here. We'll save that way. For later."

Danny and Sal looked at the plaster Sister Patricia Marie. Searching out a definite feature on which to focus, their gazes finally settled on the hollows of her eye sockets.

The second Sunday in March the temperature fell to the twenties. The wind was so strong that small troupes of litter twirled in the air at intervals above the boardwalk. Danny and Robin walked along, looking for the Polar Bears.

The night before, he had told her they had to move from Sal's. No problem, he had said, he had a tip about an apartment in a city-subsidized building in lower Manhattan. All they had to do was get food stamps, he had explained, and a world of opportunity would open up to them. They had argued. Robin could not believe Danny thought it was acceptable to live that way. He had to keep doing his art, he had explained. She answered that she saw his point, he had to keep making his art so it was okay to be a leech.

"There's Lem! Hey, Uncle Lem!" Danny projected his call through the funnel of his hands.

"It's Sal's kid," Lem cried to the other Polar Bears. "With a young *lady!* Hey, bubula!"

Down on the beach, there was much backslapping and congratulations for Danny. With his Minolta, Danny took pictures of Lem and some of the others with Robin.

Later, walking back to the high-rise, he told Robin he had an idea how he would use the pictures. "I don't think it's right to use people to make social comments," said Robin. "I don't think art justifies it."

"*I* don't do that. Jesus, I've known these guys—these women, too—I've known them my whole life."

"But your art always has to comment. It doesn't just show."

"I can't believe you're saying this basic stuff *now*. I don't have to defend what I do. I know what I'm doing."

"There's a thin line between using people to convey insights, and just plain exploiting them."

Danny could not believe this was the same woman who said she needed his irreverence. "Look who's talking!" he declared, immediately aware this was the most juvenile retort. "At least no one I know actually *suffers* from my exploitation, to use your way-off-base term."

Robin spun around. They now walked several yards apart, and had to shout. "What's that supposed to mean?"

"It means at least I don't pay poor Mexicans migrant wages and make out like I'm doing them a favor!"

They continued along, nearly sprinting. Every few seconds Danny looked to the left, to see if he had reached the next street. As if in defiance of his constant vigilance, the street he had turned up his whole life now seemed to appear from nowhere, fanning ever wider to admit him.

IT HAD BEEN a month since Otis had worked the phrase "low road" into his daily thought and conversation. When his and Nora's old friends asked him out, he answered no-thank-you, and explained that he was just taking the low road for a while. In the middle of March, at the Board meeting in Manhattan, Otis had neglected to report that Sonya Barlow had withdrawn her donation of Zavin's woodcuts from the May auction. He told himself he would get to it, he was just taking the low road for a while.

During his period along the low road, Otis began to have nightmares. He dreamed of catastrophes that resulted from his losing control. He dreamed that one morning he went to his office at Studio Hall where instead of crossing over the carpet with the Rensler crest he stepped over a plywood floor with streaks of wet tar. The floor was like a parody of an abstract expressionist painting, and its splatters detained all who tried to get to Otis. His office, too, was carpetless, and as he sat down at his desk the sound of a siren pitched him from his seat, then from his dream. A night later he dreamed he went to the sublet in Turtle Bay and found Nora, bald, talking animatedly to Barbara Ziegler whose hair remained as thick and inorganic as that of a Dresden figurine. The next night Nora appeared in the closely cropped style he had last seen, and dressed in a striking array of autumn colors. Nora's voice in this dream had a strong timbre. Over and over she declared her new-found happiness, and Otis struggled in vain to rise from the bed—to crane his neck or open his eyes onto the radiant face he saw only through the cunning eyes of dream.

Otis knew these dreams would vanish if he resumed use of his own, sure voice. If he spoke out decisions and opinions, his dreams would grow benign. If he reported to the Board the news about Sonya Barlow, he would begin to take the control that would bring his nighttime world into perspective. If he traced Nora down at the Malibu stunt man's, if he told her in no uncertain terms that he thought her giving up chemo a grave mistake (an opinion which he had every right, indeed every obligation, to express), Nora would cease to become the fading and gaining spectre of his nightmares. Yet he *wanted* to continue to take the low road. He wanted, simply, to do nothing. Whether this impulse was brave or perverse seemed oddly none of his business.

Ever since Nora had left, Otis had gone to galleries and print expos to look at, and occasionally purchase, eighteenth- and nineteenth-century intaglios. He had attended several antiquarian book fairs and had done a little trading with rare art book dealers in the Midwest, as well as with one in New Zealand. Although it was not strictly demanded of his job, he had attended professional meetings in the design fields of interiors, packaging, and print media.

The fourth weekend in March, however, Otis did nothing. He stayed in bed on Saturday morning. There was a vaguely sour feeling in his stomach. He got up after noon and wandered about the apartment. Wearing his silk pajamas, navy with gray piping, he gazed at his bookshelves. Many books there brimmed with the passion he could not muster. And it interested Otis to notice the disturbing points of view to which he had been drawn as a young man—Camus, Kafka, Celine. Although Otis had moved on to novelists who treated the problems of life in a lighter spirit, he was not proud of having abandoned his edge of nihilism. Rather than think the novels he had gravitated towards in recent years—Austen, James, Wharton, even Galsworthy—reflected an evolving taste, he felt he had lost the strength with which to accommodate the visions of, to use Galsworthy's phrase, "those who are always building dungeons in the air." Otis knew he could not today read the novelists of his youth and still go on.

In the middle of the afternoon, Otis put on his chinos, denim shirt, and tweed jacket, along with a mohair scarf, and went for a walk. Never in his recent memory had he met the day at such a late hour, and he was unhappy with the results of the broken routine. He felt he was still in a state of dreaming. Given the nature of his dreams lately, this was no sensation to relish. He felt stripped of something; he did not know what. As he walked along, he fidgeted with the fringes of his scarf, the wedding band he still wore, the tortoiseshell buttons on his tweed jacket. He needed to feel all that was readily manifest about himself. He walked along in an excruciating state of provisional enjoyment. He observed the beginning signs of spring, the crocus tips in the tiny yards of the houses on Garden Place and Grace Court, with a sense of squelched anticipation, a sense that he was ready to enjoy, if only.... When he looked up at the rooftops, at the same dormer windows that had countless times filled him with romantic notions, he felt a rising sense of welcome running headlong into a descending mood of futility. The suggestion of spring in the air confirmed for Otis that no aspect of life piqued his interest.

There was no one to whom Otis could confide his waning interest in the world. Talking to anyone connected to Rensler would be out of the question. Besides, most listeners would blame Otis's circumstances; his wife had cancer and she had moved across the country to be with another man. This was true. Yet Otis believed there were always facts with which people could design their fall from grace. The point was whether they chose to be subverted by these facts, or whether they cultivated a will to triumph over them. Otis had always viewed the will to triumph as something innately within him. Now it had abandoned him. He realized that the low road was anything but a place to coast, that if he did not turn off the low road immediately, only he would be responsible for where it might lead.

When Otis returned home, he called his internist of many years. Shamelessly resorting to the "for a friend" ruse, he got the name of a psychiatrist, one heavily involved in pharmacology, on the Upper West Side. In a choice between Upper East and Upper West, he went unhesitatingly for Upper West.

The impeccable tailoring of Dr. Ray Braun's gray worsted suit, as well as his towering height, immediately set Otis on edge. He shrank within himself at the threshold of Dr. Braun's door. There was a certain type of man with whom Otis had been uncomfortable since boyhood, and Dr. Braun was an example of this type. He had decided in his crib to be successful. In support of his decision, he had developed tunnel vision. If the points of view of others came into Dr. Braun's path, his tunnel vision preserved them while shooting right past; other points of view were flotsam for Dr. Braun. The impeccably tailored suit tipped Otis off. Then came Dr. Braun's thoroughly unctuous smile, his patronizing nods towards psychoanalysis, his habit of caressing his own hands as if he were anticipating a football game kickoff or a guillotine execution.

Otis had to admit, though, that he was in Dr. Braun's office because he himself put some faith in the improvisational cure. If Dr. Braun's personality type was fundamental to the practice of the improvisational cure, well, Otis had asked for it. Dr. Braun was frank and clear in pitching his views on depression. Otis was the willing customer waiting to be sold the solution. Although it seemed to Otis that Dr. Braun was bored, and although it stood to reason he repeated this same summary to patient after patient, he nevertheless meandered luxuriously within its explanation. He compared and contrasted antidepressants in the class of m a o inhibitor and tricyclic, and then he disclosed to Otis his rationale for prescribing each type to a number of depressives who did not have altogether typical symptoms. He strayed into an anecdotal discussion of these depressives. Otis was not surprised. Revealing select nuggets of their decision-making process was an amenity certain professional men extended to others, regardless of their field. Otis did what was expected; he nodded approvingly. Next, Dr. Braun asked Otis some surprisingly basic questions about his moods. Clearly, he had no stake in mystifying his approach to healing. After some minutes he prescribed Elavil, which Otis would take in gradually increasing dosages. Dr. Braun mentioned other options should this one not "yield results." On guiding Otis from his office, he gripped his shoulder and wished him luck. Otis felt bereft. He felt like a child who has just been given a set of explicit instructions, then told he was on his own.

After a week on Elavil, Otis began to closely watch himself. Watching himself was a luxury that at other times Otis found wasteful. And he was uncomfortable when others watched themselves. Every year at Rensler a new group of self-analyzers formed. Otis rushed past them in the halls, in Kollman's cafeteria, basking on the library steps in warm weather and huddled near the hot-air vents in the drafty old painting studios in cold weather. Generally, it was the suburbanites who self-analyzed. Among them were both superior and marginal talents, but only occasionally were there any really hard workers. Otis overheard snatches of their conversation. They confessed the most private feelings to one another, then waited with tense expressions for the confirmation "me too!" or "that's cool." Recently he had passed just such a group in the hall between the silk-screen and lithography rooms. "Okay, so if you're worried about emotional inertia, turn it around!" advised Melina Irwin, a pretty young girl from Greenwich. "Make paintings *about* inertia!"

Under the sway of his new depression, Otis began to understand why people needed to watch themselves. He did not enjoy it. He did not strictly approve of it. But for the first time in his life he saw that minute self-examination might be a process to which people are periodically driven, not the idle activity they assume for lack of better purpose. After he began the Elavil, Otis attended closely to his moods. As it began to take effect, he woke up in the morning with a vague sense of hope. The feeling was not founded on anything concrete, and it did not point to anything concrete. Yet it came after a peaceful sleep, and Otis registered it as a sign of improvement, something he could report to Dr. Braun. (Was there something subversive in the Elavil? Otis found himself eager to present Dr. Braun with the evidence upon which his self-satisfaction was based.)

The last evening in March, Otis sat by himself at a small Greek restaurant in Brooklyn Heights. He ate moussaka and flipped through the local paper. In the real estate section was a listing for fifty acres for sale in Sullivan County. There were two streams on the land, three unused barns, all accessible via a town road. Otis remembered an idea he had had months ago, right after Nora left him and before she got sick. It was an idea how he might use all the money he had invested in utilities. He decided he would call the number in the paper. Then he ordered coffee, drank half of it, and walked hurriedly home. Just before he got to his building, he made another resolution: Next week he would tell the Board that Sonya Barlow had withdrawn her offer of the Zavins. He would tell them that her teaching also reflected no investment in Rensler whatsoever. He would recommend they carefully consider her reappointment.

Later, as Otis got ready for bed, he reflected not upon his decisions, but upon the fact that he had made them. He hoped these decisions would release him from the emotional inertia he could not portray in paint or words. He swallowed the pills that would lead him into a dreamless sleep. He well knew that this manner of resisting inertia was only skin deep. He regretted this. He wished it could be otherwise. For now, though, he was in the middle of a busy semester. It seemed to Otis that if left untended his inertia could turn him into the man he saw now from his bathroom window, the thin one in the drab wool jacket who every night wandered back and forth along the Promenade.

APRIL

TO MARK HER seventy-third birthday, Sonya had some people in for lunch. Her guests did not know it was her birthday. They were there to celebrate the purchase of her apartment, the one on Riverside Drive she had already lived in for twenty-six years. Probably because it was her birthday, Sonya reminisced far more than usual. She talked of her days at the Art Student's League, her top ambassadors, her Shakespearean actors, her premier scientists. She talked of her travels in Europe and Israel, of successive portrait commissions in St. Moritz, Tel Aviv, Paris. She told funny anecdotes related to jurying sculpture exhibits for the National Academy of Design and the Chicago Institute. Sonya's guests listened attentively. Perhaps they knew it was her birthday after all. They were polite beyond all reason, considering Sonya several times let them know her real friends either lived in Europe, or were dead.

The lunch guests were women: Irene Cone, Freyda Wiltshire, and two younger women—Betty Raskin, the part-time librarian at Rensler who had in her collection every Zavin monograph, and Jessica Kitter, the lawyer who had worked on her apartment deal and who collected contemporary prints.

After lunch the women assembled in the living room. Sonya brought in freshly brewed tea. From her small collection of teapots she had selected a stainless steel one by the Bauhaus designer Marianne Brandt. A spherical shape was echoed four times within its design, yet the teapot was a study of simplicity. Her guests praised it. Then Sonya unveiled "The Spirit," which had come back from the foundry the week before. The bronzing had turned out first rate. Miraculously, the superb craftsmanship of the Freyhoff brothers had been preserved by their cynical, bifocaled successor. While Sonya had managed the intuitive balance of "The Spirit's" volumes, Freyhoff had kept her surface texture wonderfully intact.

Making the distinction between a creation and an acquisition, the women praised "The Spirit" more emphatically than they had praised the teapot. Sonya made no such distinction, but she accepted their praise.

"There is a certain indebtedness to Giacometti," observed Irene, peering closely. "A certain tension in the torso area that puts me in mind of him."

"I see more Laurent," said Jessica Kitter. "Not the surface," she said, turning to Sonya. "That is pure you. But the elegance of her lines."

Culture mavins all, thought Sonya. Each had her favorite artist, one whose work she happened to run across the moment her blood-sugar level had primed her for a revelation and, *poof,* forever after the work of that artist was the standard by which to judge all others, however remotely related.

"Zavin had some dealings with Giacometti," said Sonya. "Do you know he didn't work for months because he couldn't get the arrangement on his table right? The package of cigarettes, the saucer, the pencil—they paralyzed the poor man. Paralyzed by the search for equilibrium. Can you imagine that happening to these young artists today? Only their assistants ever see what is on their drawing tables!"

Freyda Wiltshire laughed appreciatively. She had taken a liking to Sonya ever since Roger, during the clairvoyant period of his illness, had advised her to buy the Zavin portfolio. Also, ever since she had become a widow.

"For my own part," continued Sonya, "I have the greatest respect for any man who can be paralyzed by the search for equilibrium."

"What about Zavin?" asked Betty Raskin. "What was he like? What was your relationship to him?"

Now that the Pella windows had been installed, the wind no longer rattled the panes of glass within their old sashes, and the sound of traffic no longer invaded the apartment. Following Betty Raskin's question, the silence in the living room was absolute.

Irene Cone was the first to speak. "Would mentor-student be an apt description, dear?"

"Well, really," said Sonya, "of course Maxwell was a mentor." She quickly rose with the instinct to offer something, but realized that the meal was over, there was nothing left to offer. Once up, she wandered about the room, patting the heads of her portraits, absently stroking the thigh of her sculpture of Eros. Her Eros was a full-grown man; Sonya had represented him after the birth of his brother Anteros, when, according to the legend, Eros had belatedly grown into a tall and mighty man. Sonya's fingertips lingered on the cool bronze of the sculpture's thigh. She looked blankly at the women in her living room. Irene and Freyda had both been married. Betty and Jessica were currently married. Any one of them could have been Maxwell's wife; it would not have mattered to Sonya.

The arrangement had suited her, had been good for her art. What worked, worked. Sonya was not one to undermine a glorious success with doubts. Still, there had never been an occasion in all the years when she had referred to Zavin in any but the most oblique way. Until this very moment, her indirectness had served her well.

"Your relationship must have been very exciting," Jessica remarked. "He must have just swept you away, a man with that kind of power."

"Well, of course, all of us who worked with him were very lucky," said Sonya. "Zavin could look at the pile of peas on his plate and recall the Great Pyramids. He used to say the instinct for pure form rushed through the blood of the ancient Egyptians. According to Zavin, when someone had an instinct for pure form, he had everything."

"Yes," said Betty. "Pure form was where the emphasis was placed, back then."

Sonya could not imagine the state of mind that had prompted her to invite these four women to occupy her space on the occasion of her seventy-third birthday. "And where, dear, would you say the emphasis is placed *today*?"

Recognizing her mistake, Betty looked helplessly at Jessica Kitter, the only other guest of her generation.

"My main interest is in prints," Jessica said, "but I would say that the emphasis...well, what are we focusing on, technique or theme?"

"We are focusing on what motivates!" asserted Sonya. She had dropped into the Wassily chair. "Everything else is fluff."

"We really shouldn't generalize," cautioned Irene.

Sonya flashed her a censorious look. She detested her generation's overabundance of female mitigators.

"Then it seems to me what motivates today is anger," answered Jessica.

"Exactly! But there is a vast difference between the anger of *back then* and the anger of now. Back then, there was an unspoken rule," said Sonya. "Artists made demands of their anger. There was a great deal of anger; artists will always be enraged at those who hold power over them, and artists have a way of turning fruit flies into captors. But the point is, they *transcended* their anger, they demanded that anger tell its story within the framework of forms talking to forms. They demanded their anger be exquisite. "

"Interesting," said Freyda. "And I agree."

"Giacometti is the perfect example. The man teemed with rage. His sculptures walk with unimaginable grace."

Blowing on their tea, the women did not respond. Then Betty persisted, "I understand Zavin was married to a beautiful woman, but that he couldn't communicate with her." She looked at Sonya.

Sonya rose from Wassily, covered "The Spirit" with her protective white sheet, looked at her watch, and said hastily, "I had no idea it had gotten so late. It was so nice to have you here, to celebrate my little good fortune in your company."

In less than five minutes, her guests had gathered their coats and belongings, and were hurrying down the hall to the elevator. As Sonya closed the door to her apartment, she heard Betty Raskin say to Jessica Kitter, "It's too bad she demands that her work transcend her anger. It could have saved her from becoming such a bitch."

At three o'clock, Sonya sat idly in the Wassily chair. Zavin's presence permeated the room. His presence was entirely benevolent; he had been amused by her performance with the lunch guests. He had admired her command of the situation.

Still, she had been shaken by their questions about Zavin. She had been unprepared. Yes, she had been a bitch, and she would be again. The obtuseness of people was a constant source of amazement to her—their readiness to violate privacy. Everyone reduced their most intimate relationships into lines of Madison Avenue copy. They coerced others to do the same. Married women were the worst. Married women had always tried to inveigle their way into Sonya's confidence. She had never let them. She had no need to confirm her feelings by checking them against the feelings of married women. This great urgency people had to prove they were alive by telling all—well, telling all was a messy, formless affair that did no one any good.

Yet there in the Wassily chair, Sonya could not keep back the tears. First came a pressure at the bridge of her nose, then her eyes stung, and with the tears came the inevitable blood from her nose. She arched her head back and stared impatiently at the gray plaster of the ceiling. Zavin was still with her. How and to whom could she ever represent his place in her world? Who would possibly understand what had been taken away from her when he died? She had not gone to the memorial service at the Park Avenue Synagogue. Rather, she read about it in a small notice in the *New York Times*. Hundreds had attended. No one sent her condolence cards, or baked from their hearth, or invited her to pour out her grief. Quietly, she had called the lawyer Zavin had told her to call, the one in charge of his trust for her. She had barely been able to produce an intelligible sound, but the lawyer had not said he was sorry—who knows what his type made of a woman in her position. For weeks on end, Sonya had cried. Finding the consequences of her secrecy unbearable, she had reviled herself for having lived under such a tight shroud. She resolved to be more open with people, to make a few trusted friends, to present to them the entire array of vital feelings Zavin had awakened in her, to give them the gift of his charged presence, his unflagging gallantry. But she had never cultivated these trusted friends. Rather, she returned full force to her work. She had seen this man and that one, but she had kept Zavin with her, had indulged herself in the morbidity of not letting go.

When she no longer felt the blood trickling down the back of her throat, Sonya straightened up. She'd had enough of herself. Her morbidity had become for her like the overused color she had once banished from her palette, a drab old compound that had repeatedly attracted her brush, only to later kill off her picture.

Where to, now, she asked herself. For the time being she had a tiny nest egg, but she had no trusted friends, no commissions, and few exhibition prospects. If no one was interested in accepting her gifts in art, well, she had two choices. She could lie down and die, or she could extend her gifts within the improbable context of daily life.

She went to wash up, then called Otis Daley at his Rensler office.

"I'll get right to the point," she said, perceiving shortness in the tone of his greeting. "I have not felt right since I came to your office. My position now is much more secure, and I can afford to be myself. A new sculpture of mine has just returned from the foundry, and I'd like to donate the first casting to your auction. I would be delighted if you would accept."

Otis paused, then thanked her—tentatively at first, then, as if in a dawn of recognition, with genuine enthusiasm.

Sonya had never given away a drawing or sculpture in her life. What was so wondrous about Otis Daley's thank-you was its maddening innocence. He believed that her real self was a woman of bounty. From Sonya's point of view, a person's essence was determined not by some colorless list of facts, but by the depth and breadth of illusion they conjured. At this moment, mid-afternoon on her seventy-third birthday, Sonya was a munificent woman.

SITTING IN the Saab's passenger seat on the drive up I-95, Claire had a premonition that it would take her many years to recover from the humiliation to come. She had reason to predict humiliation. The weekend before, an unusually bright first weekend in April, Melina had called very early Saturday to suggest Claire catch the 9:15 train to Greenwich. Kevin and Selina were on a buying trip, explained Melina, and Regina was being treated for depression at a facility in Westchester.

Although she was in the middle of a painting, Claire had not been able to resist the idea of Melina all alone in the Greenwich house, the idea of the two of them taking turns looking through the telescope in the gable, being silly with the cats, buying lobsters on the Irwin's account at the fish market in town, roaming the house naked all weekend. Charged with anticipation, Claire's mind wandered from the conversation to which flowers she might bring from the stand in Grand Central. Suddenly, the sound of a familiar name jolted her back. "Brad Shipley's coming over to see some rushes on Sunday," Melina was saying. "I forgot. Oh, well, that's okay." The image of irises and freesia vanished from Claire's thoughts. She told Melina she really needed to stay to work on her painting after all. She hung up the phone before Melina could say good-bye.

Now, the second weekend in April, Claire and Melina would really be alone in the house by the Sound. Already,

Claire was uneasy. In every sense, Melina was in power. As she drove the vintage Saab, changing gears with the shift attached to its steering column, Melina was the picture of control, an experienced driver capable of handling the most idiosyncratic machine.

Next to Melina on the extra high passenger seat, her feet resting like mere leaves on the floor mat, Claire felt like a child. Melina's conversation was typically warm, and she frequently reached over to squeeze Claire's hand, but the ordinary harmony of her tone sounded sinister to Claire, whose bleak thoughts careened. Moreover, they were going to the vast and opulent house in which Melina, absurd though it seemed to Claire, had been brought up. Those relentlessly cheery rooms were no place to bring up the subject of Melina's disloyalty. How could she sit with Melina under the smiling stuffed bass or the watercolor of the yacht club (the Irwins knew how to escape the aesthetic rigors of their profession), and describe her unutterable pain at imagining the two of them, Melina and Brad Shipley, together?

No, before they had even reached Connecticut, Claire knew she would never be able to balance the power, that the weekend would be spent wallowing in the horrid realization that their connection had come to be *about* power.

All Saturday and Sunday, Claire and Melina poured their affection onto the cats. In one hysterical display, they dressed them up as medieval courtesans. Outside it rained or misted, and the wind blew. When they were not playing with the cats, they ate lobster and caviar, drank vodka and tonic, made conscientious and lonely love. Before dawn on Monday morning they went up to the gable, but while Melina adjusted the telescope Claire was silenced by the first blinding pain of a hangover, a pain which seemed to mark the enormous failure before them—Melina's refusal to acknowledge Claire's openness, a refusal that did not politely turn its back but, in consort with the telescope in her hands, seemed to address its displeasure to the very heavens.

On the ride in to Rensler two hours later, Claire finally admitted, in a trembling voice, she simply could not stand it that Melina saw Brad Shipley so much.

"Hmm," Melina said, her eyes on the road, "I'm sorry. I really am. I don't really care that much about Brad. But I can't be restricted."

Claire said nothing for the rest of the trip. At the Kollman parking lot, she told Melina that she hoped her grandmother got better, she hoped the place in Westchester would help her awful depression. She added that she really liked Regina, she was moved by her. Then she smiled in a way she knew very well to be doleful, and, with the intention of never opening it again, shut the door to the vintage Saab.

Three mornings later, stunned by her inability to recall what her life was about, stunned and in urgent need of distraction, Claire invited her mother to play hooky. Wanda made it clear that leaving her nursing assignment in the middle of the week was highly uncharacteristic. She agreed, though, to meet Claire at the entrance to the Central Park Zoo. After the zoo they would poke around the shops along Madison Avenue. Claire had selected these diversions. They were going-back-to-the-womb diversions because they were Wanda's idea of a perfectly suitable way to spend an afternoon.

When Claire arrived, Wanda was already there, using a lamppost to support some exercise warm-ups. Claire rushed towards her as one might rush towards a child blithely disrobing in public—with quick steps but anxious looks into the crowd. Wanda stopped when she saw Claire's frowning face. She smiled at her daughter's severity. "Honey!" she called, rushing forth.

Again, Wanda was glowing, Claire was pale. Wanda's fuchsia lips were sticky on Claire's cheek. "We *have* to brighten you up a little," she said. "I'm so glad you wanted to take the day off like this. It was the best idea you've had in months!"

Claire felt herself stiffen. To think that Wanda assumed that if Claire expressed no ideas to her, she simply *had* no ideas! To think that Wanda imagined her always locked in an airless, turpentine-smelling room simply because she was not at the Central Park Zoo with her.

They went to watch the polar bears. One lay spread-eagle on its back in a fake glacial pond while the other slept in the sun on a slight incline several yards beyond. As they stood silently watching, Claire remembered the other Polar Bears, and began to tell her mother about them.

"They swim in December!" repeated Wanda in contrived disbelief. "Isn't that amazing! Interesting, too, a reaction against too much comfort, I bet, man's need to be adventurous, to upset the apple cart. What are they like? Have you talked to them?"

"No. Actually, I've never seen them."

"Well, but you know about them. How do you know about them?"

"I know about them—okay? Is that so amazing?"

"Claire. You asked me to come in this afternoon."

"Jesus. This guy I know knows them, all right? He just told me about them."

"*Oh*," said Wanda. "I see."

My god, thought Claire. She thinks I asked her in to tell her about Danny! A month earlier she had introduced Wanda to Danny with the intention of misleading her, but today she had no wish to plant allusions about anyone. She just wanted to be left alone. Claire rushed ahead, announcing she was going to monkey island, where there would be more action.

It was chilly along Madison Avenue later, and although they kept gathering their collars, they did not pick up their pace. This part of the visit had been earmarked as a leisurely stroll. Wanda had so far not paused once in her conversation. Now she exclaimed over a coffee maker in the window of an upscale houseware's shop. Claire told her she heard it had been designed by a Rensler graduate, but Wanda was not impressed. Rather, she responded by comparing it feature for feature with her new one at home. She went on in tortuous detail. Claire listened in a blunted, mesmerized silence. She wondered about levels of being alive. Now that she had spent time with Melina, how could she be said to be alive here on Madison Avenue with her mother? Were Wanda not her mother, she would never have occasion to know her. How odd it was to be strolling along with this woman who was so completely foreign to her, yet who was so much a part of her as to be entitled to say "*we* have to brighten you up a little." There was some glorious comfort in this paradox, some feeling Claire had determinedly sought today, and so she squeezed Wanda's shoulders and kept her arm clumsily about her as they walked along.

Claire went with her mother to wait for the bus at Port Authority. They sat on a bench drinking coffee from styrofoam cups. For a moment, Wanda Rollins stopped talking. When she turned to look at Claire her expression was serious and a bit frightened. Her lipstick had all but worn off. Claire noticed a new sagging of the skin around her jawline.

"I wonder," ventured Wanda, "if you are so reluctant to share with me because you saw how unhappy I was with Daddy. I wonder if you think that if you share with me the same thing will happen to you. That could be described as a sort of magical thinking, you know. Life doesn't work that way."

Claire shut her eyes and sighed. She wished her mother had never started with those groups—the caregivers, the weightwatchers. They amounted to the same thing: counterfeit openness. Claire had once heard her twentieth century survey teacher, Sonya Barlow, go on about the new counterfeit openness, and she had been glad to hear someone describe it—describe and publicly attack it.

"You don't have to say anything now, but I hope you'll think about it. All this keeping to yourself—it isn't good."

Who the fuck says, Claire was about to answer, but the bus to the Oranges pulled up, and so she hugged her mother good-bye.

That night, Claire smoked a joint from the stash Danny had left behind the dead radiator in his efficiency. It was potent—laced with something or just carefully cured. She put some Alice Coltrane on low and sat on the floor, propped against the single bed, gazing at some canvases that had just come back from the Presidential Gallery. All month, students had praised her. People who had never spoken to her sought her out to talk about the show, to say they really related to it. One girl, a freshman, confessed to Claire her own mighty attachment to Impressionism, as if Claire's show had made her taste respectable. By all accounts, the show had been a triumph. A *coup*, Cole would have said, and his discovery of a fitting military term would have validated Claire's ambitions. In her father's eyes, a public success legitimized the most suspect, the most ethereal effort. Sonya Barlow would say her father practiced America's true religion—worship of the product.

Each compliment had given Claire a warm but short-lived glow. Here, stoned in an increasingly disgruntled way, she had to address the part of herself that plummeted thirty seconds after each compliment. After the warm glow vanished, she had walked around feeling like the worst sort of imposter, someone who conveys unfelt joy. Her joy was not hers but that of picture subjects from another century, young ladies who were utter strangers. Claire had read about French society during the period of Impressionism. She knew that, if led away from their boating parties to be seduced by the woman who painted them at leisure, the ladies who were the subjects of these pictures would have run screaming for the hills.

Restless, Claire stood up and went to inspect the contents of her refrigerator. Nothing in it appealed to her, yet there was a gnawing at her stomach. She did not want to go out; she knew the walk to the all-night bodega two blocks away would be interminable.

From the refrigerator Claire removed eggs, a plastic bag of soggy and engorged bean sprouts, an onion with only four fresh rings, a cold boiled potato, and a pot of Boursin. She fried the potato and onion into hash browns and combined the rest of the ingredients into a huge, lopsided omelet, which she topped with ketchup. She ate these with zeal, as if the act of eating could somehow expunge all the cowardliness from her paintings. Claire reveled in the shabbiness of her supper. A realization of searing command struck her: lobster and caviar were the food of the faithless, while her meal tonight fed only the worthy. Then, seeking to extrapolate on this perception, she entirely forgot it. She stacked the dirty dishes in the sink, and watched the little insight bob and then retreat from the surface of her memory. Finally, she gave up trying to uproot it, swore she would never get stoned again and, still wearing her carpenter's jeans and black jersey, went to bed.

ANYONE WHO happened to observe Danny's explosive stride on his way to Cherry Street might have wished that he keep propelling ahead, that no unplanned stop give rise to the overflow of his rage. And it was true that Danny struggled at every stoplight, shifting from one foot to the other, rubbing his palms together in a hypertensive frenzy. At every stoplight he ventured into the crosswalk before the light changed.

The refrain "Are you talking to *me?*" from the movie *Taxi Driver* kept running through Danny's head. He and Robin had seen the movie in Brooklyn. They were no longer a couple as they watched, but they had clutched hands for as long as images filled the screen. Danny's concentration had wavered, but he had riveted on "Are you talking to *me?*" Practicing in the mirror the voice and posture of bringing off alibis, Robert De Niro had repeatedly confronted his unseen accuser: "Are you talking to *me?*"

Now, darting around cars on Canal Street, flipping his finger at a pretzel vendor whose cart dominated the sidewalk, plowing through a crowd of lunchtime office workers (the synthetic colors of their clothes an unheeded scandal), Danny responded, "Are you talking to *me?*" to all *his* unseen accusers, a faceless tribunal that ticked off the counts against him: no girlfriend, no job, no school, no belief.

Back on the "D" train, exhausted, the key to Cherry Street in his pocket, Danny silently translated all the Spanish advertisements. He persisted until he got each word of each ad. He memorized the boasts of saffron rice, mouse and rat poison, free pregnancy tests. No matter how refined his translations grew, he perceived that the ads were reproaching him, and so continued to defend himself, "Are you talking to *me?,*" all the way back to Coney Island.

At home, Sal sat at the dining table fitting model pieces together. He was building the Titanic and had just begun the hull. Etta had gotten him the set.

"You'd be better at this, babe. Yeah, I know, you think it's for bozos. But you got the facility."

Danny withdrew into the kitchen and returned with a can of Pepsi. He sat down across from Sal. "We gotta talk."

"Talk. Since Etta, all I do is talk. I didn't think about how when she lived upstairs she was probably busy talking to herself, you know what I mean?"

Etta had moved in. Now she was at her job at the Department of Motor Vehicles. Later, she would come bearing a foil-lined bag of barbecued chicken.

"Listen. I got some stuff I gotta tell you. Things are changing fast, Pop. Robin and me, well, you know, *kaput.*"

Without hesitation, Sal answered, "She was too old for you." He put his tube of cement down and looked at Danny. "It would'na lasted."

Typical, thought Danny. Sal liked Robin. All along he said she was on the ball, a real go-getter, a woman with plenty upstairs. All it took was for Danny to say it was over, and she was suddenly nothing but too old.

"The truth is, Pop, I think I let her down. I think I expected more of me. More than I could give."

"You give plenty," said Sal automatically.

"Anyhow, like I said, stuff's changing fast. I'm takin' that place on Cherry Street. Listen, it's nice, I saw it. It's gotta kitchen with a window and a whole extra room where I can do my art."

Sal sorted through the grey plastic ship parts spread over the table. "So you gonna sleep in the living room, then?" he asked. "You can get a convertible."

"A futon, I'll get. Later."

"Whad'ya, a monk? Take yourself to Castro."

"Someone left a mattress. I'll use it for a while."

"You want five hundred bucks? Get me my passbook."

"Pop. I'm fine."

"Yeah, right. There's an empty studio downstairs. I talked to the super. Wall-to-wall carpet, new fridge."

"Etta wants me out. She don't want me downstairs."

"Shit. Etta."

Honeymoon bliss, thought Danny.

Sal rolled himself away from the table, pivoted his wheel-chair so its back faced Danny. In a second, there was a click from his Zippo and a cloud of smoke appeared above Sal's head. "Whad'ya gonna do with yourself? Whad'ya think— you can sit around takin' handouts like your old man?"

"One thing at a time, you know? I'll get in Cherry Street. I'm tellin' you the leases are like gold, once you're in. More could go haywire on Sutton Place. Then I'll be in, and I'll get a job."

"A year and a half in art school oughta land you right in a board room, babe. Write your ticket."

"Pop. Since when do we make each other squirm?"

"Get me my passbook." Sal spun around. His eyes were small and glazed with tears.

"Hey. I'm sorry. You shouldn't worry."

"First you go to Mexico, now you're goin' to the jungle. Who's gonna take care of you?"

Danny could not answer. He could not say Robin, he could not say himself.

"I oughta get the mummies out first. Robin'll lend me her van." Then, wedging the tin opener inside the empty can of Pepsi, Danny added, "She didn't come home two nights last week. And listen, what's the use anyway? She wants a real life. She's already got herself a studio-plus-alcove on York Avenue."

"Get ridda her," was all Sal said, his eyes focused not on Danny, but on another time and place.

"*She* got ridda *me*."

Sal resumed his place at the table. "I ever tell you 'bout your grandfather's best buddy went down with the Titanic? 'Course, this was the maternal side, now."

Before she pulled her van out of the Cherry Street parking lot, Robin told Danny that she still loved his irreverence; if the truth be told, she still needed it.

"I'll bottle it for you," he had offered. "Fancy box with gold calligraphy. '*Irreverence* by Vincent. Smell like you've only dared dream.' You got two choices. Hog Pen or Baboon Cage."

Back alone in his new apartment, Danny went into the living room and stood by the window. From there he saw half the span of the Brooklyn Bridge. He had hung up all the *retablos* from his Rensler days; they climbed the entire wall to the right of the window. The collection of brightly colored miniatures and the wide expanse of bridge presented a dramatic abutment of forms that would attract any Rensler eye, would surely attract Claire's when she arrived.

Minutes later, though, stalking into the living room ahead of him, Claire was upset. "You were *supposed* to meet me at the subway," she said. She had tried the broken intercom, then called from a pay phone.

"So listen," he said, gesturing to the view, "would you check this out, already...is this amazing, or what?"

"It's great. Depending on how you feel about bullets in the hall."

"Amenities. The interior designer moonlights as a gang leader."

Claire had gone over to look at the *retablos* on the wall. As if she were in a museum, she clasped her hands behind her back. Danny had to steel himself against falling in love with this gesture.

"You wanna see my new *momias*? They're in here," he said, and started off to the other room.

She placed a hand on his arm. "Later."

Standing there, Danny felt his old body-consciousness return. He was helpless. When a body is wanted, it relaxes between poses. When it is unwanted, it swells and bloats, grows hairy, prickles deep inside.

"I'm sorry about those pictures Robin took," he said, his eyes fixed on the Brooklyn Bridge. He really did want to apologize. Also, though, he wanted to remind her of his body when it was wanted. "I know you think I did it on purpose, but it was honestly a mistake. I'm sorry."

"It's all right. I believe you."

Danny faced her. "Hey. Huong Fat?"

At Huong Fat, Danny and Claire's favorite Chinatown dive, the conversation turned to love. The MSG is what did it, Danny said during a lull, but neither laughed.

Danny started by talking about Robin. He told how because of Robin he knew the difference between love and need, love and a signed pact to enter into self-delusion. Self-delusion was okay, he said, he hadn't minded it, it had been interesting, he had proved he could play the game of the world. But then, it was different from love, he confessed, blowing on his eggdrop soup.

Then Claire told Danny about Melina. He looked openly at her face while she spoke. She looked in the direction of the worst wall paintings, the kitchen, the waiter. He tried to make it easy for her. He told her nothing she would say would take him by surprise.

"Okay, thanks," said Claire, her voice gaining strength. "I was in love. Maybe I still am," she said, her tone dipping again.

"But, Melina, there's a glibness there, an ease that—" she paused. "I guess maybe I don't trust anyone who's not a nervous wreck." With this, tears came to her eyes, and she bit fiercely into a steaming spring roll.

Here, Danny had to hold himself back. His opinion that Melina Irwin was a silver spoon, that she negotiated the world without a conscience, had been driven in with a sledgehammer. He continued to look directly at Claire. It was not so bad, what she told him, he thought. It was easier, less sweeping, he had to admit, than if it had been, say, Tito. He knew instinctively he must never let Claire sense that the depth of his injury had been reduced by the fact that Melina was a woman. And yet when he said, "I guess you're gonna need some guts," his voice was softer than either had ever heard it, and as full of love.

"Yes, I know."

"I think you're gonna be fine, Claire. I think you got the guts, I mean, like the style of guts, whatever it takes to be fine."

Claire opened her mouth, but the voice that came out was not her own. She paused, then tried again. "I have to tell you, I'm worried about you living down here. To me, it seems like you've done the meanest possible thing to yourself."

"It seems that way a little to me, too. I figure there was a reason. I figure I'll figure things out."

The rest of their food had come, and Claire heaped Danny's plate, a thing she had never done. "Still can't talk, can you?" she said, her voice quivering with relief.

"Nahh, hopeless. But ya know," he said, nodding, "I think I might get the real stuff yet. And you and me, maybe we can be sort of like each other's love managers, you know what I mean? That wouldn't be so bad."

Claire cocked her head and smiled. A gesture from ol' Melina Irwin, Danny recognized it, but at least it showed he had gotten over.

After dinner, Danny and Claire went to a Canal Street import shop. Danny bought himself a glazed white Buddha with a clock in its belly. Minutes later, they hugged outside the entrance to the subway. When Danny saw this hug would be different, he leaned the bag with the Buddha against a fire hydrant so Claire might feel both his arms about her. This was a hug that made each the child and each the parent, taking in and dispensing a good will so complete that Danny did not worry over its brevity, but let it tend him all the way to Building D-4, up the lurching elevator, past the corner of whispering men who traded works from hidden pockets to darting hands, and into his dark apartment where he stared at the Brooklyn Bridge, under whose shadow he must now find a life.

AT NOON ON a warm Monday in the last week of April the slender grass mall between the sculpture studio and the library was crowded with students on break or cutting classes. Briefcase in hand, Otis passed among Frisbee players, botanical illustrators, art history students cramming for a test, fine arts majors analyzing themselves in small groups. Otis loved Rensler on warm spring days. On unexpectedly radiant days the sunshine cast its balm over the most peevish students, enticing them to stretch out in luminous patches of grass.

Passing unhurriedly to his office, Otis stopped to chat with students he recognized. P.J., the one with the off-campus welding shop, had fashioned an iron windmill and had brought it out to the mall. Otis examined its ingenious design, then slapped P.J. on the back. Next, he ran into Claire Rollins. Her

Impressionist-like paintings in his gallery had turned out to be a fine success. "Great day," Otis said, approaching her. "'Sunday Afternoon on the Island of Grande-Jatte.' Right?" Otis expected Claire to beam in approval. Rather, she looked embarrassed. He complimented her on her success, then asked if she had seen her friend Danny Vincent, if there was any chance she could lure him back to Rensler. Claire turned to look at the library. Her face was red. "He'll come 'round when he's ready," Otis said, squeezing Claire's shoulder.

Not in the mood to enter his office, Otis looked ahead for other students he knew. He saw none. Rather, Sonya Barlow appeared before him. She had a thick sheaf of papers under her arm. Only lately had she begun to carry around class papers and exam books. Only lately had Otis observed her talking to students outside class.

"Hello! I passed around the slide of your new sculpture to the Board last week. I wish you could have heard the oohs and ahs."

"How nice. How really very lovely."

"I hope you'll come to the auction. You could get a look at some of your bidders."

"I could write you a tome on that type."

"I suppose there is a type," Otis said. He did not, however, want a discourse on it.

"Isn't this a perfectly glorious day!" Sonya narrowed her eyes and looked about her shrewdly. Suddenly, in the most pointed of gestures, she directed Otis's eye between two branches to one sun-illuminated scroll on the cornice of the old library roof. "There's no doubt where the focal point is in *that* composition," she declared.

Otis probably would not have noticed how beautifully the scrollwork showed up on the library cornice today. Still, he was not sure if he appreciated Sonya's guidance. She was one of those artists who felt free to commandeer the observations of everyone else. He worried that she did this with her students.

"You must be off to your day, and I won't keep you," said Sonya quickly, "but I hope you don't mind if I ask you how your wife is. I have felt for you since our little lunch in January."

Otis was also not sure if he appreciated Sonya's having felt for him since January. "Oh, things are fine," he answered before he could think. "Fine, arrested, everything's fine." The words rushed together.

"I'm delighted," declared Sonya, and waited for more.

Otis held up his hand in farewell. On the way back to his office he made himself face the question of what, beyond the excesses of her carefully crafted persona, so bothered him about Sonya Barlow. It occurred to him in a flash that what bothered him were the deep creases in her face, and the immodesty, the defiance of those gray orthopedic shoes that declared, "I'll be damned if I can't be old around you!" It was an unseemly thought, and he quickly supplanted it by examining the handful of messages Lily handed him as he walked past her desk.

Among the pink slips Lily had passed to him for years had always been ones that said only "your wife." This morning, Otis was not so jolted by the unexpectedness of the message as its words. What was "your wife" but a vacuous term in an antiquated nomenclature? The women's caucus of the spring before had taken up the taxonomy of relationships—how we pigeonhole ourselves upwards of a hundred times a day. Otis had been impressed with some of their points. On the pink slip, it was the "your" that offended. Otis's gut response was that he did not want to be responsible for this "your." He and Nora had lived close to each other's side for twenty years, yet

Otis's heart beat a little less resolutely at the sight of this "your," as if by possessing her more he would possess himself less. Here it was, though: "your wife" spelled out in Lily's painstaking cursive. All that distinguished it from countless such notes over the years was the phone number of the sublet in Turtle Bay.

Otis shut the door to his office and sat thinking in his chair. Until this very month, he never would have been able to articulate, even to himself, how nervous he had felt at the sight of the term "your wife." Things had happened quickly this month. When built to its therapeutic dose, the Elavil had left Otis drowsy and dry-mouthed. He had called Dr. Braun to tell him he had decided to go it alone, then called several of the postgraduate institutes in Manhattan to seek recommendations for "someone to see." The action itself, like the completion of any decision these past months, had been salutary. And Otis had been amazed at his need to tell.

When Beth Mazur had greeted him in the small vestibule of her Upper West Side apartment, he had thought he would never be able to talk to someone so young. She could not be more than thirty. From years of being president of Rensler, Otis had an almost mechanical response in the face of youth; it was his role to promote for them their wondrous potential. Tirelessly, he pointed out ways in which they could make their existence and their unique talents felt. Otis had counseled the most phlegmatic and jaded young people that if they could only develop faith in their voices, their voices would be heard. What, then, did he have to offer this young Beth Mazur, already so receptive and possessing such a clear voice?

At their first appointment, Otis had told the events of the preceding several months: Nora's leaving, her mastectomy, her love affair with the stunt man. He had been amazed how much could be told in so little time. He was adamant with

Beth Mazur that what he really needed now was to plot where to go next. He was willing to look back later, after he had gotten himself to a point where he could look forward.

In a quick succession of appointments, Otis had discovered what he had to offer were musings on the same questions *he* so loved to ask: Forget what the culture would have you think, what do you really think? It was just this mode of inquiry from Beth Mazur that made Otis scrutinize the term "your wife." There was something so wildly permissive in her pose as she leaned forward in her leather chair to ask him what he *really* wanted, that Otis, hunched around a fluttering in his chest, said, "What I really want is to buy a large tract of land and raise a good deal of money to build a place, a *colony*, if you will, and recruit artists from all the wrong places: Zimbabwe and Appalachia and the most god-awful outposts you can imagine."

Otis had said this, then colored deeply for having allowed himself to be led into such an unseasonable realm as that of the wish. Yet on the weight of Beth Mazur's prompting ("call it a harmless exercise"), he had gone home to call the number he had saved from the paper. This coming Saturday afternoon, Otis had an appointment to see the fifty acres still for sale in Sullivan County.

Lily knocked at the door to remind Otis it was time for the bimonthly faculty meeting. Trailing behind her, Otis made his way through several corridors to the faculty lunch room, where the coffee urn was flanked by two platters of assorted pastries. He took up his position at the round table in the middle of the room. From there, without ceremony, he delivered the news that seniority and merit raises would have to be postponed. Cost of living increases would hold, but at one percent lower than he had hoped. The other increases must wait until after Rensler got some results from new strategies to increase its revenue. There were no poker faces among his faculty. Otis was sure he saw a woman in the art ed department mouth the same *fuck you, Daley* he remembered from a student protest years before.

Minutes later, crossing the campus to get his car and drive to the Upper West Side, Otis was struck by the glare of the sun. Its rays stung his eyes and he felt a swell of irritation at the sight of so many students cutting classes.

"I can appreciate your dilemma. Her message must have thrown you for quite a loop."

Otis dropped his eyelids. He kneaded his temples. "I'll have to call her when I get back. Or tonight, at the latest."

"Why?"

"*Why!?*"

"Let's look at this. Nora has been quite satisfied to be independent of you for—"

"She has cancer," Otis said. This, he thought in a rush of panic, was the problem of Beth Mazur's age. Youth is apt to turn its back even on malignity.

"So because your estranged wife has cancer—and you don't know the details of her health—because she has cancer, she is not responsible for her behavior. Because she has cancer, you must put your own plans aside."

"I have no plans."

"Oh. No?"

"The colony idea is not realistic in any sense of the word. And I can't tie up my capital now. I'm going to cancel my appointment."

"It seems to me," said Beth Mazur, sitting back in her chair, "that as president of an art school you must be quite capable of turning the infeasible into the real."

"I'm fine at Rensler. For now."

"During our last session, you—"

"Ignoring her call is not within my ken."

Beth Mazur said nothing.

"I'm sorry, but what you're suggesting, what your silence is suggesting, is monstrous by my standards. How do I know she has anybody? How do I know what she's been through?"

"Have you considered what *you* have gone through? Let me add, Otis, I would never pose this question to a man who clearly loved his wife, and was loved by her."

"I have considered what I need to consider!" In saying these words, Otis drew upon nearly every important value he had exercised as an adult. With each syllable, he perceived himself careening at ever greater speed from Beth Mazur's world.

After a pointed silence, she said, "It's your life." She did not pronounce it in the usual dismissive tone, but with gathering momentum, so that "your" was emphatic, and "life" quite nearly hysterical.

They met for dinner at an Indian restaurant on East 28th Street. Over the phone, Otis asked Nora if high seasoning was the best thing for her. She had answered that it was the very best.

At the restaurant, Otis handed her a plate of *poori*.

"You're still wearing it," she said, referring to his wedding ring.

"I'm literal. Don't you think I'm a very literal man?"

"Not unless you've become so," she said. "I have personally become less."

Otis tore off his own piece of bread. He did not want to hear how she had become less literal. What the stunt man might have done to effect this particular change in Nora was too much for Otis to contemplate. He watched her eat. She looked terrible.

"I have had a lot put into me these past months, and a lot wrung out."

"Do you want to talk?"

"No. I don't see how it can be avoided, but no."

"I've had some therapy," he said.

"Really?"

"She was not terribly positive about my seeing you. Of course, she's very...what they apparently call directive."

"Otis. I can't believe you, of all people, would resort to that shabby trick of letting your therapist speak for you. I may as well be back in Malibu."

"I'm sorry," he said.

The waiter came to take their order. Nora had a smile for him Otis had never seen. It had a readiness about it, yet still it trembled.

"How was the Knox's anniversary?" she asked after some time.

"I didn't go. I'm afraid I took the easy way out by way of a gift. Roses." Otis reviled himself right as he said it. His need of Nora was dispensable; why show her otherwise?

"Malibu, if you haven't gathered, was a mistake."

"I'm sorry. I hope he was at least good to you."

"That's a matter of interpretation."

"Nora. What do you want?"

So different, thought Otis, from Beth Mazur's "what do you *really* want?" He was not plumbing the depths; he had no hope of attaining them.

Nora, who had been gripping the edge of the table, suddenly pitched forward, doubled over, and vomited onto the glistening terra cotta floor.

Otis jumped up, but Nora would not let him near her. As she bent unnaturally forward, Otis saw that her short hair, so resembling the style he had last seen, was a false piece. She was back on chemo.

Otis sat back in his seat, while a busboy appeared and began frantically mopping. As Nora fled to the bathroom, the busboy cast Otis a furtive look of alarm. Otis sat still, breathing shakily. In a moment, he placed a fifty-dollar bill under a water glass. By the time Nora reappeared, he already had her coat. He threw it over her shoulders, and kept his arm tightly in place. Slowly, they walked out to Lexington Avenue. In the lulling rhythm of one uttering a mantra, he turned the same phrases over in a low voice: "You need to be safe, you need your things, you need me." He heard with remoteness the great intimacy of his tone, as if it were delivered by the brazen rush of passing traffic.

MAY

THROUGHOUT THE semester, several instructors had approached Sonya to substitute teach their classes. She had politely refused them all. Accordingly, she had not had the luxury of approaching them, and so had twice been obliged to teach with a bad cold. On this Tuesday morning, a month away from the close of the spring semester, she filled in for a painting instructor, Jack Kaiser. Between classes the week before, he had complained of an important appointment that conflicted with his first section. When Sonya offered to take over his class, he had looked at her in open disbelief.

The students were working on a sustained pose, Jack had explained, and the model Natasha, whom the kids called Tash, would be there for her third and final session. Jack briefed Sonya that several students had a particularly hard time conceiving of the whole. Try though he had to get these students to loosen up, to think of Tash as the composite of her volumes, Jack complained that some still insisted on niggling over the creases of her elbows, the texture of her upper lip. "I've done timed gestural poses," said Jack, "and I've taped charcoal sticks to dowels and had them draw from a standing position. Nothing's worked with these few kids. You'll see who I mean. I tell them over and over, use your whole arm." When Sonya had heard Jack's reverence for the essential gesture, she nodded her head vigorously. She had strained higher so that he might see the affirmation in her eyes. Well, she thought, perhaps he's not one of the ones out to kill off the rest of us.

When Sonya entered Jack Kaiser's class, Tash was assuming her place on a metal folding chair on top of a plywood platform. She and a student in the first row of easels were laughing. There were chalk marks on the platform floor, indicating where Tash's feet should go. She was making a production of stamping her feet precisely within these marks. The student laughed nervously. Sonya remembered as if it were yesterday her initial embarrassment in relation to the League's models decades before. It was not particularly their nakedness that had thrown her, but their role as art's functionaries—how they permitted the mystery of their bodies to be transferred from their ownership to the anonymous clutter of canvases before them. If Sonya lived to be a hundred and fifty, she would never forget her second anatomy class at the League. A pinch-faced little instructor had asked the disrobing model to turn around before the class. With a grease pencil, he had marked up her back and buttocks, dividing them into sections. She may as well go off to be drawn and quartered, Sonya had whispered to her neighbor. As the instructor drew, he described the muscle groups within each of his sections. This, Sonya had thought, was the method by which she would learn to draw the human being in all its subtlety. Were Maxwell Zavin not also teaching at the League, she might have walked out that day, never to return.

Sonya introduced herself to Tash. For a moment, their gazes locked. Sonya wore one of her knit tunics. She wore a black skirt, black tights, and her dear beasts. She wore her lark-in-ascent pin. Tash wore a battered felt hat with a badge displaying a coat of arms, a thick smear of lipstick, and nothing else. She was Rensler's old lady model. Her toes jammed together, their nails calcified. Blue veins, submerged in the legs of younger women, swelled to the surface of Tash's. Her breasts began where younger ones peaked. Tash's skin bore patches of psoriasis, deep white dimples, secret furrows. The music of the human form, Zavin had once exalted. Sonya had heard Tash made her living circulating between art schools and art departments in the tri-state area. Everyone's old lady model.

"I know you have all been deep at work," said Sonya, standing directly in front of Tash. Students were opening their paint boxes, pouring turpentine into coffee cans, adjusting their easels. "But this morning I implore you to go deeper. Some of you know a good deal about anatomy. You know how the clavicle and scapula function, and how the hip joint fits into the pelvis. You know exactly where the head is set on top of the spinal column. But don't let what you know rule you. Look for the structural continuity of the figure. Forget the skin over her knuckles. Turn the thing into geometric action. Get to its humanness."

"What if we don't finish today?" asked a girl from the back of the studio.

"Oh, *finish*," answered Sonya. "What is finish?"

"You know. For Mr. Kaiser. Get everything in."

Sonya sighed. She could not expect instant gratification from this new plan to extend her gifts within the context of daily life. "I think you might want to take that up with Mr. Kaiser. For my part, I am curious to see how you do with this model's essence."

Sonya stepped aside and revealed Tash, who had relaxed her pose, and was reading a paperback Stephen King. She replaced the book to her handbag and glared at Sonya.

Sonya smiled politely and turned away. She circulated among Jack Kaiser's students. She spotted Claire Rollins and went to stand behind her painting of Tash. Claire was not one of the ones who niggled. "I like this very much," said Sonya. "You have come to grips with the form. There is geometric action here."

Claire wiped her brush against the side of her can of turpentine.

Sonya pointed to Claire's handling of the wall and windows behind Tash. "You put in just the angles to bring forth the model's angles."

"Thank you." Claire paused. "What's 'geometric action'?"

"Oh, dear. There is no textbook definition I know of. It is just the right balance and movement of forms. In painting, the clunkiest forms must move."

Claire looked at Sonya. "Oh."

Give these children confidence, thought Sonya. Give them voice for their convictions.

"I must tell you, I saw your exhibit at Otis Daley's gallery. You are quite a talented young lady, but it is time you turn your energy to finding your voice. The French Impressionists made many fine and delightful pictures. They indulged a great many people. But, *please*. They are not here, and they are certainly not now."

Claire turned towards Sonya. Her light brown hair was disheveled, and could use, thought Sonya, some good quality highlighter. Her eyes were bloodshot. The intensity of concentration in her expression showed no hope of softening. The hormones that make these young people suffer so, thought Sonya.

"It's funny you said that. I'm working on changing my direction. It's just that...well, it's powerful stuff. It might alienate people."

"Good! I'm delighted. Let it."

"You think?"

"Yes, I most certainly think. I should remind you how the Impressionists alienated their public. What shocks one generation comforts the next."

"Generation?"

"Half generation. Is that more palatable?"

"I guess you don't think I should care if I never get to be known," said Claire.

"Oh, I wouldn't be so glib as all that. But you must try to fight it, this great hunger to be known. So much is a fight, don't you think?" Sonya could not help but give Claire a squeeze.

Claire blushed. "*Yes.* I'm beginning to see that."

"We're in agreement, then. Isn't it interesting how people come to their solitary conclusions only to find out they are in agreement with one another? That is the way of harmony; it can't be sought. It is the same in painting. You design your subject matter to be harmonious, and *presto*—you have an absolutely banal statement. Harmony exists despite us, dear. It wants only for you to trust it." With these last words, Sonya wandered off, fingering her lark-in-ascent pin.

During her half-hour break, Tash approached Sonya, who stood looking out the window at the chimneys and water towers and exhaust vents that cluttered distant rooftops. Tash wore a cotton kimono. Cheap, thought Sonya, from some place like Harrington Import/Export. She held a styrofoam cup of steaming coffee. She assumed a place beside Sonya, and looked where she looked. Sonya was not used to such invasions. Students wandered in and out.

"I liked that about my 'essence,'" said Tash. "Very sweet."

"Please. I'm sure you have a story to tell, but—"

"My story robbed me of my essence. Yours is different. I like your pin. A lark?"

I won't walk away, thought Sonya. I'll stand here.

Tash reached inside her kimono to scratch her breast. Sonya saw the large left breast collapse into the right one, saw folds of skin deepen. Her own breasts were small and still quite firm—from yoga, she was sure.

"What brings you to Rensler?" Tash asked.

A neutral enough question, thought Sonya. Still, she held her body stiff. "They recruited me."

"*Oh*," said Tash. "Do tell."

"If you'll excuse me—"

"Why'd they recruit you?"

Sonya traveled about the city at all times of the day and night. When trouble threatened, she set her jaw firmly and coached herself as to her own invincibility. Now, trapped beside this old lady model, her pulse raced and her body grew hot.

"You'd have to ask them," she answered.

"I hope they treat you better than me." Tash grew closer. Her shoulder knocked against Sonya's.

"I don't dwell on how people treat me."

"You don't have to."

"I've always thought we can *will* how others treat us." Sonya looked at a particular water tower as she said this. Its appearance immediately became charged, as if it held not water, but Sonya's present words.

"That's interesting. We can will how others treat us." Tash balanced her now empty coffee cup in the cradle she made of her palms. She rested the back of her hands on the windowsill. The hazy noonday light fell upon the row of blue numbers on the underside of Tash's left arm, the same arm that had been folded across her stomach as she posed.

I must not leave, thought Sonya. This woman has come into my orbit and she has brought her history. "You are a good model," she said, her tone unconvincing.

"I'm too old to model. I have no business modelling. At my age, the world should pose for me."

"I don't believe there is any such age," said Sonya despite herself. "To partake is a privilege."

"Who *are* you?" demanded Tash.

It occurred to Sonya that her experiment with daily life could simply fail. Tash had abandoned her coffee cup on the windowsill and put her hands inside her deep kimono pockets. The numbers disappeared. It was up to Tash to walk away, but she did not. Clearly, she waited.

Sonya swallowed so awkwardly that her eyes filled with tears and she was forced to re-swallow several times. Finally she managed, "That was inappropriate. About partaking. I'd like to...to *retract* that, if I may. Please. It was obtuse."

Without a trace of hesitation, Tash removed her right hand from her pocket and extended it for Sonya to shake. It was a large hand whose blunt fingernails were dotted with chipped polish. I will try this thing, thought Sonya; I will experiment with this thing. She strained on tipped toes to look into Tash's eyes, then grasped her hand with both of hers and shook it with resolve, as she had done countless times with her statesmen, her actors, her premier scientists.

When all the students were back at their easels, Sonya addressed them. "You perhaps felt trapped, stuck within the problems of composition, and you had your break. It is good you went away, but now you are back. Look at your pictures. Look directly at what you are most afraid of in your composition, look right where it is most lily-livered. Keep looking. I bet, I *know*, you will open a dialogue with this part, and it will point the way for you."

From behind Sonya, Tash made a sound that could only be described as a snort. Ordinarily Sonya would have identified the sound as one to be summarily dismissed. The world was full of snorters; whole populations survived by snorting at other people. Today, though, Sonya heard Tash's snort as an alarm. It signaled the unmistakable ring of cant in her own words. She heard her words as Tash heard them, and they became worthless pieties, romantic sentiments that still attracted her but also marked her as a woman who refused to come to terms with reality—a truly old lady.

Sonya looked out at the students to see which had impressed them more—Sonya's words or Tash's snort. Their expressions did not give them away. Unlike herself, these young people respected the equality of all vantage points. Sonya recalled that she had long ago acknowledged the equal worth of all outlooks. She recalled it not through the memory of her brain, but through the more incantatory memory of her gut. She looked out at Jack Kaiser's students and saw in a jolt of clarity that each possessed a singular future.

Early that afternoon, in the studio of her apartment on Riverside, Sonya was greeted by "The Spirit." Later this month art truckers would crate her up and take her downtown to Rensler's pre-auction exhibit. Sonya fetched a chamois cloth from the hall closet, and set about dusting her bronze surface, getting between her toes and fingers, and over the hollows beside her breastbone. She could not conceal from herself her great sadness at the prospect of "The Spirit's" departure. Never attach to objects, Zavin had warned, but through the years Sonya had found herself professing fidelity to each of her sculptures in turn. Always, she had to remind herself that neither clay nor bronze was flesh, she must not wait around gazing with expectation at the likes of "The Spirit."

At 3:00, by prearrangement, Sonya met Irene Cone and Freyda Wiltshire at the 72nd Street entrance to Central Park. It was time for the spring walk, and Irene had asked if she might bring Freyda along.

The weather was warm and dry, and Sonya was pleased that they walked at a good pace. They touched upon many subjects. Irene and Freyda traded the latest news of their children. Freyda told Sonya she had recently been to a show of American Modernists in Paris, that Zavin was prominently featured at this show. They spoke of a particular antique shop in Bridgehampton, the abrasive voice of a new public radio announcer, the efforts of Greenpeace.

Not far from the East Side, Irene and Freyda sat down to rest. Sonya paced a bit, but finally settled with them on their bench.

From her brocaded handbag, Irene removed the paper bag. She tossed some breadcrumbs considerably short of a group of pigeons far to the left. Without a word, she handed the bag to Freyda, who passed it to Sonya, who sat closest the pigeons. The crumpled bag remained open on Sonya's lap.

"Who are you working on these days?" asked Freyda.

"No one. People don't commission anymore. I have decided on another route. Otis Daley, the president of Rensler, has been after me for years to come teach there. So I have decided to start in the fall. They have a talented young crop of students, and I would hate to have them eaten by the art wolves when they could learn to see instead."

Freyda and Irene looked at each other doubtfully. They used a secret language to prepare the response that would not reflect their real opinion. Meanwhile, Sonya took a handful of crumbs from the bag. She cast them fully out. Many pigeons flapped their wings and scurried forth, impervious to the attention they drew to three old ladies on a bench, particularly to the one who had thrown the crumbs with a bold, impossible vengeance.

CLAIRE AND Danny sat at a booth by the window of Benno's. It was Saturday morning, and Danny had taken the subway from the Lower East Side. Claire had walked over from Kollman. The coffee shop was crowded with Rensler students and neighborhood workers off for the day. Claire did not think Danny looked well. He still wore his serpent ring, but the fancy belt and leather boots were gone, his hair was unwashed, his beard scraggly. She thought she saw the yellow tinge of a faded bruise on the side of his head.

"Remember Tash?" asked Claire.

"You mean Lady Natasha of the heraldic insignias?"

"She was in the camps."

"Jesus. Really?"

"I saw the numbers on her arm. She picked her pose to hide them, but I saw them when she was talking to Sonya Barlow."

"Old twinkle-toes? There's a dynamic duo."

"It *was* weird. I have to tell you, I feel really lousy, like I was duped. If I had known about her, I would've painted her differently."

"You should always paint people like they've been in the camps," said Danny.

"That's crap. I hate artists who appropriate suffering."

"Yeah, so what about artists who appropriate 'people at leisure'?"

"Listen, Danny, let's talk about artists who appropriate disasters and miracles in flea-bitten eighteenth-century Mexican pueblos. Let's talk about appropriating the preserved rib cages of nuns and *bish*ops, for Christ's sake! I can do this, too."

"Okay, I'm sorry. We just got different ideas about how to paint people, you know?"

"That's all right, we should."

"You're right. We should." With half an English muffin, Danny sopped up the runny yellow of his egg.

"At least I would've taken the rosebuds off her cheeks," Claire continued. "That's the direction I have to go in; I have to take the rosebuds off all their cheeks. Why's that so scary?"

"Look at it this way," said Danny. "It's not as scary as being jumped and dragged into a broom closet and given the once over, all for three bucks and a unicorn belt buckle."

"Danny!"

"No lie."

"When're you coming back to Rensler? What're you trying to prove there, anyway? I know about an apartment on Dawson, practically around the corner from Studio Hall. Two bedrooms. If you don't mind giving me the one with north light, we could, you know, *take* it."

Danny flushed and looked with some astonishment at his plate, as if it had become empty of its own accord. After a moment he said, "No offense, babe, but I don't know if I wanna be around while you're takin' the rosebuds off their cheeks."

Claire folded her arms across her chest and looked at Danny. It was true; she was about to take herself down to the bone and she had wanted him around while she did it.

"Wise boy," she said. She was certain that before her eyes Danny had performed a prelude to some stunning new maturity, one that already left her without the slightest consolation, either this morning amid the cross-yelling at Benno's or, it seemed, along her vista.

Claire knew her memory of the apartment on Dawson, which she had seen several days before, was enhanced by desire. Its contours, particularly those of the front bedroom whose bay window faced north, had taken on a soft-edged definition. Within these contours Claire could see a more ephemeral version of her own image, amassed from the brush strokes of Pissarro or Signac, moving from one canvas to the next in absolute self-possession. The room had plank floors painted white. It had a ceramic tile fireplace boarded up with sheet rock and guarded by the leering cement gargoyle crouched on its hearth. It had tin ceilings and silver radiators that glowed. Although there were also peeling plaster, one mustard-colored wall, a crumbling section of corkboard above the mantelpiece, and windows that rattled even in a breeze, Claire was still drawn to the place. She had never felt such affinity with a room, a prescience that she was meant to be contained within it. Having sheltered so many Rensler students, she reasoned, the room innately supported the most dismal of private flounderings.

Claire wanted to move at the end of May, when Kollman closed for the summer. As for a roommate, the only person who had asked to live with her was Trudy Barnes, who had found a summer job as an apprentice pattern-maker on Seventh Avenue.

The prospect of living again with Trudy had a perverse appeal. The remorseless femininity of Trudy's nightgowns, her habit of grabbing her hair at the least suggestion of a problem, her apparent belief that the details of fashion models' costumes gave the earth its gravity—all made Claire feel oddly secure. And it was the glassy-eyed and impassive Trudy who had said, "Your father, Claire. Your mother said he died." There was something too riveting there: her own name, the reference to both her parents, the news itself. Running into Trudy lately, Claire behaved with a guilty obligingness, as if she must repay Trudy for the discomfort of having to produce such a stark and desolate set of words.

The afternoon Claire had showed Trudy the apartment, Trudy declared, "Oh, imagine one of your paintings there!"

She had pointed to a wide blank wall in the kitchen. Claire said nothing; she could not deny the sweet rush, the effect of Trudy's admiration. Yet she must be prepared. She knew her paintings would lose favor.

They arranged with the super to sign the lease on Monday. When Claire got back to Kollman, she called Danny. "Picture this," she said. "Me and spacey Trudy Barnes."

"All right, now you're rolling. An invisible roommate who pays rent."

Claire was in bed, reading *The Horse's Mouth*, when Wanda knocked at her door on Sunday morning. Claire thought it was Trudy, who said she would stop by to plan how they would furnish the apartment on Dawson. She had told her they would naturally each be responsible for their own rooms, but Trudy had reminded her there was common space, too—the kitchen and bathroom and an especially large entry hall. Claire dreaded their meeting today. Trudy's room at Kollman was decorated with a crepe-paper sun that fanned out from two Popsicle sticks and a profusion of stick-on stars that glowed in the dark. "Come on in," she veritably barked at the sound of the knock. "It's open."

"You don't lock your door?" came Wanda's incredulous voice.

"Jesus, Mom! What're you doing here?"

Wanda gave a meek smile. "That nice guard downstairs said I could park by the curb," she answered, as if in explanation.

"You couldn't have called? You asked me to get a phone, so I got a phone. Why didn't you call?"

"Oh!" said Wanda, waving away the question. "You're not out of bed, yet? What're you reading?"

Claire's deepest inclination was to jump up, put her hands on her hips, and demand to know what gave Wanda the right to barge into her room, rousing her from the time and place she had so deliberately sought among the pages of Joyce Carey. But she could not jump out of bed. Below her T-shirt emblazoned with the Rensler crest, she wore nothing. She was not ready to assert her voice while her naked body mocked her words.

"Please go into the bathroom," Claire said, stressing each syllable. "I'll yell when I'm ready."

"I'd like you to look at these," said Wanda after Claire's call had released her. She had removed a handful of brochures from her canvas tote bag. She sat down on the bed and patted the place beside her.

On the top brochure, "Imbibe the Grandeur!" was printed over an aerial view of a gorge. Inset boxes along the right edge showed a shooting geyser, rushing waterfalls, a tree trunk that dwarfed the family posed beside it.

"I thought we could go out west this summer," Wanda said. She touched Claire's thigh.

"Mom, no. I can't. I know you can get at that money that's there for me, you know, from Daddy. I already committed to rent an apartment. I just want to paint this summer."

"You talk about painting, but you haven't *seen* anything, honey! We could have a marvelous time. It's so lucky, you know, that money is there. You can paint all next year."

"It's different. I want to paint on my own."

"I'm not going to beg," announced Wanda, tossing the brochures back into her bag. "I'll go with Amanda."

Little did Wanda know how much Claire wavered. Little did she know how reassuring was the prospect of guaranteed grandeur contrasted with that of redirecting the entire course of her painting. Claire was just about to offer a wan afterthought, a tired and graceless reconsideration, when the phone on the floor beside her drawing table rang.

"Hello!" she declared. The moment she heard the voice at the other end, Claire's face blazed.

Wanda leaned forward to study her daughter. She narrowed her eyes as if to examine something vital—a chrysalis at the vital moment of its transformation.

Claire spun around, turned her back to her mother. "Hi. No, not now. Why there? Okay, what time? Okay, I have to go."

Wanda looked up. Filled with delicately nuanced paintings, Claire's room was no setting for this present string of laconic replies. When Claire hung up, Wanda met her head on.

"There is something so arrogant, Claire—there is no other word for it—about how you protect your privacy. As if your inner world were sacrosanct, as if it were superior to mine and everyone else's." Wanda's voice was sharp; it was building momentum to sustain her attack.

Claire looked at the pink stripes on Wanda's new sneakers. She was silenced by her secret acknowledgment of her mother's courage.

"I don't know who that was, but don't think I'm so naive. I know what's going on with you."

"What?" Claire challenged.

"Come on, Claire. I can put two and two together. You've been resisting since you were eight years old. It all fits."

In this sentiment was the true line of demarcation. To Wanda, Claire painted because she resisted experience. Now, it seemed, Wanda perceived she moved towards women because she resisted men.

"You don't know what you're talking about," said Claire. She hated herself for visibly trembling.

All at once, Wanda softened. Her face, the new puffiness now fully established at her jawline, might have been that of a priest giving absolution. Tears collected, and they were the tears of one burdened by love for the universe. All that saved Claire was projecting into her next conversation with Danny: Father, I have sinned. Go gently, my child.

"Honey. It makes no difference to me who you love. It only matters *that* you love."

Claire nodded slowly. All right, she thought. Mark these moments. Each arbitrates a new struggle. Each struggle imagines its divine solution. "Thank you," she said. "Thank you for saying that."

"It would've killed Daddy. He hated them, you know. Especially the men. He called them the worst names, and once at a party he did the most humiliating imitation."

Mark each moment, thought Claire. "My new roommate is coming down. We're going to talk about the apartment. I really don't have any more time."

"Honey. I'd love to meet her. Really. If not now, then whenever you're ready."

The idea of herself and Trudy Barnes as a couple was so jarring that Claire, walking over to her sock drawer, tripped and fell back onto Wanda's lap, which gave way under Claire's weight and the vibrations of their exorbitant laughter. The sound of this laughter reached out to the hall. It became part of Kollman's communal wildness, the boisterous commotion of young people who lingered endlessly in small, rotating groups.

Seated on the circular bench of one of the enormous planters in the Great Hall of the Metropolitan, Claire read the same paragraph of *The Horse's Mouth* over and over. Every time she looked up, she lost her place. Finally, seven minutes past their appointed meeting time, Melina appeared in the crowd that streamed through the vast doors atop Claire's favorite stairs in New York City, the regal fan of steps that she associated with public buildings in cities possessed of distant history.

Claire always had the feeling that she had accomplished these steps by a fluke, that the keepers of majesty had turned their backs while she, in jeans and worn black jersey, had stolen past them to the threshold. Watching Melina approach from this same threshold, Claire saw too well what divided them. Melina entered the Met with no doubt that she belonged there. Her cheeks were flushed from the climb, her eyes were bright, her tan Burberry coat was open and billowed around her stride.

When Melina reached Claire, she smiled in that crooked way that had months ago absconded with Claire's sleeping and waking sanity. Melina shook her head slowly, as if amazed at the unfolding increments of their brief, sweet history.

They went to the dining hall, where Melina ordered them both cappuccino. Claire watched Melina sprinkle cinnamon on her mound of froth, then scoop up tiny peaks with the pointed edge of her spoon.

"I thought you'd like to know that Grammy's back home."

"How is she?"

"Dazed, I'd say. Overmedicated in the mornings. She asks about you all the time. She really took a liking to you."

Claire said nothing. She, too, was dazed. She had a life-long habit of growing sleepy at pivotal moments.

"She'd love to see you. She'd love for you to come out."

Claire could hear Danny: "She's usin' the old lady as bait. Hey, come on, she's letting the grandmother *pimp* for her!"

But Claire knew that Melina put her deepest wishes into the mouths of others. It was a twisted, peculiar grace that had repeatedly distanced Claire. Yet when Regina or Luisa or one of the Greenwich cats had begged to see her, Claire had been touched despite herself.

"My parents are going to Argentina this week, but they left the spring bulbs for Grammy. She would love it if you could come over. We could plant all Saturday, and then Sunday you and I—"

"I *can* be restricted." Claire heard herself say. "I know you can't be, but I can. It may be sick of me, but there you have it."

"Well, I wouldn't call it sick, it's just.... Claire, you, I miss— I miss your painting."

"You miss my *painting*?"

"Oh, come on," said Melina, dropping her tone to its most conciliatory. "I didn't mean it that way. And maybe I was wrong. Maybe, if there's enough there, I could be restricted."

"I can tell you right now, take it from someone who intimately knows, there's not enough there."

Melina, forbearing, cocked her head.

Claire waited for her own anger to pass, but it swelled with each new moment. It was unlike any other anger she had known. All her old furies—at Cole, at Wanda, at Danny— were mere flares of indignation at being wanted beyond her means to give. This was far different. Her heart knocked in her breast, her stomach tightened as if within a vise. It was she who wanted, she who was being told her wanting was unseemly, she must "have enough there" to be found worthy of her inordinate readiness.

Melina waited still, her head held poised and alert.

Without a word, Claire shot up and turned to go. She rushed through two rooms of ancient Greek and Roman friezes and of marble busts, out again to the Great Hall, up yet more steps, and through a maze of galleries. She glanced at the paintings she passed, but could not reach out to the noble themes of other centuries. When finally she landed upon the Impressionists, she made herself stop. She stopped before "The Monet Family in Their Garden" painted by Eugene Manet. There beneath a shade tree was Madame Monet. Her son Jean, strangely invertebrate, was stretched over her outspread skirt. There was a rooster, a chick of wispy strokes, a gardener tending to his work. Claire was not deceived by them. She saw how they basked in their agreeability. Charging restlessly about the gallery, she paused only at "The Sofa," Toulouse-Lautrec's brothel scene of two old whores despairing of their lives. At least he knew to take the rosebuds off their cheeks, thought Claire. Still dissatisfied, she roamed further, through cavernous galleries, until she came upon a Hans Hofmann, the painter whose name Sonya Barlow had invoked all year long.

"Deep Within the Ravine" was huge, tawdry with primary color, defiant. It had been painted with a knife. Claire stared at a smooth patch of bright orange for many minutes, until she had to admit she no longer knew what was beautiful.

The ringing of chimes alerted visitors the museum was about to close. Melina had long since gotten into her Saab and driven off. Claire's pulse was calm. The most marked difference about her as she walked down the Met's steps was her new inability to identify beauty. Just as she stepped onto the Fifth Avenue sidewalk a vague tremor of excitement came over her. It was as if the fresh breeze had perceived that something of value had left Claire, and it rushed to fill the empty space with a senseless thrill.

"HEY!" SHOUTED Danny. He had just finished his second ear of sweet corn when he spotted Lem coming through the door of Nathan's. He beckoned him over. "Look't this," he said, "the ol' patron saint of friendship crossed up our paths!"

"To tell the truth, bubula, your old man told me you'd be here. I ran into him and Etta at the A&P."

"Oh, yeah? I had to leave. Shopping for Spam shoves me straight into domestic hell."

"Yeah, well, we both know they only serve beef bourguignonne here. Hold on, I'll be right back."

Lem got a styrofoam cup of hot water and a Lipton bag, then returned. "So how's tricks?"

"Tricks've been better."

"Sorry 'bout Robin. She wasn't a bad looking girl."

Danny shrugged. "I think we'll probably be friends. The rest wasn't in the stars."

"Friends? Christ, who stays friends with them? Whatever happened to that other one, the one who didn't give a flying fuck about the Polar Bears?"

Danny laughed. "Actually, we're friends."

"I know how it is, bubula. She was *really* the one, wasn't she?"

The simple truth of Lem's statement, combined with the fact that he had driven out of his way to come to Nathan's, led Danny, despite his reservations, to say, "Yeah, well, I don't know, but she likes women, anyway."

"A lezzie?! Look, it's not your fault, bubula. What the hell's the matter with people? I told Sal not to send you to an art school. It's good you're outta there." Lem put his broad hand on Danny's shoulder and squeezed. He was shorter than Danny, and had to look up to meet his eyes. Once a pure cornflower blue, Lem's eyes were cloudy behind the cataracts whose seriousness he dismissed. His eyebrows were white; some hairs strayed from the sweep. Perspiration had filled the wrinkles on his forehead. "You're a good kid, like I always told you. Whad'ya doing now?"

"Oh, you know. Keepin' on. I got these new things, the *momias*, and I'm trying to get a show. And a job. There's a place that uses artist-types to make denture molds. If that doesn't pan out, I know a kid who does photo retouching for good bucks."

Lem was not listening. "Your old man know about the lezzie?"

"He wouldn't care. He's okay."

Lem muttered something Danny could not make out, but he thought it was "pussy."

Danny wiped his mouth with three napkins. "They must make these for midgets' faces," he said, pointing to the pile of napkins still before him.

"I've been thinking, bubula. My Bushwick man, God help him, just gave notice. He's had emphysema for ten years, but it finally got him, he can barely get a sentence out. So I got a job to fill. Most of them start from the bottom, but I'd train you myself. Special."

Lem owned three dry cleaners. One in Coney Island, one in Flatbush, one in Bushwick.

Danny had been paying homage to Lem and the other Polar Bears since he was ten. It never occurred to him that one day Lem might give him the dubious privilege of rejecting the way he lived. He blushed furiously.

"Think about it. You don't have to tell me anything now. I just think it wouldn't hurt you to be a little set up, you know what I mean?"

Danny could only nod.

"Good to see you, bubula." Then, with the air of one dispensing sage advice: "Hang on to that youth."

Back on Cherry Street, Danny was steeped in remorse for his desertion of Claire, who had asked him to live with her, his betrayal of a dawning sense of who in the world is right and who in the world is wrong, when he realized he was being followed down the hall to his apartment. No one but his pursuer was in the hall, and if he turned to go back down the elevator, he would certainly be trapped by him. His only choice was to enter his apartment as stealthily as possible. The problem was that he had already violated Sal's only admonition about living on Cherry Street: Always have your keys in your hand half a block away. Danny's keys were in the outer pocket of his backpack, which was still slung over his shoulders. He removed the pack and felt a knife point at the small of his back. "I bet you got more than a lousy belt buckle in *there*," came the voice from behind him. The man rapped on the door to Danny's apartment.

"Not much," said Danny.

"Open up. I'll be the judge. Course, you're free to call the cops, but I don't think you want the city knowin' who you paid off to get into this place. They hate you middle-class sponges even more than they hate us downtrodden underclass."

There had been key money to the super. Sal's five hundred dollars. Another few hundred from Rick Falzone, now a plumber in Bay Ridge, who had bought a *momia*. A good luck check from Lem. Danny just stared at his accuser.

When Danny was a little boy he had fantasized about talking some scamp out of butchering him, then guiding the lost soul on the road to self-respect and lawfulness. Feeling the cold tip of the knife under his denim shirt, Danny at once abandoned his missionary courage. The pursuers from his boyhood fantasies were mere tramps and ne'er-do-wells who secretly waited to be converted to the virtuous life. The pursuers from his boyhood were children's book characters whose destinies Danny had extrapolated upon—out-of-work chimney sweeps, rag sellers on a bender. They were not the pursuers of Cherry Street—the wife beaters, the heroin addicts.

"Okay, all right," said Danny.

The man took Danny's backpack and, with a bow, handed it to him. Once inside, he threw the pack against a wall. "Shit!" he yelled.

There was nothing in the living room but the wall of *retablos*. Just below, the ceramic Buddha with the clock in its belly ticked loudly.

The man caught Danny in a half-nelson. Slipping the knife under Danny's shirt, he forced him into the bedroom. Along the wall was the regimen of plaster *momias*—bishops, nuns, friars. On the linoleum floor was a Salvation Army mattress covered by a blanket. The only other furniture was the cable spool table, on top of which sat a Gallo jug fit with a black candle. "Come on," he whispered into Danny's ear. "Whad'ya got?" His breath was agreeably sweet as a baby's.

"Nothing."

The man pushed Danny onto his bed. Danny squeezed his eyes shut. No mission on earth was as vital as that of not pissing in his pants. When he opened his eyes, the man was attacking the other side of the mattress. He slashed through the powder blue blanket Sal had bought Danny the week before and the Calvin Klein sheets, seconds, sold cut-rate from a vast bin on Canal Street. The man's neck grew sinewy, his jugular vein pulsed, his tongue clicked against the roof of his mouth. The knife slit the ticking and burrowed through layers of cheap cotton wads to clink discordant notes against the springs. The vehemence of the slashing, the intense focus of it, allowed Danny to roll himself off the mattress. Whatever he might have looked like doing it, he pictured himself a cool character.

From his perspective on the linoleum floor, Danny reasoned in a magical way. He equated the destruction of his mattress with his own salvation. The poking and shredding

continued. The man grunted. His nostrils flared. Danny
rolled out to the living room. From there, he ran out of the
apartment.

Rushing down through the stairwells, he suddenly remembered Mexico—San Miguel, Guanajuato, Mexico City. Before
that Taxco, Oaxaca, San Cristobal. Never once while in Mexico
had Danny been threatened by another human being. *Familia*,
he reminded himself. They all had *familia* to throw them out,
to take them back, to curse them, to become them. Who did
the man slashing the mattress have? It seemed to Danny that
no one in lower Manhattan had anyone. He ran through the
parking lot to the corner public phone. When he reached it,
he did not know who to call. As he leaned against the phone
booth to catch his breath, Danny for the first time knew it was
imperative that he marry someone.

Uncertain where to go next, Danny took the "2" train
uptown. He was not literally searching for a wife, but only
putting himself in the frame of mind of belonging to someone
in more than the halfhearted way he had belonged to Robin,
in far more than the chimeric and doomed way he had belonged to Claire. In his high-top sneakers, Danny stepped
lightly from street to avenue on the Upper West Side, following couples, contemplating their lives with a mix of contempt
and amazement at the apparent ease with which they bought
into the world. At first he followed a couple wearing trench
coats. The woman carried a briefcase. They stopped to look
in the window of an antiques shop on Columbus Avenue.
Danny looked with them. The man wore tinted aviator glasses.
An asshole, thought Danny. A sleaze—he probably owns a
Baskin and Robbins franchise and docks the pay of every
Puerto Rican scooper who comes in ten minutes late. Danny
could not stand the way the man kept pushing the glasses up

his nose with his beefy thumb, but the woman *liked* it; she
finally pushed the glasses up herself and kissed him on the
mouth. Danny's stomach rumbled loudly. The horrible scare
on Cherry Street had done something to his digestion. He
hoped that the horrible scare had not also knocked off his
standards. He had to get control of himself, put things in pro-
portion. Just because he wanted to get married did not mean
he would start buying tinted aviator glasses or running after
sallow-faced girls who looked like they were born to be CPAs.
Danny's stomach rumbled again. The couple stared at him.
He left, turned down 73rd, and walked towards the park.

On 73rd he followed a couple who gave him more hope.
The man wore jeans and a chamois jacket. The woman wore
jeans and some kind of peasant blouse. They held hands. They
talked about a mutual friend, speculated if all the acid trips he
had taken several years before had done something to his mind.
They both knew that acid could have residual effects, but they
did not want to blame Kyle's wild spells of rebellion on his
acid days—that was a trap and an oversimplification; Kyle
had a touch of the mad prophet in him way before he dropped
acid. This point of agreement about Kyle prompted the couple
to drop hands and put their arms around each other's waists.
Danny was heartened. He watched with a benevolent sense
of approval as the couple ran up the steps of a limestone building, then disappeared inside.

It was suppertime, but Danny did not want to leave the
Upper West Side. If he stuck to the tree-lined side streets and
Central Park West, this part of town had a higher percentage
of solid citizenry than did Cherry Street. The trees had bloomed
in April and early May. Their tender shoots gave off a compelling fragrance. Some apartment windows were open and
Danny smelled spicy, aromatic dishes—complicated dishes
that mocked the foil-lined bags of barbecued chicken and

cartons of pork lo-mein that doubtlessly sat open on three-quarters of the tables in Coney Island at this very moment.

Danny went to a small restaurant called The Middle Eastern Kitchen. He ordered stuffed grape leaves, humus, tabouli, chilled yogurt. He ate slowly, then wandered out to Broadway where he drifted in and out of the brightly lit record and clothes stores. Finally, as dark descended, he took the subway all the way back to Coney Island.

When Danny arrived at Sal's, careful to knock and wait to be received, Sal and Etta were playing cards at the dining room table. The smell of fried Spam lingered in the air.

Danny unlaced his high tops, worked them off, and flopped down on the old corduroy chair. He crossed his feet on its matching hassock.

Sal kept looking over at Danny. Several times, Etta asked Sal if he thought he was such a shark he didn't have to pay attention to his hand.

"I changed my mind about Cherry Street," Danny said at last.

"It was the futon I couldn't understand," said Sal. He turned to Etta. His voice was ebullient. "He's sleepin' on this *futon* like some kind of a monk. What's he done that's so terrible? First a futon, then a bed of nails."

"I never got the futon."

"So what's next? We saw Lem in the A&P. He told us about Bushwick. Hell, imagine you in Bushwick with people's laundry."

"I'm going back to Rensler. And I'm going to switch my major. I'm going to major in product design. There's a guy who just got outta Rensler last year. Three companies were fighting over his coffee maker. Now it's in every department store in the country. I think Europe, too. He bought a co-op. One year outta Rensler."

"Danny! You don't give a shit about co-ops! You don't care about coffee makers! What about the *momias?* What about the little miracle paintings?" Sal stared at Danny.

Etta stared, too. She can't wait, thought Danny. She can't wait for me to say forget the *momias*, forget the little *retablos*, they don't mean anything.

Unable to think clearly, Danny stood up. He paced around. With his toe, he poked at a matted section of the old brown shag carpet. Goddamn Rensler, he said to himself. The goddamned Rensler taste had gotten to him; there was a small but tenacious part of Danny that now criminalized Sal for his lousy taste. Danny looked around the room. There was still the pinball machine with its sawed off legs, all the rococo furniture, the ornately framed pictures of relatives Sal and Danny never heard from. On every available surface Etta had put one of those textured white glass bottles with the skinny necks; they held bunches of plastic flowers with stiff nylon leaves. Plates from Atlantic City and Asbury Park were displayed on the wall next to the kitchen. Real stuff, of course; Sal knew nothing of kitsch's irony. Try though he did to prevent it, Danny felt a swell of revulsion. He fell back down in the chair. He could not say anything. He could only think, hey, what's next, I'm going to turn into a room snob, I'm only going to sit in rooms with lots of wood and glass and skylights, rooms laid out with modular furniture and ficus trees.

"Danny. Answer your old man. What's going on with you? Why're you doing this to yourself?"

"What'm I doing to myself? I'm just making some decisions, here. Cherry Street's no good for me. Don't you want me back at Rensler? Don't you want me to make some bucks?"

Sal looked at Etta, then back at Danny. "Bucks are only the half of it."

"Lemme sleep here. Please. In the morning—then I'll de-cide what I'm going to do." Danny's voice cracked over the word "decide." He turned his head away, then found himself looking at the front door with its police and chain locks in place for the night. Etta laid her winning hand down in one triumphant slap. She reached into an open can of Planter's mixed nuts. Sal, his unshaven face gone pale, continued to watch Danny, who after some moments got up and walked back to his old room.

THE LAST SATURDAY in May began for Otis at 7 a.m., and he did not lie down beside Nora, still under seda-tion, until after two the next morning.

All day, Otis had directed preparations at the Manhattan gallery where the auction pieces were to be previewed. Al-though he and Sid had planned carefully, had recruited sev-eral student volunteers to receive and log in art works at the gallery, there was chaos throughout the day. Despite prom-ises to the contrary, two artists had submitted their paintings without frames. Otis had to arrange with a Tribeca framer to rush the jobs for hanging that night—paying him almost double from Rensler's tight auction budget. One of the student han-dlers had dropped a framed lithograph, shattering the glass so that a shard became embedded into the pale, serene center of a color field. Sid and Winnie had carefully removed the frag-ment of glass, but the damage was irreparable. Otis had to call the artist. From the auction emergency fund that Sid had insisted upon, Otis offered a price halfway between the piece's low and high presale estimate. The artist, a printmaker on the

Rensler faculty, told Otis the point of the auction was for Rensler to raise money, not lose it. In a voice perilously close to breaking (his mind had wandered to thoughts of Nora at home), Otis told the printmaker he could think of few people who would take that attitude, that it was moments like these that defined the real person.

Although he was tense throughout the day and evening, frequently calling over Sid and Winnie for quick, troubleshooting conferences, Otis was also exhilarated far beyond what he had felt at openings or graduations. Some of the older alumni who came to personally deliver their work had gained international reputations. Several made it a point to meet Otis, to introduce themselves and deliver short, heartfelt speeches about Rensler, to memorialize some instructor whose wisdom to this very day informed their proudest solutions. Until late afternoon the gallery filled with work donated in the greatest good will.

At midnight, Otis, Sid, and Winnie strolled around the two huge rooms hung high with the work they had solicited over eight months. The rooms were now a treasure trove. Winnie had given Sonya's "The Spirit" a special place on a carpeted platform at the rear of the gallery. Studies for final products—the original design of the signature upholstery pattern for a major airline, the first tracing paper sketch of the famous Rensler coffee maker, an animation cell from a classic cartoon—all lent the auction a wonderfully intimate, in-process look.

After one o'clock, as Otis started home, he was still under the influence of a heady feeling of privilege, the effect of his long day's proximity to the first-rate auction pieces. He was wide awake at two a.m., when he tiptoed by the spare room in which the nurse from the agency slept, and into bed beside Nora, heavily sedated on tranquilizers and painkillers.

Two days earlier, when Nora had leaned over to draw her bath water, one of her ribs had snapped in two. The cancer had spread to her bones. Beside her now, Otis could not calm himself from the day. His energy was galvanized for the next question, the next exigency, the next storm of praise. He tried to ease himself into sleep by matching Nora's deep breaths, but her breathing was far too drawn-out for the world of the waking. He listened, dismayed. When he reached out to hold her it struck him that his same touch was now brutal, and so he withdrew.

A month earlier, in the cab speeding down Lexington Avenue after the incident at the Indian restaurant, Otis had methodically listed to Nora all the reasons why she should return to the apartment on the Promenade. It might have been that Nora could think of nothing beyond her churning stomach, but the utter compliance in her face had terrified Otis. He was not afraid of Nora's return, nor the details of her care, nor even the inexplicably rapid plunge of her health in an era when so many hung on; it was simply Nora's passivity that set off in him a wild dread. He went to see Beth Mazur the next morning.

"This is no time for grace," Otis had protested. "This is no time to step back and let the guest have his say."

"Otis. Tell me about your wife."

"I am telling you about her. She's keeping her manners! Can you imagine keeping your manners?"

"Perhaps her manners are vital to her."

Otis could not understand. Had his wife's detractor become her defender? He found he could bear neither stance. He asked Beth Mazur outright.

"I'm not her detractor *or* her defender. You made the decision to invite Nora to come back home. This was not an easy decision for a man in your position. There are many shades in the spectrum of this conflict. You had finally learned you were unable to accept Nora, unable to accept your life together, and now—"

Otis winced. This neat little summation seemed unnecessarily explicit, its message foreboding. He looked at Beth Mazur. "I feel like *I* have stopped fighting," he confessed, his voice dim.

She nodded, a nod of deeply commiserative grief. It was beautiful, and it set Otis to weeping. At the end of their session, Beth suggested that they increase their hours together, that however Otis felt, he was in a circumstance that warranted the extra hours. Otis agreed.

The next day, the day he had to arrange for a nurse to be on hand in the hours he could not be home, Otis sat in his Rensler office and conjured Beth Mazur's deep nods and their great, consolatory force. In addition to recalling the exact angle of Beth's head when she nodded, Otis lingered over her stockings that reflected the glare from the track lighting above, over the one high-heeled shoe balanced casually off her toe. He well knew that in the end this memory would be replaced by Beth's reasonable, workaday self. In the end, Otis would see Beth as a vital agent in helping him get through a difficult time. But today in his office, Otis dwelled upon a transcendent few minutes during their last session, when above Beth's fallen pump her perfect foot had drawn circles as she described a particular moment of love in her life, a lavish moment she could not help but share with Otis.

Now it was Sunday and Nora's cancer had spread to her bones. As had become her ritual, Nora reached for her pills the moment she woke up. When she saw Otis sitting on the bed at her feet, she closed her eyes. Her lids fluttered against the chance of real sleep. He wanted to make breakfast for her, but she was not interested. He suggested they try one of the board games he had bought from the section labeled "Sophisticated Games" at a local book store. Nora looked at him incredulously. They exchanged no words, but he knew he had blundered badly in offering her these diversions for the briefly ill. Nora sat up. With some difficulty, she went into the bathroom. She was there for a while. When she emerged she was wearing lipstick. Otis had never before appreciated the transforming power of her lipstick, a shade called Sucre she had worn for years. Or maybe it served her more faithfully in illness; the lipstick suggested that the hollows of her cheeks were part of a calculated new look. Otis reached out his hand, and Nora latched on for support. She touched his shoulder and told him, gently, that he should go about his business. A terrible thing this was, this compelling him to promote the tasks of the day to false prominence.

Later that afternoon he brought her soup and crackers. She ate little. When she was finished, Otis lay down beside her. He tried to explain away the letter he had sent to her in November. Nora tried to explain away the stunt man. She did not reach further back, to her leaving Otis. She told Otis of the stunt man's coarseness. She smiled a little. Otis petted her with skittish fingers. He was reminded of Nora's own, overly delicate touch from years before.

When Nora drifted off again, Otis left the apartment. He walked for a while along the Promenade, then stopped and rested his arms along the balustrade. Quite oblivious to the docks and the river and the oblong bubbles of the Wall Street Tennis Club way beyond, he thought about Nora, asleep stories above. He thought about her daily steadiness and wondered who among the dying waits for catharsis, and who simply waits.

There was much to discuss with Beth during their next session. Otis talked to Nora's doctors—the oncologist, the radiologist—about her physical care; he talked to Beth about her emotional care. He sought from her suggestions how he could help Nora to make peace with herself without intruding on her privacy. This seemed to Otis to be his chief responsibility. Beth maintained it was Nora's. Otis complained that Nora's self-restraint masqueraded as peacefulness, and asked what he could do to lead her past it to genuine peacefulness. At this, Beth abandoned her sympathetic expression. She asked Otis why it was so important to him to mediate Nora's unexpressed conflicts, if his own peacefulness might possibly be at question. There was a predictability, an obviousness in this response against which Otis recoiled, but he quickly judged it within himself to pursue Beth's line of thinking, to work with her until their collaboration resulted in the return of her animated expression.

At 7:30 on the night of the auction, Otis stood at a phone booth in front of the restaurant where the benefit supper had been held. Just before the two of them were to leave for Manhattan, Nora had said she could not make the dinner, that the sight and smell of all those courses would just be too much. She planned to take a cab to the auction. Now, her sentences punctuated by sighs (the effect of Valium), she told Otis she could not make the auction either.

Board members and Rensler donors emerged from the restaurant and onto the street. Seeing Otis on the phone, they nodded and smiled. Brad Shaw, apparently pleased at how the benefit was going, poked Otis's arm to get his attention, then smiled at him.

"I'm coming home," said Otis.

"Denise has me under control." Nora permitted Otis to hear the irony in her voice. "Do you want to talk to her?"

"No. I want to talk to you. You seemed pretty strong before."

"I'm not pretty strong now."

"All right. It'll just take me a minute to get the car."

"Otis, please," she said.

This "Otis, please" was twenty years old. It was short-hand for "please stop aggravating me."

To his amazement, Otis was overtaken by a swell of rage. In a second's flash, he realized the rage was somehow connected to what had occurred over the last month in Beth Mazur's office. Yet he could not bear the timing of this anger; he put his mouth closer to the receiver. "Darling. How do I know you'll be all right?"

"Because I'm telling you," answered Nora. "I'll be fine."

Otis heard Denise in the background. She had come into the bedroom with a tray of something.

"I wish you success," said Nora. She hung up.

Off the phone, Otis did not move. A young man in a bomber jacket stood inches behind him, jiggling change in his pocket. Otis forced himself to step aside. He leaned against a signpost. She had wished him success tonight, and she had been sincere. The prospect of his success remained for her a greater comfort than his actual presence. Otis went into the bar directly across from the signpost. He ordered a scotch and soda—his drink, when he drank.

A gold-and-white hand-lettered banner hung above a table crowded with champagne bottles and rows of stemmed glasses. It hung freely from the ceiling, and it announced Rensler's seventieth anniversary. Two Rensler insignias flanked the letters. They were painted in gold leaf. Each time the bartender's head grazed the banner, the insignias twinkled. They winked at Otis as he came in from the narrow cobble-stone street of dark warehouses and newly converted loft spaces, a once menacing street that now offered style as its chief commodity.

The auction had already begun. Weeks before, Otis had decided he would not watch the bidding, which now took place in the rear of the second gallery. Still, the auction refused to be discreet about its success. Spatterings of applause continually broke from distant corners. Board members with beaming faces ducked in and out of the crowd.

Otis stationed himself at a massive, enamel-painted pillar in the center of the first room. He watched a group of students by the champagne table—a clique, really—Tito and Sandy and P.J., Claire Rollins. Otis saw that Danny Vincent was among them. They all wore their particular uniforms, but each with a twist. Sandy had clipped a rhinestone Statue of Liberty to the bib of her overall. P.J. wore his usual khaki work shirt but also a white tuxedo waistband. Along with his paint-splattered Levis, Tito wore a burgundy smoking jacket with grosgrain lapels. Claire had draped a bright silk scarf over the shoulders of her black jersey. She had exchanged her sneakers for dark red ankle boots. Otis was surprised to see that Danny had trimmed his beard to look almost professorial, that instead of the embroidered Lucifer jacket he wore a Harris tweed blazer. When Danny spun around, though, a garish paisley ascot confirmed he still held himself at arm's length.

"Man of the hour!" shouted Tito. The group moved towards Otis. In turn, Sandy, P.J., and Tito shook his hand, pumped it in violent swoops. Hanging back, Claire smiled at him, a lovely smile that she had clearly designed to override her shyness. As if presenting an offering to Otis, Tito pushed Danny to the center of the group. "Guess who's back?" he said.

"I'm delighted, Mr. Vincent." Otis affected a courtly bow. "I've missed your *retablos*. I look forward to seeing them around again."

At this, P.J. and Tito hooted.

"Jeez," said Sandy, and rolled her eyes.

It seemed to Otis that Claire's smile dimmed.

"You wouldn't believe it, Daley," said Tito. "He's switching to *Product* Design."

"Yeah, right, I can see it," P.J. said. He framed an imaginary headline: "Vincent Dustbuster Takes Staten Island by Storm."

"Up yours," said Danny.

Ignoring this exchange, Otis squeezed Danny's shoulder. "I'm delighted you're back. We'd love to have you in Product Design."

The sound of cheering in the rear gallery overtook their conversation. The radiant group that emerged from the back surrounded Sonya Barlow like an aureole. From somewhere among them, Brad Shaw came forth, heedlessly stepping in front of Danny and P.J. to whisper a number in Otis's ear. Like loyal attendants, the group parted so Otis could congratulate Sonya.

For a moment, Otis was baffled. For one disorienting moment he could not for the life of him see any connection between sculpture and money. The two seemed to inhabit different universes. Coming perhaps too abruptly to his senses, he threw his arms around Sonya Barlow. When he released her, neither of them had quite latched onto their roles. Sonya recovered first. "How very nice that it worked out," she said, "that 'The Spirit' has had some small effect."

P.J. and Sandy rushed behind the table to help the bartender uncork champagne bottles. Otis spotted Sid Casner across the room and sought out his eye. They both smiled, managing to communicate their relief at the success of the auction as well as their wariness of overreaction.

As he stood on the street, Otis heard the dim but communal shout: "Rensler lives!" He'd no idea that over the months students had worried over Rensler's survival. It had not occurred to him until now that Rensler's exact combination of petty and grand struggles had made it an intimate stronghold, a preserve worthy of defense. These kids, thought Otis, these kids with their rhinestone pins and satin smoking jackets, their howling and cursing and backslapping—these kids had suffered the threat to their home in silence. The sounds of their elation followed Otis as he turned around the unlit corner. Their cheers hovered in the air far beyond the point at which Otis expected them to die, all the way to the next corner, where he had to turn to claim his car. He would go back to Nora, to a voice submerged, a laugh no longer able to exceed its mark. He would announce his great success of the evening merely by running his fingers along her thin cheek, a sign that really nothing momentous had happened, a night like any other had occurred and tomorrow would be—please—a day like any other.

CLAIRE AND Danny stayed behind. The gallery had been lent for the whole evening, and Claire roamed about as the crowd thinned out, taking off her new boots to coast along the bleached and glossy pine floors. Danny joined her. He coiled her silk scarf around his wrist and put his ascot around her neck. They glided together in their stocking feet into a back room where huge paintings leaned upright within slatted chambers. Carefully, Claire pushed back an unframed abstract by one of the gallery's best known painters. Tiny, precise ellipses ran in currents, opposite directional forces. The painting was many shades of gray. Claire opened her mouth to comment, then found she did not have the slightest notion what she thought of the painting. This frightened her because next week she would move into her new apartment and begin to change the course of her own painting.

"I don't know," she said. "What do you think?"

Danny stood on tiptoes. He strained forward. "What can possibly be said when all has been said?"

Claire jabbed his arm and gestured to the front room, where she had just seen Sonya Barlow. She looked through the open door. People gathered empty champagne glasses and tossed them into trash bags. It struck Claire that she and Danny might be friends for many years.

Danny mouthed an apology. Barlow had come through big time tonight; he really didn't want to offend her. Especially now that he was back at Rensler. Tomorrow he would reclaim his Kollman efficiency, pay a special price for the summer while he worked at Lem's Bushwick place, making money for next year. He looked at Claire, at his satin ascot crumpled about her neck. She was still trying to construct an opinion about the ellipse painting. He didn't understand the urgency she felt about the forming of aesthetic opinions. It wearied him to contemplate the pressure she placed upon herself. Maybe he wouldn't see so much of her this summer. Next fall, maybe they would just run into each other once in a while.

"Wanna go to Benno's?" he asked now. "No-ice-cream shakes and greaseball fries?"

It was late when Sonya passed Claire Rollins and Danny Vincent along their way to somewhere. Lights surrounded them—the street lamps and car beams and the pale bulbs in remote corners of stores long closed for the night. When they congratulated her, their hushed voices signaled that they stood in a new perspective to her. They were in her debt, for "The Spirit" had become an item of barter, and it had played its part in securing their future. Sonya joined them along their way. For several minutes she walked between them; she felt the new balance of the composition they made together, there on Mercer Street. She became the solid form towards which they gravitated. She was both within this composition and outside it, and found both standpoints pleasing. They laughed together for half a block, and then Claire and Danny fell out of step, perhaps distracted by the thought of their destination.

At the intersection, they stopped. "Thank you for coming," Sonya said, as if the corner of Mercer and Houston were her vestibule. She smiled and then hurried north into the late night, certain she didn't have a moment to lose.

ABOUT THE AUTHOR

PATRICIA GROSSMAN is the author of the novel *Inventions in a Grieving House* and two children's books, *The Night Ones* and *Saturday Market*. She lives in Brooklyn, New York.

Selected Titles from Award-Winning CALYX Books

NONFICTION

Natalie on the Street by Ann Nietzke. A day-by-day account of the author's relationship with an elderly homeless woman who lived on the streets of Nietzke's central Los Angeles neighborhood. *PEN West Finalist.*
ISBN 0-934971-41-2, $14.95, paper; ISBN 0-934971-42-0, $24.95, cloth.

The Violet Shyness of Their Eyes: Notes from Nepal by Barbara J. Scot. A moving account of a western woman's transformative sojourn in Nepal as she reaches mid-life. PNBA Book Award.
ISBN 0-934971-35-8, $14.95, paper; ISBN 0-934971-36-6, $24.95, cloth.

In China with Harpo and Karl by Sibyl James. Essays revealing a feminist poet's experiences while teaching in Shanghai, China.
ISBN 0-934971-15-3, $9.95, paper; ISBN 0-934971-16-1, $17.95, cloth.

FICTION

The Adventures of Mona Pinsky by Harriet Ziskin. In this fantastical novel, a 65-year-old Jewish woman comes of age, facing alienation and ridicule, and ultimately is reborn on a heroine's journey.
ISBN 0-934971-43-9, $12.95, paper; ISBN 0-934971-44-7, $24.95, cloth.

Killing Color by Charlotte Watson Sherman. These compelling, mythical short stories by a gifted storyteller delicately explore the African-American experience. Washington State Governor's Award.
ISBN 0-934971-17-X, $9.95, paper; ISBN 0-934971-18-8, $19.95, cloth.

Mrs. Vargas and the Dead Naturalist by Kathleen Alcalá. Fourteen stories set in Mexico and the Southwestern U.S., written in the tradition of magical realism.
ISBN 0-934971-25-0, $9.95, paper; ISBN 0-934971-26-9, $19.95, cloth.

Ginseng and Other Tales from Manila by Marianne Villanueva. Poignant short stories set in the Philippines. Manila Critic's Circle National Literary Award Nominee.
ISBN 0-934971-19-6, $9.95, paper; ISBN 0-934971-20-X, $19.95, cloth.

POETRY

The Country of Women by Sandra Kohler. A collection of poetry that explores woman's experience as sexual being, as mother, as artist. Kohler finds art in the mundane, the sacred, and the profane.
ISBN 0-934971-45-5, $11.95, paper; ISBN 0-934971-46-3, $21.95, cloth.

Colophon

The body text is set in 11 point Optima.
Section titles are set in 18 point Parisian.
Typeset, layout, and production provided by ImPrint
Services, Corvallis, Oregon.

Light in the Crevice Never Seen by Haunani-Kay Trask. The first book of poetry by an indigenous Hawaiian to be published in North America. It is a revelation about a Native woman's love for her land, and the inconsolable grief and rage that come from its destruction.
ISBN 0-934971-37-4, $11.95, paper; ISBN 0-934971-38-2, $21.95, cloth.

Open Heart by Judith Mickel Sornberger. An elegant collection of poetry rooted in a woman's relationships with family, ancestors, and the world.
ISBN 0-934971-31-5, $9.95, paper; ISBN 0-934971-32-3, $19.95, cloth.

Raising the Tents by Frances Payne Adler. A personal and political volume of poetry, documenting a woman's discovery of her voice. Finalist, WESTAF Book Awards.
ISBN 0-934971-33-1, $9.95, paper; ISBN 0-934971-34-x, $19.95, cloth.

Black Candle: Poems about Women from India, Pakistan, and Bangladesh by Chitra Divakaruni. Lyrical and honest poems that chronicle significant moments in the lives of South Asian women. Gerbode Award.
ISBN 0-934971-23-4, $9.95, paper; ISBN 0-934971-24-2, $19.95 cloth.

Indian Singing in 20th Century America by Gail Tremblay. A brilliant work of hope by a Native American poet.
ISBN 0-934971-13-7, $9.95, paper; ISBN 0-934971-14-5, $19.95, cloth.

Idleness Is the Root of All Love by Christa Reinig, translated by Ilze Mueller. These poems by the prize-winning German poet accompany two older lesbians through a year together in love and struggle.
ISBN 0-934971-21-8, $10, paper; ISBN 0-934971-22-6, $18.95, cloth.

ANTHOLOGIES

The Forbidden Stitch: An Asian American Women's Anthology edited by Shirley Geok-lin Lim, et al. The first Asian American women's anthology. American Book Award.
ISBN 0-934971-04-8, $16.95, paper; ISBN 0-934971-10-2, $32, cloth.

Women and Aging, An Anthology by Women edited by Jo Alexander, et al. The only anthology that addresses ageism from a feminist perspective. A rich collection of older women's voices.
ISBN 0-934971-00-5, $15.95, paper; ISBN 0-934971-07-2, $28.95, cloth.

CALYX Books are available to the trade from Consortium and other major distributors and jobbers.

Individuals may order direct from CALYX Books, P.O. Box B, Corvallis, OR 97339. Send check or money order in U.S. currency; add $1.50 postage for first book, $.75 each additional book.

CALYX, A Journal of Art and Literature by Women

CALYX, A Journal of Art and Literature by Women, has showcased the work of over two thousand women artists and writers since 1976. Committed to providing a forum for *all* women's voices, *CALYX* presents diverse styles, images, issues, and themes which women writers and artists are exploring.

"The work you do brings dignity, intelligence, and a sense of wholeness to the world. I am only one of many who bows respectfully—to all of you and to your work."
—Barry Lopez

"It is heartening to find a women's publication such as CALYX *which is devoted to the very best art and literature of the contemporary woman. The editors have chosen works which create images of forces that control women; others extol the essence of every woman's existence."*
—Vicki Behem, *Literary Magazine Review*

"Thank you for all your good and beautiful work."
—Gloria Steinem

Published in June and November; three issues per volume.

Single copy rate: $8.00.
Subscription rate for individuals: $18/1 volume.

CALYX Journal is available to the trade from Ingram Periodicals and other major distributors.

CALYX is committed to producing books of literary, social, and feminist integrity.

CALYX Journal is available at your local bookstore or direct from:

CALYX, Inc., P.O. Box B, Corvallis, OR 97339

CALYX, Inc., is a nonprofit organization with a 501(C)(3) status. All donations are tax deductible.